CROWN OF SECRETS

THE HIDDEN MAGE SERIES

Crown of Secrets
Crown of Danger
Crown of Strength
Crown of Power

And set in the same world:

THE SPOKEN MAGE SERIES

Voice of Power
Voice of Command
Voice of Dominion
Voice of Life

Power of Pen and Voice:
A Spoken Mage Companion Novel

CROWN OF SECRETS

THE HIDDEN MAGE BOOK 1

MELANIE CELLIER

CROWN OF SECRETS

Copyright © 2020 by Melanie Cellier

The Hidden Mage Book 1
First edition published in 2020 (v1.2)
by Luminant Publications

ISBN 978-1-925898-49-1

Luminant Publications
PO Box 201
Burnside, South Australia 5066

melaniecellier@internode.on.net
http://www.melaniecellier.com

Cover Design by Karri Klawiter
Editing by Mary Novak
Proofreading by Deborah Grace White
Map Illustration by Rebecca E Paavo

For the newest member of my family,
my niece, Annabeth Jasmine,
whose birth coincided with the birth of this story.
I hope you will enjoy reading it one day.

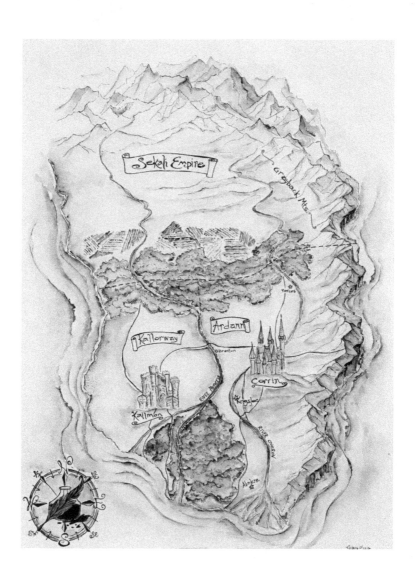

CHAPTER 1

Something hit the side of the carriage so hard it tipped to one side, teetering for a moment on the verge of falling before crashing back onto all four wheels. Our forward momentum lurched, slowed, and halted completely as the carriage continued to shudder and rock.

I picked myself up from the far side of the vehicle, where I had been thrown by the violent movement. Thankfully I was riding alone, or I would have ended up with a pile of others on top of me.

If any of my family members had accompanied me—as they had wanted to do—they would no doubt have now told me to stay safely inside while they investigated the disturbance. But since they weren't present to baby me, I thrust open the carriage door and clambered down without obstruction.

"Your Highness! Get back inside!" barked a familiar voice.

I sighed. I wasn't entirely free of cautious protectors yet.

"What was that?" I asked Captain Layna.

When a scan of the immediate area didn't reveal any obvious sign of attack, I frowned back at the side of the carriage. The section that had taken the hit was easily visible, the paneling splintered and caving inward. The damage stopped just short of an actual hole, faint traces of power lingering on the wood.

I spun back around. "Mages? An attack?"

I gave my surroundings a more thorough examination. Although there was no visible sign of it in the air, I could sense the power that now enclosed us in a large bubble. As royalty, I was so used to being shielded that I had hardly registered its presence earlier. No doubt the captain had released a shielding composition the moment after the attack hit. We hadn't been expecting trouble on our own side of the border, or we might have already had one in place.

"Princess Verene, I really must insist you return to the carriage," Layna said in a pained voice.

I continued to ignore her. Nothing lay ahead of us on the road in the direction of Bronton, no enemies appearing to spring an ambush or follow up their attack. I looked back the way we had come instead and recognized our location.

I frowned. "That's the Wall. But I thought they cleared this section already. And we didn't leave the road, so it should be safe anyway."

Ever since we left the capital, we'd been surrounded by ripe fields, stretching out on either side of the West Road. But here, the ground lay barren for a wide strip, spearing out on both sides, perpendicular to the road.

I winced at the sight of the dark, dead land, so stark after the colorful growth we'd been passing through for so long. Here was a visual reminder of why I was being sent away from my home and everyone I knew and loved. Even after more than twenty years of peace, a barrier lay between my home kingdom of Ardann and our western neighbors and long-term enemies, Kallorway. But as the aging Head of the Armed Forces liked to remind my parents, the war had raged for longer than the peace had so far held. It took time to heal such scars.

Time, and apparently effort and sacrifice. And I was the chosen sacrifice.

I shook my head at the morbid thoughts. I should be grateful my aunt, Queen Lucienne, had finally found a way I could be useful, however unpleasant this particular prospect seemed.

I refocused my attention on the strip of land that had once been the Wall. It had taken a full twenty years of peace for the people to be ready to see it dismantled, so the work had only recently begun. I had come this way with my family a few times as a child, on our way to visit the fortified border town of Bronton and the Abneris River which was the official border with Kallorway.

I called up a picture of how the Wall had looked then: a wide stretch of jagged rocks butting right up to the road on either side, the stones too large and sharp to allow either vehicles or horses to cross. And while I had never ridden its whole length, I knew it had once stretched all the way along the river from the great northern forests to the tip of the southern forest. Only Bronton and a few border settlements, instrumental to the war effort, had stood between the Wall and the Abneris. The barrier had funneled all traffic to the border through this one road and had been the only reason Ardann had managed to keep the war contained to the border region for so long.

The clearing efforts had begun at the road and spread outward, and only a scattering of smaller rocks were left as far as I could see southward. But when I squinted north, I could see a patch of cleared dirt that grew steadily more rocky. Several distant figures milled around the point where the stones grew to full size. It looked like on this side, at least, the clearing crews were still within sight of the road.

The six people had stopped whatever work they had previously been engaged in and were milling together in what looked like confusion. One had an arm raised, pointed in our direction, and despite the distance, I thought I could see concern on their faces. After another moment, they all took off together, in a huddled mass, jogging in our direction.

I watched them come warily. Something wasn't right with the scene, although I couldn't put my finger on what. Beside me, Captain Layna stirred uneasily.

"Where's their mage?" she asked, identifying the wrong note with the scene.

The Wall had never been merely a collection of sharp rocks. Such a barrier couldn't have hoped to keep back the might of the Kallorwegian war mages. It had been created not with the labor of commonborns but with the effort of a hundred creator mages. When they moved the stones into place, they had bound them and strengthened them with power. And in the three decades of war that had followed, every newly graduated mage in the kingdom had spent a two-year term at the front lines, adding their own workings to the ones left by the creators of the Wall. Over the years, it had become a patchwork of power—a death-trap with no key or even record of the deadly dangers lurking within.

There was a reason—beyond our mistrust of the Kallorwe-gians—that no one had been eager to attempt dismantling it. And there had certainly been no talk of assembling a hundred mages to undertake the difficult task. Mage numbers were too few to be diverted for such a purpose during times of peace.

But the work had been going on for many months now, a slow and steady process undertaken by teams of commonborns working with a mage. The commonborns did the physical work of moving the stones only after the mage had painstakingly cleared each small portion of lingering workings. But the men racing toward us were clearly all commonborns, and I could see no sign of a mage robe anywhere.

My muscles clenched, and I rose onto my toes, poised for action, as the reality of the situation hit me. We hadn't been attacked at all—at least not with any intent. The commonborn clearing team had triggered an old working, and we had been the unfortunate targets of its aggression.

My eyes picked out one of the commonborns who lagged well behind the others, both hands clutched around his chest. It looked like we weren't the only victims. And if they had reached an untouched section of the Wall, then there could be more danger still to come.

I took several steps toward the approaching workers, who were still outside the protection of our shield, but Layna darted forward to stop me. Using her unique privilege as my personal guard, she grabbed at my arm, pulling me to a halt.

"No, Your Highness," she said firmly.

No doubt she had intended to follow the words with a lecture about my safety, but her words stopped, both of our heads whipping toward the approaching workers, although there was nothing to see but their running forms.

They neither slowed nor flinched because they couldn't feel what Layna and I could—a swell of power growing behind them at the edge of the Wall.

"They're nearly here," Layna said in a strained voice. "They'll make it into our shield. Although it may not be strong enough."

Diverted by this thought, she let me go and thrust her hand inside her gold robe, searching for another shield composition.

"The injured one won't make it," I said, my hands moving as fast as hers.

At my words, she looked back at me, her own hands stilling on the small roll of parchment she now held.

"No, don't—" She lunged forward and tried to pry the scrap of paper I had retrieved from my hand, but she was too late.

Ripping it, I released the power stored inside the written composition, flicking it toward the still-unaware workers. The shield raced out to enfold them, reaching for the injured man just as whatever attack had been building at the Wall unleashed.

Raw power, stronger than the bolt which had hit our carriage, rolled toward us. It engulfed first the injured worker and then the others, only half of whom were within the guards' shield.

The strength in the attack composition broke through the extra shield I had worked, but the wave of its power had already passed the injured man before his defenses failed. Layna, her eyes widening, ripped the composition still in her hand, surrounding all of us, including the five closer workers, in a second layer of shielding. This new protection held when the attack broke through her old one, the power of the unknown composition from the Wall dissipating into nothing. I still had no idea what it had been designed to do, and I was more than glad not to find out.

The commonborns had stopped, panting and regarding us with wide eyes. They may not have been able to feel the approaching power, but they could see the compositions in our hands and feel the tension radiating from our bodies.

I took several deep, steadying breaths, although I had undertaken no physical exertion. As a princess, I was always surrounded by guards and defenses. I had never before personally unleashed a shield composition in anything other than training.

"What were you thinking, Verene?" Layna snapped, clearly equally overcome by the unexpected emergency. It wasn't like her to forget her usual formality. "We are here to protect you and are well-stocked with compositions. You, of all people, should know better than to use your own personal stores unless to protect yourself from direct and immediate threat."

My sympathy for my guard fell away at the words *you, of all people*. I knew her concern was for me, but I didn't need a reminder of why I was unlike any other royal charge she might have been assigned—unlike any other in history.

The other three royal guards who had accompanied us at the insistence of my parents had now drawn close. Each of them held a piece of parchment, their eyes focused on the distant Wall. If there was another threat, they would have us protected in layers of shielding before it could reach us.

The squad of commonborn guards in their red and gold uniforms formed a wider circle, enclosing us, the carriage, and the commonborn workers. They were my honor guard, but they had been chosen from among the Royal Guard's finest.

The attention of the workers, however, was all focused on Layna and me. One of them stepped forward, visibly trembling as he looked from the royal insignia on the side of the carriage, to my white robe, to the golden circlet nestled in my dark hair.

He dropped to one knee, and the other workers all followed suit.

"P...Princess Verene," he gasped. "Our apologies. We don't know what happened." He glanced over his shoulder to where the injured worker had apparently given up on joining us and sunk to the ground, his face white. "Johnson said something hit him, but none of us saw anything." He glanced uneasily back toward the Wall.

I opened my mouth to assure him we were all unharmed and bid him relax, but Layna spoke first.

"That is because he was hit with a bolt of raw power," she said. "A similar one to the missile that hit our carriage. I don't know if they were targeted toward movement, or whether they just speared out in all directions and we were unlucky enough to be hit. The more relevant question is what were you doing working on an uncleared section of the Wall? Where is your mage?"

The man's face whitened, his color now resembling his injured companion.

"Uncleared?" He licked his lips. "This section was supposed to be cleared. The mage assured us..." He pulled two torn scraps of parchment from an inside pocket. "I worked this myself, Your Highness."

He held out the pieces to Layna, the movement highlighting the complex pattern of darker skin pigmentation around his wrist. He was one of the lucky sealed commonborns then, able to safely read and write and therefore to handle written compositions.

The captain stepped forward and retrieved the two halves of the parchment, holding them together so she could read the words of the now-released working. Her face grew darker, and she bit back a curse.

"I repeat, where is your mage?"

The man swallowed. "In Bronton, Sir. He came out this morning, but he doesn't like to spend his whole day standing around in the fields. He always goes back to Bronton in the afternoons."

"Does he now?" Layna asked, her dark voice laden with dire threats. "Then I think we had better continue on to Bronton."

CHAPTER 2

 $\mathcal{I}$ jumped in quickly, directing my words at the worker. "That is not your fault, however." The poor man clearly expected some sort of terrible punishment for placing a member of the royal family at risk.

I peeked over Layna's shoulder and scanned the composition, ignoring the clenching in my stomach. I never liked interacting with compositions—not when I was the only mage in history unable to create one.

Since the beginning of recorded history, the act of writing words had allowed humans to access power—power that could be shaped to an untold number of different tasks and purposes. But people had always been divided into two groups—those who could control the power the writing unleashed and those who could not. And for those who could not—the commonborns— any attempt to write would result in an uncontrolled explosion of pure power that brought death and destruction to the writer and all those around them.

And so, for uncounted generations, commonborns had been forbidden all access to the written word. Because everyone knew reading led to writing. With so many lives at stake, it was too dangerous to risk someone absentmindedly tracing a word with their finger or being tempted to test their limits. If common-borns never saw the written word, if they never read, then they could never write. We had an entire discipline of mages—the Seekers—whose role was to prevent any illicit access to words.

Meanwhile, those who could control the power—the mages—formed themselves into disciplines, learning how to strengthen and refine their natural control. They ruled Ardann—as they did Kallorway and the northern Sekali Empire—and their power allowed the kingdom to prosper. The growers and wind workers ensured the crops flourished. The creators built roads and public buildings, and the healers ran healing clinics that even common-borns could access for a fee. It was a system of vast inequality, but one dictated by birth not will.

Everything depended on your bloodline. Mages handed down the ability to control power to their children, as the common-borns handed down the lack of ability. And because some mages had more natural strength and control than others, mages formed marriage alliances designed to increase the future strength of their families. And none had more carefully culti-vated generations of strength than the royal line. Being born as royalty ensured a birthright of great power.

Until me.

Here I was, child of our current queen's younger brother, daughter of two of the strongest mages ever to live, and I was utterly without access to power. It was a great accomplishment, really. The first child ever born to a mage not to inherit their ability. I'm sure the Royal University would have loved the chance to study me. Thankfully my royal status was enough to prevent that, at least.

But I had received the education of a princess, even if I could not use all of it, and I easily understood the import of the compo-sition in Layna's hands. The mage assigned to this team had cleared this section of wall of old workings and then left. In what he no doubt felt was an abundance of caution, he had provided the commonborns with one of his compositions—a working designed to give a section of rocks a final check before the workers began clearing it. The sealed commonborn probably had a small stack of similar, unworked compositions in a pocket somewhere, to release as they progressed with their work.

Once such a thing would have been impossible. Commonborns were not allowed to possess written words. Only the richest among them could afford to purchase compositions from the poorest and least powerful of the mages—the only mages who would stoop to such a degradation as selling compositions. And these purchased compositions were carefully sealed and color-coded for purpose, ensuring a limited range of use.

It was my parents who had changed all of that. They had traveled to the previously closed Sekali Empire and discovered a different world there. A world where all commonborns were sealed as young children, their access to power blocked, allowing them free access to the written word.

The discovery of the sealing composition had rocked both Ardann and Kallorway. But neither of our kingdoms could follow in the footsteps of the Empire. The sealing composition drew directly on the energy and power of a mage, and when it worked its purpose, it sealed the mage as permanently as it sealed the commonborns. In the Empire, whole clans were devoted to this purpose, the sealed mages raising their unsealed children in the knowledge that by one day taking their turn to seal a large collection of commonborn children they would serve their people and bring honor to their families.

But the enmity between the two southern kingdoms was of long standing, and centuries ago we had decimated our mage numbers in ancient battles. We didn't have enough mages to make the sacrifices of the sealed Sekali clans, even if we could have convinced or compelled enough mages to do so. And so my parents had suggested a compromise.

Instead of imprisoning mages who had failed the Academy and proved themselves unable to control power to a sufficient degree, those mages would conduct sealing ceremonies instead. There were not, of course, a great many failed mages, but their numbers were joined by those mages who had misused their power in severe enough ways to warrant permanent imprisonment. Now we could imprison their power instead of their bodies, clearing the mage cells and benefiting the commonborns at the same time. Sealing ceremonies were much rarer in Ardann now, but they had been common at the beginning, thanks to the traitorous mages who had attempted to help Kallorway seize control of our kingdom.

I had no way to know if this man was recently sealed or had been sealed two decades ago while young. Many of the sealed now worked as teachers in the commonborn schools, served as officials at the palace and among the disciplines, or worked for the rich commonborn merchant families. But others, like this man, chose to ally themselves with mages, working in partnerships.

I considered the man in front of me. His bearing proclaimed him a soldier.

"Let me guess," I said. "You've recently finished with the Armed Forces?"

The man looked surprised, some of his color slowly starting to return now that I was showing no sign of handing out angry punishments.

"Aye, that's right, Your Highness. His Lordship and I heard there was better gold to be had with the clearing teams." He referred to his mage partner using the general honorific awarded to all mages. "I'm not getting any younger, and I have to be thinking about laying something aside for retirement."

Layna sighed, speaking quietly, her words directed at me.

"That mage still should have known better. He would have been fully briefed."

I shrugged. "We'll have to ask him when we get to Bronton."

In the Armed Forces, many tasks were completed by sealed commonborns without the physical presence of their mage partner. But Layna was right. This mage should have known the same principle didn't apply here where maintaining his post at the Wall offered only boredom, not danger.

Sealed commonborns might be able to safely read and use compositions provided by mages, but sealing didn't grant them the mage ability to sense power. The mage should have known that some of the compositions embedded in the Wall might have been crafted to resist probing compositions such as the one he had provided to his team. What those compositions could not do, however, was hide their own power. The mage needed to be present so he could feel any lingering workings he had initially missed. He would have felt the power and, if he didn't sense it in time to dismantle it, he would have been able to protect his men, at least.

I frowned, my eyes wandering to the injured man who was now being tended by one of his worried-looking companions.

"We can't leave yet, though. We need to heal that man first."

Layna grimaced, looking from the worker to me. "You know my compositions are all keyed to you specifically, Your Highness."

I narrowed my eyes and drew myself up to my full height—which wasn't saying a great deal.

"Yours may be, but don't try to pretend all of theirs are." I gestured at the three mage officers still surrounding us.

As my personal guard, Layna keyed her compositions to me—both to render them useless if they fell into other hands and to make it easy to resist temptations such as this one. She had been trained to keep her whole focus on her charge. But the same wasn't true for the other guards who had been assigned just for this journey. And I knew one of them was only on assignment to the Royal Guard from the healers.

"That man was injured in service to Ardann—and due to the negligence of the mage entrusted with his care. He's a laborer, so there's every chance he can't afford a healing clinic. And clearly we can't trust the mage in charge of this team to do the right thing by his workers. So it is left to us to act. And if you won't, I will."

I reached slowly for one of my internal pockets, the movement making my position clear. I wasn't in imminent danger which meant I far outranked Layna—she had no authority to prevent me using one of my own stored compositions. But neither would she want to see me deplete my supply—not when I was the only royal in Ardann who lacked the capacity to restock. Every one of the compositions I carried for my protection had been provided to me by others.

The captain blew out an exasperated breath. "Very well. We will heal him and then make all haste to Bronton."

She gestured at one of the mage guards, and he broke away from us to jog toward the injured man. I watched him go, my bottom lip gripped between my teeth. How wonderful it must feel to know that you could bring healing and relief with the stroke of a pen.

I shook off the thought, looking back at the man still kneeling before us.

"You were following orders, and this situation is not of your making," I said. "But it is not safe for you to work out here without a mage present. I assume you're also staying at Bronton?"

The man nodded.

"Once your companion has been healed," I continued, "you must assist him back there. By the time you arrive, we will have had the opportunity to talk with your mage. This situation will not happen again."

The man swallowed but nodded, not voicing any protest.

"I will be passing back this way soon," Layna said in a deceptively soft voice. "So you may be sure that I will follow up the instructions I give to this mage. And those instructions will make it clear that the blame rests solely on his shoulders."

"Thank you, Captain, Sir." The man clambered back to his feet and saluted, clearly still a soldier at heart.

Layna gestured a dismissal and attempted to herd me toward the carriage. I complied, softened by the reminder that she did care about these people. She just cared more about her job, which was protecting me—however unworthy of such protection I might be.

My parents had gone to great lengths to impress on the court that, power or not, I remained a representative and symbol of the crown. And when your mother was the most powerful mage in history—famous throughout Ardann, Kallorway, and the Empire —people tended to listen when she spoke. Maybe my lack of power wouldn't have galled me quite so much if it wasn't for the constant comparison with her. The one and only Spoken Mage.

When he was younger, Lucien, my older brother, had petulantly pointed out that he was a spoken mage as well. He had inherited my mother's unique ability to access power through spoken compositions. But when I tartly reminded him that he was heir to the throne and should be content with that, he had fallen sheepishly silent. Perhaps he had remembered who he was complaining to.

I sighed as I reluctantly climbed back into the carriage. I had never blamed my brother for the occasional outburst. He and I each had our own burdens to bear, and we had no one else to safely vent with outside of each other and our younger brother, Stellan. Royalty weren't permitted to whine about the burdens of their position to others.

In the privacy of the carriage, I rubbed a hand over my face, more tired than I had reason to be after the brief excitement. I needed to pull myself together before we reached Bronton. Layna was on the warpath, but we didn't know how senior the mage in question might be. If he had spent many years in the Armed

Forces, he might be inclined to look down on a captain of the Royal Guard.

He would not, however, look down on a princess of Ardann.

I sometimes thought my parents had put more effort into teaching me how to wield authority like a weapon than they had with my brothers. They rarely spoke of my deficiencies, but I could see how my lack had motivated so many of their actions.

The carriage rolled through the open gates of Bronton, the sounds of the bustling town filling my ears. Bronton had grown larger and more prosperous since the war ended, bursting at the seams of its sturdy walls. Once a center of war, it was now a center of trade, no longer surrounded by an Armed Forces tent city. When we were children, Lucien had often requested stories from the time our parents spent here in their youth. He had favored the tales of battle and cunning, while I preferred the ones of true love, promises exchanged, and a glittering Midwinter Ball.

Even then, I had sensed that I would never wield the sort of power required to triumph on a battlefield. If I wanted to make use of what birthright I possessed, I would have more luck in the politics of the ballroom.

The ability of a mageborn child to control power stabilized at age sixteen, so it was only in the months since my last birthday that my parents had been able to conduct a full range of private tests with me. But mages had early means of probing their children's future strength. And my parents' extensive testing had only confirmed the early indications—I was in every way like a sealed mage. I could safely write but not because I could control the power my writing released. I could safely put pen to paper because I could not access power at all.

I had avoided Lucien for a full two weeks after my parents finally gave up their efforts. But eventually I had relented. It wasn't my brother's fault he had inherited both our father's ability to write compositions and our mother's ability to speak them, while I had inherited neither.

With the ability to both write and speak compositions, Lucien's power almost rivaled our mother's. Mother was limited by her inability to prepare compositions in advance, an impediment that meant it was difficult for her to work complex compositions quickly. But she retained one skill my brother had not inherited.

A mage's ability to compose was limited by their energy reserves. Accessing power burned energy—just as running or lifting heavy stones did—and if a mage poured too much energy into a composition, they could incapacitate themselves for days, or even die. To prevent this, mages rarely wrote open compositions that drew on their energy once released. Instead they limited their workings to the power they could store in the parchment at the time of crafting the composition. Mageborn trained for four years at the Royal Academy to increase their skill and stamina so they might maximize their natural limits for both strength and complexity in a working. And still some workings remained outside our grasp, their scope too great for any mage.

Mother, however, could use her power to access the energy of others, making her personal capacity almost limitless. It was the one skill my brother had not inherited. But even without it, he was incredibly powerful, having not only dual abilities but also the natural strength he inherited from both our parents.

He was the culmination of everyone's expectations. Even my father's older sister, now queen, had anticipated unprecedented power in the children of a royal prince and the Spoken Mage. So great was her certainty and her dedication to the crown that she had given up the possibility of a family of her own.

Queen Lucienne had made Ardann strong despite the tumult of great change and social upheaval brought about by the end of the war and the discovery of the sealing composition. And she had done it through unstinting sacrifice. She would not weaken

Ardann by producing heirs to the throne who would be over-shadowed in power by their cousins, her brother's children. Instead, she had remained single, and when Lucien showed early signs of inheriting the strength of both his parents, she had promptly named him her heir.

Sometimes I wondered what would have happened if I had been born first, a universal disappointment. Perhaps it would not have been too late for her to marry still at that point. But then, perhaps I would not have been so powerless if my brother had not received both of my parents' abilities before I ever arrived.

I stomped on the resentment before it could blossom in my mind. I only had to look to my aunt to know that a royal had no business wallowing in self-pity when her kingdom had need of her. And I was determined to prove myself as capable as her, even if I didn't have access to power.

As the cobblestones of the town clattered under the wheels of the carriage, I allowed myself a single moment of disgruntlement. Did my sacrifice really have to involve spending four years among our enemies?

CHAPTER 3

The carriage came to a halt, returning my thoughts to the immediate moment. Layna's face appeared at the window.

"Stay here," she said before disappearing again.

I peered after her. The Armed Forces still had a major headquarters in Bronton, and she had led us into the courtyard of their building. Mages drawn from all disciplines, as well as retired mages, were being used in the effort to dismantle the Wall, but the Armed Forces were overseeing the task.

I could hear Layna shouting something across the courtyard, sending gray-uniformed commonborn soldiers scurrying before her. She stopped outside the large double doors, glancing back at me and making no move to enter the building.

After several drawn-out minutes, a grumpy-looking mage appeared. He wore the silver robe of a mage officer in the Armed Forces, but from Layna's expression, he was the retired officer we were seeking.

He eyed her up and down, his eyes narrowing at her gold robe.

"Who are you?" he asked, his voice carrying to where I sat. "Is this commotion really necessary? I was resting."

Layna crossed her arms and snorted contemptuously. "Yes, resting on the job. I didn't realize the Armed Forces had grown so lax after two decades of peace." She paused to glare at him. "And I am Captain Layna."

The man drew himself up, chest puffing out. "You're in Armed Forces' territory here, guard," he spat at her. "And General Griffith himself is in residence at the moment. You should watch your tongue. A bit far from your jurisdiction, aren't you?"

I straightened my circlet and pushed open the carriage door. The movement attracted the man's attention, his eyes flying to the vehicle which he had apparently failed to note previously.

I stepped down with full dignity, moving slowly and purposefully, my eyes not leaving his face. I was already dressed in the white robe of an Academy trainee, but it was the gold circlet on my head and the insignia on my carriage that proclaimed my true rank.

"The captain is exactly where she is supposed to be," I said, ice in my voice. "Unlike you."

The man swept into a deep bow. "Your Highness, I didn't realize you were here."

"Evidently." I looked down my nose at him—an impressive feat given he was significantly taller than me. "And I am glad to hear that the general is in Bronton at present since it seems I will need to call him to order for the control he exercises over his subordinates."

All color drained from the man's face. The elderly general, past due for retirement, ruled his discipline with an iron fist. He had spent a lifetime building his position at court and would not treat kindly a mage who earned him a royal rebuke.

He was also, officially, my grandfather. But our rather complicated relationship—one that had never included any great affection—was irrelevant here. When I spoke with the authority of the crown, I spoke with a voice far older than even the seventy-year-old hardened general.

The mage bowed again. "I can assure Your Highness it is not necessary to—"

"I will decide if it is necessary," I cut him off sharply. "You have neglected your duty and those above you have failed to ensure your competent completion of your task. The resulting error has placed a member of the royal family, as well as a member of your own team, in physical jeopardy. My guards have been forced to expend a large number of valuable compositions due to your negligence, and I demand recompense."

"I..." he spluttered, looking desperately between me and the unyielding Layna. "Of course. I..."

"You are fortunate no one died," I told him. "I will leave the details to my captain. I trust I will not be kept waiting long."

"Yes...I mean, no..." The man cut off his own words with another bow as I turned and swept back to my carriage.

I shut myself inside and leaned my head back against the seat. Now that she had my authority behind her, I trusted Layna could arrange matters without my further interference. I just hoped she could manage the situation without involving the general. I really didn't have the energy to deal with him today.

Some time passed before Layna appeared again, climbing into the carriage and rapping on the roof. We began to move as she gave me an amused smile.

"That was nicely done, Your Highness. Thank you."

I grinned back at her. "It's the most entertainment I've had in days, truth be told." My expression soured. "I hope you wrung him out for everything you could."

The captain nodded. "Naturally. He won't be neglecting his duties again." She gave me a knowing look. "And I reported the matter to the major in charge of the Wall dismantlement. I did not happen to cross paths with the general."

I blew out a breath of relief. "With any luck, he won't hear I'm in Bronton until we've already left in the morning."

Layna hid a grin, although I couldn't believe she relished the thought of running into him any more than I did.

"I suspect that if he does hear of the happenings today, he won't be overly eager to seek you out," she said.

I straightened. "Yes, of course. You're right. He'll be afraid I might give him an official reprimand. Can you just imagine how much he'd hate receiving one of those from a sixteen-year-old?"

"Almost makes you wish he would come to see you," Layna murmured, a wicked glint in her eye.

I shook my head at my captain. "I, for one, just want my bed. The day has been quite long enough."

We had left at first light to reach Bronton in time for darkness to fall, and the long hours in the carriage had made me weary and irritable, even before the happenings at the Wall. But no doubt I would have to sit through a formal meal with whichever senior mage had been nominated to host me for the night. I didn't need any more hassles with the Armed Forces on top of that.

The next morning we departed at a more reasonable hour, having less distance to travel. I had slept poorly, though, and faced the day with trepidation.

We reached the Abneris River all too soon, crossing it on a wide, sturdy bridge that hadn't existed in the days of the war. Now, however, we were joined in our crossing by a party of merchants in a cluster of carriages, and a farmer with a horse and cart. The politics between Corrin and the Kallorwegian capital of Kallmon might still be strained, but trade between our two kingdoms was well established.

While I had been to Bronton before, I had never crossed the river and entered the kingdom of our old enemies. None of the royal family had since the days of the war, just as none of the Kallorwegian royals had visited Ardann. We left the business of diplomacy to various representatives, a sign of the ongoing mistrust between our kingdoms.

Until now. As of this moment, a princess of Ardann had not only crossed into Kallorway but was taking up residence there. Such a thing had not been done in living memory. My father had told me that when his own father—the old king—was young, there had been talk of him doing an exchange year at the Kallorwegian Academy. Apparently it had been a common practice in ancient times to foster ties between the kingdoms. But King Osborne had ascended the throne in Kallmon before the plan could come to fruition, inciting war with Ardann rather than seeking peace. The subsequent war had dragged on for thirty years, and he had eventually been killed by rebels of his own kingdom who were sick of the bloodshed and loss. His son, King Cassius, sat on the Kallorwegian throne now.

But no Ardannian royal had ever completed their entire education in Kallorway. As far as I knew, no Ardannian mage had. While we had no reason to mistrust the competency of the Kallorwegian mages, Ardann still wanted its most important members schooled within its own borders.

Which is why it made sense for me to be the first. My education mattered little. I was to attend the Academy because it was mandatory that every mageborn start at the Academy the autumn after their sixteenth birthday. Occasional exceptions were made regarding the start date, such as in the case of my father who had started a year late due to his participation in a delegation to the Sekali Empire, but no one could avoid attendance altogether. And my parents had always insisted I be treated like any other mageborn.

I had dreaded starting, knowing that my inability to compose would only be more stark at the Ardannian Academy than it was at court. And at the Academy formality was put aside in an effort to encourage year mates to make bonds regardless of their respective families' positions. My own parents had met during their years there and remained close to many of their year mates. Those bonds were one of the reasons my mother kept assuring me the Academy was about more than learning to compose.

But the formality of my rank was the only protection I had ever had in a court that valued strength and power above all else. My parents claimed those values had improved since their own youth—that the court recognized different types of strength now in a way it had never done before. But the only strength I had was my royal blood, and at the Academy that would matter less than ever before.

Perhaps it was my own earlier arguments on the matter that had helped sway my parents when Aunt Lucienne suggested I attend the Kallorwegian Academy instead. But replacing one unwelcome school for another had not been my intention. I recognized her genius, however, and didn't put up a fight. Here at last was a way for me to help the crown—a task I was uniquely suited for, if only by my lack of ability. I was determined not to waste the opportunity I had been offered.

More fields greeted us on the far side of the bridge. It was unsettling how similar the landscape looked to the road from Corrin. I had built up Kallorway in my mind as an unfamiliar place, but the land itself knew no such distinctions.

Unlike in Ardann, where the Royal Academy had been built inside Corrin, right beside the palace, in Kallorway it occupied a remote location, closer to the border with Ardann than its own capital. It was a relief that I would not be facing King Cassius and the cutthroat Kallorwegian court. At least, not yet.

All too soon, we were passing through a village, and I glimpsed the forbidding walls of the Academy rising in the distance. There was no elegant white marble here, but instead gray stone, both for the wall itself and the building that rose behind it. It was an unwelcoming prospect.

My honor guard still rode in front and behind my carriage, accompanied by Layna and one of the other mage officers at the front, and the remaining two mages at the back. On the empty road we had made an impressive cavalcade, but riding through the looming gates of the Kallorwegian Academy, we looked small and outnumbered.

I straightened, telling myself not to be so fanciful. Stuck inside the carriage, I could hardly judge what sort of impression we made. I touched the circlet on my head for reassurance. I carried the weight and authority of a crown and a kingdom with me. I didn't need platoons of guards as well.

My confidence faltered when it came time to descend from the carriage, but my training helped me keep my trepidation from my face. The courtyard in front of the vast building was paved in a lighter gray stone but lacked the decorative touches of the entry to the Ardannian Academy.

The Academy building itself stood freely in the middle of the walls, facing south toward the capital. But a number of substantial outbuildings pressed against the other walls, their form suggesting they were barracks or housing of some kind. It fit with the briefing I had been given. The Kallorwegians did not ascribe to the informality of the Ardannian Academy, and no doubt they did not wish their servants to live in the same dwelling as their own important selves.

I suppressed a sigh. Here my royal blood would count for more than it would have at the Academy at home, but the thought of all the formality brought me no joy.

I ascended the grand stairway to the wooden doors which swung open at my approach. Inside, I found an enormous entranceway that at first glance appeared filled with people.

Only my years of royal training stopped me from faltering at the intimidating sight. Instead I raised my chin slightly, my eyes falling on a tall young man who stood at the front of the crowd.

He met my gaze without hesitation, a glint reflecting in his eyes in response to my slight movement. But a moment later I was sure I had imagined it. His face remained cold and impassive, his eyes too dark to shine in such a way, although they made an impressive contrast with his light, sandy hair.

The young man stepped forward, inclining his head in my direction. "Welcome to Kallorway, Princess Verene."

I realized at once who he was and was even more certain I had imagined the appreciative glint. He looked not much older than me and wore a white robe like my own, so if he was taking the lead in welcoming me, it could only be because he was Crown Prince Darius of Kallorway himself. And everyone knew the Kallorwegian crown prince kept his emotions well in check and far from view.

I gave him a half-curtsy in response as befitted a junior princess to a crown prince.

"Thank you, Your Highness."

An older man stepped forward to join him, giving a proper bow. "And welcome to the Kallorwegian Royal Academy. We hope your time here will be fruitful and your learning deep."

I gave him a regal nod. This man I recognized. Duke Francis—Head of the Academy. He had personally traveled to Ardann over the summer to reassure my parents as to the arrangements in place for my stay. His gray hair was just as I remembered, and his face as carefully neutral as ever, despite now being in the comfort of his own domain.

Now that I had a moment to take everything in, I realized the crowd of people was carefully organized. No other white robes were in evidence, but silver-robed figures formed several lines to the duke's right. To his left, an even larger number of servants, dressed in dark green uniforms, formed neat, still rows. I gave a shallow nod in their direction before focusing my attention on the silver-robed instructors.

Their presence had given me a jolt at first, the color of their robes signifying officers of the Armed Forces at home. But here in Kallorway, the instructors and academics wore silver instead of the black they wore in Ardann. I hoped I would adjust to the change soon and not continually imagine myself surrounded by hostile soldiers.

Other than the duke himself, the Academy had six senior positions, presumably the six mages standing in the front row, their junior instructors behind them. One of them drew my attention, standing out from every other mage present due to his gold robe. Duke Francis had assured my family that his trainees were protected by a sizable guard, and this must be their captain. Officially, the Academy Guard were an offshoot of the Kallorwegian Royal Guard, and their captain would therefore dress in gold.

The man gave me a measuring look before his eyes moved on to Layna. When she met his gaze, her own expression cool, he gave her a solid nod as if to reassure her he was ready to take on responsibility for her charge. Now that it had come to it, I didn't find his confidence reassuring. I wished my own captain could stay.

But King Cassius had insisted that if I was to attend his Academy, I must do so alone as every other trainee did both in his kingdom and in Ardann. Not even royalty brought their own guards to the Academy. Such a thing would be an insult of the highest order to the Head of the Academy—a position just as senior as the Head of the Royal Guard. The Academies of both kingdoms had protected and trained their future kings and queens for generations beyond count, and if Cassius's own sons were not permitted to bring guards, I could not do so either. I suppressed a shiver and wished my father had prevailed when he had argued with my aunt that the cases were not the same.

I understood why she had not given ground to the natural worries of a parent, however. How could we hope to forge the much-needed new bonds of trust and connection if we began with an unforgivable statement of mistrust?

It made sense, but that didn't mean I liked it. I gazed around the large space, carefully keeping my face impassive while my insides roiled. The next morning I would bid farewell to my guard, and I would be left behind, alone in the heart of our rival's stronghold, a trainee like any other. Welcome to the Kallorwegian Academy, indeed.

CHAPTER 4

*D*uke Francis hosted a formal evening meal in a small dining room that was part of a suite of chambers belonging to the Academy Head. Layna was invited to accompany me, although she was seated at the other end of the table, beside the Captain of the Academy Guard, who I learned was named Vincent.

I kept a subtle eye on them throughout the meal, noting the way Layna seemed to relax as time went on, even giving the occasional smile by the time sweets were served. My captain had always proved an excellent judge of character, and if she was favorably inclined toward this Vincent, then it was a count in his favor as far as I was concerned. The thought gave me more relief than I had expected.

I had assumed all six senior Academy staff would join us, but only two more were in attendance. They were the only ones who looked old enough to have been at the Academy for the current duke's tenure—a span of several decades—and were introduced as a couple. The man, Hugh, greeted me with true welcome in his voice, a far cry from the cold formality I had thus far received, and I couldn't help smiling at him. He was named as the head of the library and his wife, Raelynn, as the Academy healer.

Her position surprised me. In Ardann, the Academy healer was a junior position within the healing discipline, not a senior Academy position. Yet another subtle reminder that I was no longer at home.

Raelynn spoke quietly, but with as much warmth as her husband, the two of them carrying the conversation at our end of the table. I replied to them both with as much enthusiasm as my rank allowed, attempting to signal my gratitude for their manner. As the time drew nearer for my own people to leave, I grew more and more desperate to find some spark of friendliness in this unfamiliar place. It had been one thing to anticipate my solitary state from the comfort of home, but the reality was hitting me harder than I had expected.

As I stole surreptitious glances at Prince Darius across the table, my mood didn't lift. He, more than anything, was the reason I was here. The news he was finally to start at the Academy—two years late—had weighed heavily with my aunt.

One day he would be king in Kallmon, and that day might be arriving sooner than the usual course would suggest. Rumors had long reached us that King Cassius intended to abdicate in his unsealed son's favor as soon as Darius was at full maturity and power. And yet our intelligencers could tell us little about the crown prince's opinions or intentions. The unexpected opportunity to have one of our own spend four years as his year mate had been greatly alluring to my aunt.

But there was nothing in his face or voice to suggest he was likely to be any more friendly or open with his year mates than he was with his court. He ate with focus, replying when spoken to with precise, short answers. He volunteered nothing and never smiled at anyone.

Given the stories of his ruthless and cold father, and of his own inscrutability, Darius was hardly a surprise. But my heart sank just the same. Passionate hatred would have given me something more to work with than this stony facade. I had clearly imagined that initial glint, desperate to see the beginnings of a connection between us.

I took another bite and complimented the duke on the food, wondering if it was possible to sound more inane.

"I will pass on your compliments to the chef," Duke Francis replied. "Of course, once the year starts officially on the morrow, both you and Prince Darius will eat with the other trainees in the dining hall. But you may expect to find the food of a suitable quality even there."

"I look forward to meeting my fellow first years," I said.

A slight movement on the other side of the table drew my eyes. As soon as he felt my gaze, the prince stilled again, whatever emotion had caused him to stir already hidden. I looked back down at my plate but couldn't resist giving him subtle glances through my lashes. Was it my presence in his Academy as a first year that managed to elicit a response, or was it his own long-delayed enrollment that weighed on him?

I might be focused on the small differences, but most elements of the disciplines and Academies were the same between our two kingdoms. It made sense when our abilities were the same. And power stabilized in Kallorwegian mages at sixteen, just as it did in their Ardannian counterparts. They started at their Academy at the same age we did.

But the Kallorwegian crown prince was not sixteen. He had celebrated his eighteenth birthday over the summer. By rights I should be year mates not with Prince Darius but with his younger brother, Prince Jareth.

As if my thoughts had composed him into being, the door to the private dining room opened, and a young man stepped into the room. Everything from his features to his sandy hair proclaimed his relationship to the prince across from me, although the newcomer's lighter brown eyes gave his whole face a warmer look.

Inclining his head in a deep nod toward the head of the table where Duke Francis sat, the newcomer smiled.

"Please excuse my tardy arrival and accept my sincere apologies." His eyes fastened on me, and he gave a proper bow. "And especially to you, Princess Verene. I had hoped to be here to greet you on your arrival."

Darius gave him a look that was half disapproving, half long-suffering. "We expected you here hours ago, Jareth." He turned to me. "Your Highness, please allow me to introduce my younger brother, Prince Jareth."

I considered standing so I could curtsy properly, but that would only send everyone else at the table scrambling to their feet. Instead, I settled for inclining my upper body in his direction.

"You may consider your apologies accepted, Prince Jareth," I said. "I was just saying to the duke how much I look forward to meeting my year mates, and here you are."

The younger prince smiled and slipped into an empty seat beside his brother. A servant appeared and put a place setting down for him, a hot plate of food arriving a moment later. I eyed it curiously. Was the kitchen equipped with compositions to ensure guests at the duke's table were always supplied with hot food, regardless of how late they arrived?

"I have been no less consumed with curiosity to meet you, I must confess, Princess Verene," he said. "It has been many long years indeed since Kallorway hosted a foreign royal at our Academy."

I smiled at him. "It is a great honor to be starting with both Kallorwegian princes. I value the opportunity to get to know both you and your kingdom better."

I surreptitiously watched Darius out of the corner of my eye, wondering if my reference to all of us starting together would garner another reaction from him. But he had himself under better control now, or else I had misunderstood his reaction earlier. The Ardannian court might guess at the reasons why the crown prince of Kallorway was two years late starting at the Academy, but it looked like I wasn't going to have those theories confirmed or denied by the prince himself.

I suppressed a sigh.

"I confess to great curiosity about Ardann," Jareth said, starting enthusiastically on his food. "I hope you will share about some of the differences you see here."

"Most gladly." I started to feel a little more hopeful.

The reports that Jareth was more open than his brother appeared to be true. I had been sent to understand not only the future king but all those of his generation who would shape the Kallorwegian court of the future. Perhaps my opening would be through the younger prince.

The rest of us returned to our sweets, giving Jareth a chance to eat his meal. Raelynn began a conversation with the duke about the various classes that would be starting the next morning, and I knew I should take the opportunity to learn what I could. But I struggled to focus on their words, my attention instead taken by the two princes now sitting directly opposite me.

Darius leaned toward his brother, murmuring something in a voice too quiet for me to catch. Jareth looked at him, replying with what must have been a quip, a ready laugh in his eyes.

The crown prince shook his head, but a slow smile spread across his face, the first I had seen on him. He was intimidating when serious—even to me who had grown up among royalty— but he was striking when he smiled.

"You're hopeless, Jareth," he said softly, under the other conversations in the room. "I don't know why I put up with you."

"Because I'm a better-looking version of you?" Jareth

suggested. "I remind you of what you might one day hope to become."

I choked down a snort, and both princes looked in my direction. I quickly pretended intense interest in my plate. When I glanced back up at them, Jareth had returned to his meal, although a smile lingered on his face. Darius still watched me, however, his face shuttered, and his eyes once more dark.

The effect was even more intimidating after seeing him transformed with his brother, but I met his eyes, not backing down this time. I quirked an eyebrow upward, an unspoken challenge. Impossibly, his expression grew even more closed, and he returned his attention to his plate.

I sighed and glanced down the table at Layna who was deep in conversation with Captain Vincent, her brow furrowed but her pose open and engaged. At least one of us was making some progress.

When the meal at last concluded, a servant appeared to show me to my suite. Layna followed along, a single pace behind me, her presence reassuringly solid at my back.

"What did you think of Captain Vincent?" I asked, not turning to look at her. Layna had been my assigned shadow for long enough that we were used to these sorts of conversations.

"Not what I expected," she said. "But I feel better about having to leave you now that I've met him. I thought he was a little young for such a senior post, but apparently he only took up the position at the beginning of the summer. He was appointed directly by the king, and I suspect he was sent here in anticipation of the princes' arrival. The Academy is remote, and it would be easy to grow complacent at a post like this. And complacent guards are sloppy guards. But Captain Vincent is fresh from the capital and has spent the summer improving the state of the Academy Guard." Her voice turned sour. "I don't think I would have liked the old captain he replaced."

"It makes sense King Cassius would take the safety of his sons seriously. Especially since they're both here at the same time. Kallorway is less stable than Ardann, even after so many years." I paused. "I just hope he feels the same dedication toward protecting me."

Layna hesitated, and I felt guilty, knowing how much it pained her to leave me behind without her protection. When she did eventually speak, she sounded thoughtful.

"I sincerely hope his resolve on that matter will never be tested. But he sounded sincere when he spoke of his duty to his charges—all his charges. I believe he would consider it a dishonorable failure to allow harm to come to any member of the Academy—trainee or instructor."

The servant in front of us had stopped at a plain wooden door, so I didn't attempt to reply. The older woman dropped a simple curtsy.

"This is to be your suite, Your Highness," she said. "All the royals have suites on this corridor, along with the senior staff. The other students are higher up on the first year level."

I nodded and thanked her, although I was distracted by her words. When she said all the royals, did she just mean the two princes and me? What other royals were there?

She bobbed another curtsy and disappeared down the corridor. I watched her go, blinking in confusion. That was it? I needed more information on the Academy than that. I didn't even know how to get to the dining hall in the morning.

But it was too late to go chasing after her demanding a more thorough introduction, and I was exhausted after our journey. Pushing open the door to my suite, I took a single step into my new room before halting, my hand still on the door, my body blocking the opening.

I hadn't expected the Academy to provide as luxurious accommodations as a palace, but I had been expecting a suite assigned to royalty to contain basic, pleasant furnishings and some kind of simple decoration. What greeted me was utter mess and chaos.

Overturned furniture filled the floor space. Chair legs poked up in every direction, and my scattered belongings decorated the carpet. Something white and soft—at a glance it looked like feathers—had been thrown over everything, and words glimmered on the far wall in a sickening red.

I didn't take the time to absorb their meaning, spinning around and shutting the door sharply behind me. I tried to slow my racing heart, not letting any of my emotions show on my face.

"You know, on second thought, maybe it would be best for us to say our farewells here and now," I said to Layna. "The Academy officially begins in the morning for me, and you will no doubt be off early."

Layna narrowed her eyes, looking from me to the closed door. After a loaded pause, however, she nodded and bowed.

"If that is your desire, Your Highness. It has been an honor to serve you, and I would gladly resume the role on your return to Ardann."

I tried to pull my whirling thoughts into order, pushing away images of the room behind me so I could give her the farewell she deserved.

"You have shown yourself to be both loyal and skilled, Layna. I could not have asked for a better guard. I thank you, most sincerely, for your service."

She bowed again, and when she straightened, she had something in her hand. She held it out to me, and I saw it was a stack of parchments.

"I hope it will not be impudent of me to offer you a parting gift, Princess. I thought these might come in useful...given the circumstances."

I frowned, taking her offered gift slowly. My family had

already ensured I was supplied with a collection of compositions designed for my protection and safety, created by some of the strongest mages in Ardann. What did my personal guard feel I still lacked?

I glanced down at the first line of the top parchment, and something in me lightened. I looked back up at her.

"A locking composition?"

She grinned. "Not exactly. This is actually a working of my own design. I have been perfecting it for some time. A locking composition is valuable, but to be sure it is effective, it needs to be created with great power. And it would need to be refreshed every time it was challenged. Otherwise it could be circumvented with brute force. This is something a little...neater. If I may say so myself."

My brow crinkled, and I scanned the rest of the words.

"Oh. I see." I looked up at her. "This working has all the subtlety of a senior mage, Layna." And I didn't just mean in the complexity of the composition itself. The idea behind it demonstrated a clever mind—the kind that was likely to succeed in the hierarchical world of the mages. Perhaps when I returned to Ardann I would find Layna had already been promoted to a more senior position.

She smiled, clearly pleased at my words. "I knew you wouldn't be able to create or refresh any protections for your room yourself, so I wanted something that could last you the whole year. I've created a whole stack of them, so it should be more than enough. The beauty of this composition is that it doesn't require a lot of power, so I was able to make a plentiful supply."

"No, but it clearly requires control," I said. "It is a most generous gift, and I thank you."

The natural strength of a powerful mage was required not just to complete workings of significant power, but also to build greater complexity into their compositions. Mages didn't study compositions until the Academy, so I didn't understand the specifics of how it was done, but the stronger and more skilled a mage, the more complicated they could make their compositions and the fewer words they needed to use in doing so.

"I will admit there are a few other surprises built in that I didn't write out," Layna said, the pride in her voice making it clear she couldn't resist the small boast. "But the main purpose is there for you to read. The composition won't prevent access to your room, but it will alert you to an unauthorized entry and mark anyone who enters without your express permission. If you want someone to have ongoing access without your presence, you'll need to place your hand on the protected door along with theirs and speak their name."

I nodded. "Thank you. That inclusion will make it much easier to get my rooms cleaned."

"The most important thing," Layna said, "is that even the most inexperienced trainee here will be able to sense that your room is protected by a working. If they are a fool, they will blunder in anyway, and their identity will then be revealed. If they are not a fool, they will first use compositions of their own to attempt to decipher the nature of the power coating your door. I have specifically crafted this working to defy such attempts. Circumventing it would be far beyond the capacity of any trainee."

"This is incredibly thoughtful of you," I said, my voice soft. "I don't quite know what to say."

"Your thanks is already enough," she said. "In truth I greatly enjoyed the challenge of creating such a working. And who knows when it will come in handy in the future? If it proves of value to you, I may perhaps put it forward to my own general for broader use within our discipline."

"An excellent idea," I said. "I'll be sure to report back to you on the matter." I liked to think that her efforts might prove of benefit to her and increase her standing within her discipline.

She bowed a final time. "I wish you all the best during your first year, Princess," she said.

"And all the best to you," I replied.

I watched her disappear down the hallway, off to join the rest of my guards, I assumed. When she reached the central stairway and disappeared from view, I let out a long sigh and turned back to the mess behind me.

CHAPTER 5

I let myself into the room and closed the door. Pausing to rip one of Layna's compositions, I flicked my fingers toward the wood. Only when the comforting feeling of power enveloped the doorway did I turn to survey the room itself.

Now that I had time to focus, I read the words on the far wall.

Welcome to Kallorway, Princess.

The words themselves were inoffensive, but somehow they made the whole message more threatening. I forced my brain to consider the scene logically, however. My earlier assessment, made in a moment, had been right about the feathers. Soft, fluffy down covered everything. But my reaction to the red of the letters had been instinct rather than reasoning. They were written in bright red paint, not the dark reddish-brown of dried blood.

I rubbed at my temples and tried to decide what to do next. Telling Layna had been out of the question. She would be duty-bound to report the incident back to my family, and I didn't know what trouble that might cause. I might feel alone here, but I remained determined not to fail at the task my aunt had entrusted to me.

Ever since my family got the first indication of my lack of power, they had ringed me around in a protective presence. I appreciated their love, but their concern only increased my feelings of uselessness. And now my aunt had found a way I could serve our family, the crown, and all of Ardann. A purpose that was open to me precisely because of my lack of power. I didn't mean to throw the opportunity away before I had even begun.

And letting my parents know about the *welcome* I had received in Kallorway risked doing just that. Because my aunt might have sent me here for the good of Ardann—it was the only reason she did anything—but my parents had sent me here out of love for me.

In Ardann, among the mageborn, only failures, criminals, and traitors were sealed. With only a very few, unique exceptions, no sealed mages were accepted in society or among the court. By cooperating with the sealing ceremony, they won physical freedom, but that didn't grant them a position among us. But in Kallorway it was different. In Kallorway, no one dared openly shun sealed mages—not when King Cassius himself was sealed.

That had been the price of peace with Ardann twenty-one years ago. Cassius had been permitted his throne only under condition that he seal himself. And in exchange for accepting his rule, the rebel leader who had overthrown him, General Haddon, had been given the right to choose which mages would be sealed alongside him. The fractured Kallorwegian court remained littered with sealed mages.

And so my parents hoped the children of those sealed mages might hold a different view of my powerless state from my peers in Ardann. I had suspected from the beginning that my being both royal and Ardannian would outweigh any such influence, and it appeared I was right. But I couldn't let my parents find that out. Not yet, when I hadn't had a chance to prove I could be of value after all.

Which meant I needed to deal with this problem myself, and I needed to do it quietly. Stooping to pick up a crumpled gown from the floor, I held it up and examined it critically. Feathers clung to its length, but as I picked them off, I noted no actual damage had been done to the garment.

And with every chair that I righted and dress that I gathered, I found the same thing. Even the tapestry on the left wall—which would not be nearly as easy to wash as the stones—had been left untouched. It appeared I wasn't the only one interested in keeping this welcoming gesture from gaining too much attention.

I could not complain to the Academy Head that anything had been damaged, nor claim any reparation for lost possessions. It seemed my enemies were as cautious about this new situation as I was. Perhaps this was a test, meant to see how I would react.

I paused, a dress dangling from my hand as I considered this option. If it was a test, what message did I want to send?

Slowly I gathered the last of my belongings, picking the feathers off them and piling them on a soft sofa upholstered in pale green. Putting my hands on my hips, I looked at the room through critical eyes. I couldn't guarantee the furniture was all back where it had started, but it was arranged sensibly enough. The receiving room held two pale green sofas, four chairs, two side tables, and a writing desk which I had placed against one wall near the curtained window. When clean and tidy, it would be a lovely room for entertaining guests—if I ever had any guests to invite.

Leaving my things in the haphazard pile, I explored the room through the door on the right wall. It opened into a spacious bedroom, the same pale green theme carrying through with hints of gold. A smaller bag sat intact on the four-poster bed. I didn't need to examine its contents to know it held the few items I considered truly precious—most notable among them my small personal book collection. Even here among my unknown enemies, words were valued too highly to be cast carelessly about.

My visitors had kept their presence to my sitting room, it appeared, since nothing in my bedchamber looked out of order. A pile of parchment on a side table by the bed drew my eye, and I hurried over to examine it.

Relief filled me at the simple, familiar words. No doubt these basic compositions would be replenished, as they were in the palace at home. I tore one without hesitation, imagining I could hear the distant tinkling of a bell, although the servants' quarters were no doubt too far away for that to be true.

I crossed back through to my sitting room to await the servant's arrival, rehearsing my planned words in my mind. Soon enough a sturdy knock sounded at the door, and I opened it to find the same woman who had shown me here from the duke's dining room.

She dropped into a curtsy.

"You wanted me, Your High…" Her eyes widened, her words trailing away as she took in the sight of the remaining mess. She gulped. "It didn't look like this when I was in here earlier, Your Highness, I assure you!"

She turned nervous eyes on me, and I forced myself to laugh.

"I'm sure it did not! But as you can see some of my fellow trainees wished to leave me a welcome. It was most diverting of them, but I'm afraid they haven't given much thought to the mess they've left behind."

"N…no, Your Highness," the woman stammered, her eyes lingering on the words inscribed on my wall. Her shock seemed genuine and reassured me that her earlier hasty exit hadn't been on account of the surprise awaiting me.

It occurred to me suddenly that I might have made a mistake in allowing her access to a room where such visible writing was displayed. I examined her wrist but could see no sign of any markings there. I was about to hurry her back out the door when she moved her head to examine my piled belongings, her hair flicking backward to reveal part of her neck.

I paused, my eyes held involuntarily by the complicated markings that ringed her neck. I swallowed, telling myself it resembled a necklace more than a collar.

"You're sealed, I presume?" I asked, my words coming out more tentatively than I had intended.

Her eyes flew back to me. "Yes, Your Highness. Else I wouldn't have been given the task of caring for your room." Her shoulders straightened, and her look grew proud. "Only the sealed may serve in the rooms of royalty. How else would we refresh your supply of bell compositions?"

"Of course. Then it shouldn't be a problem for you to clean my wall. And I'm afraid my wardrobe has suffered badly from the journey. Everything will need to be cleaned and pressed."

I kept my tone even, neither overly friendly nor harshly demanding. I didn't want to earn a poor reputation among the servants, especially not with one specifically assigned to my care. But neither did I want word to pass around the Academy that the foreign princess was weak and disrespectful of her station. It was a balancing act I was well used to walking.

"Yes, of course, Your Highness. At once, Your Highness." The woman dropped into yet another curtsy, and I had to refrain from rubbing my now-pounding head. I was finished with formalities for the day and more than ready for my bed.

"I intend to retire to my bedchamber," I said. "You may feel free to come and go as you need. At least until that wall has been cleaned." I let a note of humor enter my voice. "It seems your mages are more careless in Kallorway than they are back home."

"I...I couldn't say, Your Highness," the woman said, clearly thrown off balance and uncertain what response was safest.

But my words hadn't been for her. I had no doubt that every

aspect of this interaction would get back to my unknown adversaries. My words were for them.

"I'll be back with cleaning supplies," the woman promised, backing out of the room.

"Wait," I called after her, and she froze. "If you're to be in charge of my room, then you'll need permission to access it when I'm not here to let you in. What's your name?"

"Ida," she said warily.

I directed her to place her hand on my door and did the same myself, speaking her name clearly. The power surrounding the door rippled slightly.

"Now you can enter freely," I told her. "But you'd better warn the rest of the servants not to try."

She nodded, and this time I let her hurry away. Hopefully she would only help spread the word that my rooms were now protected.

Retrieving a crumpled nightgown, I retreated to my bedchamber. As I sank into the comfortable bed, my mind was left to dwell on one important fact.

Someone had written words on my wall.

It was highly unlikely that a servant would have dared such a stunt with my room. The most obvious culprit was another trainee—or perhaps a group of them. None of whom were sealed. Which meant it didn't matter what medium was used. Writing always released power. My chilling welcome message had been a composition. And there had been no sign of the binding words usually used at the start of a composition to contain the power until all the necessary words were completed. Such an unbound, short composition was dangerous, requiring skill and strength. And this one had no obvious purpose for the power released.

So two burning questions remained. Could it have been done by a trainee—or was someone far more powerful letting me know I wasn't welcome here? And how had the unknown writer directed the power the words unleashed?

I could come up with no satisfactory answers before my exhaustion overwhelmed me.

～

I woke the next morning with startling clarity. Leaping from my bed, I raced out to my sitting room, the bell that had woken me still tolling. Throwing open the green curtains, I let bright sunlight spill into the room.

No sign of the message remained, although one section of the wall gleamed compared to the surrounding areas. The feathers had likewise disappeared, along with most of my clothing. But a small selection of clean, neat garments had been draped over the back of one of the sofas.

I hurried into a practical gown, pulling my white robe over the top. It didn't take me long to make myself presentable, my only hesitation coming when I looked at the golden circlet on the table beside my bed. In Ardann I wouldn't have dreamed of wearing it at the Academy. I was supposed to be a trainee before I was a princess. But here?

I pictured Prince Darius from the night before. His sandy hair had been unadorned, and his white robe as plain as mine. So the same tradition must exist here, despite the increased formality of their Academy. I secured my dark hair in a loose plait, letting it hang down my back, and hurried out of my suite.

Duke Francis had said the trainees ate meals in a dining hall, and I wanted to make sure I was out of my room quickly enough to catch one of the other trainees heading for the meal. After my discovery the night before, I was determined not to be found wandering around lost on my first day.

I paused outside my room, glancing up and down the empty corridor. But I didn't have long to wait, the sound of an opening door making me sigh with relief.

I had been prepared to greet one of the princes, but a young woman in a white robe emerged, catching me by surprise. I had a brief moment to examine her, the girl too busy closing her door to notice me.

She was tall, a contrast to my own diminutive height, and she carried it well, moving with an elegant, predatory grace. Her golden hair had been braided and wound into a practical bun on her head, and when she finally turned in my direction, I was confronted with sharp, green eyes.

Some would no doubt call her beautiful, although the overwhelming impression I received was one of practicality and determination. This girl didn't look the type to let anything or anyone stand in her way.

She faltered for the briefest moment, her eyes taking me in as quickly as I had just assessed her. Her brows rose up the tiniest fraction before she gave me the most shallow of half-bows.

"Princess Verene, I presume. I heard you arrived yesterday afternoon. Welcome to Kallorway."

I regarded her through narrowed eyes, her final words making me pause. But I gave myself an internal shake. It was a phrase I would no doubt hear again many times. My unknown harasser had chosen their wording well, and I did not intend to give them the satisfaction of throwing me off balance.

"Thank you." I inclined my head in her direction. "But I'm afraid I don't have the pleasure of knowing your name in return. I was told last night that this hall was reserved for royal suites, but I was unaware Kallorway had a princess."

The faintest flush colored the girl's cheeks at my words, which had been delivered in my most innocent tone.

"I'm Dellion," she said. "Niece of Queen Endellion and grand-daughter of General Haddon."

"It's a pleasure to meet you, Dellion."

So she belonged to the second power faction in Kallorway. General Haddon might have once led a rebellion, and half the kingdom might still look to him as their true leader, but officially he had always been nothing more than Head of the Royal Guard. His family's only claim to royalty came from his having forced Cassius into a political marriage with his daughter immediately after the young king's coronation.

It meant Dellion, only niece to the queen, had no true claim to royal status. Did her lack of a title embarrass or anger her? From her uncomfortable expression, she was aware it was a stretch for her to claim a suite on this hall. Although the sour note that lingered behind the discomfort on her face told me she thought she belonged here. Did she resent a true princess enrolling in her year? Enough to leave an unwelcome message in my room?

I straightened my spine. Regardless of whether or not she had been involved in the incident in my rooms, I didn't intend to back down before her. Like it or not, she was no princess—a title claimed by birth or marriage—and certainly no duchess or general—a title won only by ascending to head of a discipline. She wouldn't even officially earn the general honorific of Lady until she graduated from the Academy and became a full mage.

I gave her my best court smile even as I reminded myself not to underestimate Dellion. Her grandfather had been Head of the Kallorwegian Royal Guard for longer than I had been alive, with the seat on the Mage Council that position afforded him. And he had held that position for all those years in opposition to the king he was supposed to be dedicated to protecting. He had been the one to negotiate with Ardann for peace, a king-slayer who managed to hold his post despite perpetrating the greatest treason a royal guard could commit. Only the strongest and canniest of players could have held onto power as General Haddon had managed to do. How much it must gall King Cassius not to be able to trust the head of his own guard.

Dellion, clearly named for her royal aunt, was the oldest child of Queen Endellion's younger sister. Was her placement on this hall a sign of the power wielded by the old general through his daughter, the queen? Or was the honor only because she happened to be attending the Academy at the same time as her two royal cousins?

Another door opened, breaking what seemed about to become an uncomfortable silence. But again, it wasn't either of the princes who appeared. The young man who joined us in the hallway carried himself with an arrogant air, his face seeming set in lines of faint displeasure. He nodded curtly at Dellion and then regarded me with a long, calculating look.

After a noticeable pause he gave me a full bow.

"Your Highness. Such an honor." His tone made a mockery of the words, although there was nothing overt for me to take exception to.

Once again I was reminded strongly of the message left in my room. But clearly there was no love lost between these two, and I couldn't imagine them conspiring together to sneak into my room while I sat at the evening meal. They couldn't both be responsible.

"And you are?" I asked, letting my voice remain cool and unimpressed. "I'm afraid I find myself woefully ill-informed. It seems the definition of royal is held much more loosely in Kallorway than it is in Ardann."

The boy's eyes narrowed, but he swallowed whatever retort he clearly wanted to make.

"I'm Royce. My father is cousin to the king."

"Ah yes." I let the faintest hint of amusement tinge my voice. "King Cassius's cousin I have indeed heard of. We are year mates, then, I believe."

Was Cassius's cousin still his right-hand man, as he had been in their own days at the Academy? It might explain Royce's insolent, arrogant air, a somewhat surprising attitude given both his parents were among those sealed.

Royce glared at me, apparently bereft of words, but Dellion spoke, making no effort to hide the amusement on her face at Royce's discomfort.

49

"We are all year mates, along with Darius and Jareth. Is it not most delightfully arranged?"

I frowned slightly. Arranged? Was she merely referring to Darius's delayed start and my attendance? Or had our year been manipulated in some other way? I had been briefed on the state of Kallorwegian politics before coming, but I hadn't even made it to breakfast, and I was already aware of how many subtleties were missing from the reports of our diplomats and intelligencers.

"Enough of this," Royce growled. "It's too early in the morning for your jabbering, Dellion. Not without food inside me."

Dellion raised a single, elegant eyebrow.

"I believe it would take a great deal more than a single meal to improve you, Royce. But then I've always thought so."

He smirked at her. "At least I'm free to enjoy my meal. I hear you've been given babysitting duties." He sent a significant look in my direction before stalking away down the corridor.

I turned silently to Dellion. Babysitting? I wasn't going to dignify that comment by asking her about it aloud.

She glared at Royce's disappearing back before turning reluctantly to me.

"Duke Francis has requested that I guide you around the Academy for your first day. We should head to the dining hall for breakfast."

"Very well." I kept my voice neutral.

My aunt had sent me here because she wanted more information on people like Dellion and Royce. The opinions of their generation hadn't made it into the reports of our intelligencers, but in four years they would graduate alongside both of the Kallorwegian princes. My year mates were the future court of Kallorway, and I was here to find out where their loyalties lay.

So far, it appeared they followed the established lines of enmity set down by their parents, but it was much too early to draw any proper conclusions. For now, I needed to somehow maintain the dignity and authority of the kingdom I represented while also not accidentally alienating either side.

Dellion began walking down the hall, and I had to hurry to keep up with her long stride. When we reached the staircase, she descended, slowing enough for me to catch up.

Waving up the stairs, she said, "The other trainees are all housed up there. Each year has a level, plus there's a level for the junior instructors." It was clear from her dismissive tone that she anticipated no need to ever climb upward herself.

"The head's rooms are on the opposite side of the stairs to us. Trainees are rarely invited into that wing." She gave me a veiled look. "But perhaps it will be different for you."

Yes, she was certainly resentful of my rank. I would have to step carefully with her.

We passed the level below our suites but didn't stop.

"This level is the library and all the other instructors' offices," she said. "There's nothing on the ground floor but the dining hall and the classrooms."

"What of the kitchens and the servants' quarters?" I asked, although I already suspected I knew the answer.

She gave me a slightly incredulous look. "They aren't in the main building. They must be in one of the outbuildings, I suppose." She had clearly never given the matter any thought.

I sighed internally. It was amazing how many people forgot my mother was a commonborn, the daughter of two shopkeepers. When she was my age, she had known nothing but a life of illiteracy. Even her dreams of the future had been marred by the specter of conscription. Others might have forgotten her roots given what she had become, but she had made sure her children did not.

While many of the older mages in Ardann still thought as Dellion did, I was used to associating with those closer in age to myself. We had grown up surrounded by sealed commonborns, with a commonborn princess at the center of our court. In

Ardann, the lines were no longer so clear nor the hierarchy so rigid as it had once been. I only hoped Dellion wasn't representative of every mage in Kallorway. Given how many mages had been sealed after the war, they must have plenty of sealed commonborns among them.

We reached the bottom of the stairs and the large entranceway. The hubbub of many voices could now be heard, and I no longer needed Dellion's leading to find the double doors that opened into the huge dining hall.

Four long tables lined the room, and my eyes latched on to two sandy heads at the table furthest to the right. Royce was already seating himself beside the two princes, confirming my impression that the far table belonged to the first years.

My stomach, which had started to rumble on the way down the stairs, seized strangely at the sight of the tallest first year, his back ramrod straight and his eyes too dark to read. Why did Darius already look so familiar after only a single meal spent in his company?

He saw me but offered no sign of recognition or greeting, and I forced my eyes to move on, skimming the rest of the table. I didn't absorb the faces seated there until my gaze latched on to one that was truly familiar.

I gasped. "Bryony?"

CHAPTER 6

"*V*erene!" The petite, wiry girl tumbled from her seat and threw her arms around me. "I would have come and found you last night, but they told me you're not on the first year floor with the rest of us, and I haven't properly found my way around the inside of this awful old place yet."

She spoke with abandon, oblivious of any audience, almost vibrating with energy, just as she had always done. She had been raised far from any court, and I loved the lack of restraint it allowed her.

"Can't you just imagine me stumbling into Duke Francis's bedchamber? What a scandal." When she grinned impishly up at me, I felt like crying at the unexpected sight of such a friendly face.

"You're welcome to stumble into my bedchamber," said a boy sitting at the table behind us with a wink.

"Ugh, don't be disgusting, Wardell," said a girl sitting across from him. "As if anyone would want to stumble in there."

Wardell just laughed. "Would you rather go accidentally bumbling into Old Francis's lair, Ashlyn? At least I don't skin people alive."

The girl, Ashlyn apparently, rolled her eyes and turned to whisper to another girl beside her.

"Ignore him," Bryony told me, pulling me further down the table to a stretch of empty seating. "The duke may be stiff and rather rigid in his ways, but he has a reputation for being fair." She gave me a significant look. "And neutral. Father would never have sent me here otherwise. He says he sacrificed enough years of his life to the machinations of the court, and he has no interest in our family getting involved now."

"What *are* you doing here?" I asked. "I thought you were all still living in the Empire. No one said anything about you being here."

She grinned at me, bouncing in her seat. "It all happened quite at the last minute. Mother and Father had mentioned the idea a few times, in their usual vague way, and I thought it sounded interesting, but then the news finally filtered through to us that you were going to be here. As soon as I heard that, I insisted they send me, although there was barely time left for us to scramble down here before the start of the year. It's a good thing they're so desperate for energy mages that they were happy to accept me no matter how late I enrolled."

"I couldn't be more glad to see you," I said. "Truly."

"Mother and Father both brought me, and Father delighted in showing me all around the grounds, but they've already left. They were disappointed to miss you, though."

"I would have loved to see them," I said. "But I'm more than content to find even one familiar face."

There was no blood connection between Bryony and me, but strange twinings of unusual power connected her father, Declan, and my mother, and the two had always claimed a kinship. Although she had never lived at the Ardannian court, Bryony and I had been raised to regard each other as cousins, and it was impossible not to love the irrepressible Sekali girl.

Bryony's father, Declan, was an energy mage. He had once

54

been the only energy mage in the kingdoms, his existence a closely held secret, and even now few knew of his true status. When it had been revealed that my mother could use her power to access the energy of others, it had rocked the world of the mages. But it had been nothing to the rediscovery of energy mages.

Power mages—the only kind of mage our people had known existed for generations—could shape power to complete almost any task. But they could not use it to affect energy—not their own, nor that of others. It was their greatest limitation. They could not store up their own energy for later use nor pool energy to fuel more complex compositions. And a person whose energy was utterly depleted could not be healed.

But it turned out that many generations ago, power mages had lived alongside energy mages. This second type of mage also passed down their abilities through their bloodlines, and they claimed they had once held almost equal status with power mages. But while the cause of the change was lost to history, something had turned the power mages against them. They had banished their energy mage cousins, driving them into exile in the inhospitable Grayback Mountains.

Energy mages were like me—their access to power naturally sealed at birth—but unlike me, their energy was more than just fuel. They could write compositions that made direct use of it. The feats such compositions could perform were severely limited compared to the use of power, able only to complete tasks directly related to energy. And, on top of that, each energy mage had limited abilities, determined by their bloodline. But thankfully the most common ability was also the one most valued by power mages—the crucial capacity to give energy to others.

This one ability was most likely the reason they had been welcomed back down from the mountains when their existence was rediscovered. One such energy mage could allow a power mage to complete a composition twice as powerful as any that could be done in the past. It was a valuable ability and had won their whole people a place among the mages.

"I wasn't aware you know our resident energy mage," Dellion said from behind me.

I turned, having forgotten all about her in my excitement at seeing Bryony. She was watching the two of us with an expression I couldn't read.

"We're family," I said. "In a way. But I didn't realize she was going to be here."

"What a delightful surprise," Dellion drawled. "It looks like you won't have need of me, then."

She strolled away without waiting for any sort of acknowledgment, heading toward the obnoxious boy, Wardell, and his table companion.

"I hope you know your way around better than me," I said to Bryony. "Because I think I just lost my guide."

Bryony just laughed. "Good riddance, I say. Us foreigners can stick together."

I smiled back at her, but inside I felt less sanguine. Bryony had been welcomed as a foreigner because of her great value. I had been accepted because there was no politically acceptable way to refuse me. So far Dellion and Royce had combined to show me that the Kallorwegians didn't view me as an appealing addition to their year. And if my initial impressions were true, and they followed the political leanings of their parents, their attitudes didn't bode well for Kallorway's current or future interest in securing a closer relationship with Ardann.

I suppressed a sigh and reminded myself I had four years to work on them. For now I was just going to be grateful that Bryony was here. Thanks to my mother, the energy mages at least viewed me as a welcome connection, if not truly one of them.

My mother wasn't a true energy mage—she accessed energy through the use of power, not directly, the way an energy mage did—but her history was bound up with them. And while I might be a disappointment in terms of my ability, I had at least proven the unpredictability of my mother's bloodline, so no one was surprised to discover my younger brother, Stellan, was an energy mage despite our older brother being a power mage. I knew for a while my parents had hoped I might still turn out to be like him, but I had proven as unable to make direct use of my energy as I was unable to access power.

My siblings and I were all utterly unique. Lucien was a power mage, but one able to use both written and spoken compositions. I was an oddity, a born sealed mage, utterly useless. And Stellan was a spoken energy mage, as exceptional in his own way as my mother—and as unable to safely write as she was.

Stellan had a soft heart and would sometimes try to comfort me by reminding me that there was one thing, at least, I could do that he could not. The thought had never brought me much comfort, though. I would gladly give up my ability to write if I could live up to the vast expectation that my birth had shattered.

Servants quietly served a steaming hot meal, and both Bryony and I ate hungrily, fitting in our questions for each other around full mouthfuls.

"Are you the only energy mage in our year?" I asked. "I didn't expect there to be any."

She shook her head, pointing down the table to where a boy sat alone, his attention on his plate. I had never seen anyone so pale-skinned—even his hair was so pale blond it looked almost white. He made a stark contrast with Bryony's warm, golden skin and dark coloring, but she smiled at him fondly as if he were kin.

"That's Tyron. He's an energy mage as well."

He must have sensed our gazes, because he looked up and smiled, revealing green eyes, startling in their intensity and depth given his overall lack of coloring.

"Are you related?" I asked. "I don't remember you ever mentioning him."

"Oh, no, I only just met him when I arrived here," she said with unabated cheerfulness. "He's from the far east of the Empire."

When they were rediscovered and welcomed back, the energy mages had chosen to settle throughout the Sekali Empire. Over my lifetime, however, a few had gradually found their way south and settled at the Ardannian court in Corrin. They were drawn, I suspected, by the unique energy abilities of my mother and younger brother.

I didn't think many had made it to Kallorway, however, so I wasn't surprised to hear the only energy mages in our year came from the Empire. Bryony's father, however, had been born Kallorwegian and lived here for much of his life, although his abilities had remained secret, and even he had not known of the existence of energy mages. He had believed his family to be the only ones to possess their unique type of ability, and he was the last of his family's line.

According to my mother, he had rejoiced when she brought him the startling news of a full tribe of energy mages in the mountains—the Tarxi, as they called themselves then. As soon as he heard they were settled in the Empire, he had eagerly traveled north to meet his long-lost brethren.

Welcomed as one of them by the first few he met, he had fallen in love with a Tarxi and started a family in his later years. His ability remained a secret from most, however—too powerful to be safely revealed after he discovered he truly was unique. Which meant few knew that Bryony had inherited it. Thankfully she didn't need to reveal her father's status to claim a place at a mage's Academy.

Her mother's more common energy mage blood was enough to ensure her a place in any mage training facility. But it must be her connection with her father that had brought her here to Kallorway. Her mother was Sekali in ancient heritage as well as current residence—the source of Bryony's black hair and golden skin—but her Kallorwegian father had spent many years of his life as a groundskeeper of sorts here at the Academy. I didn't know why it had never occurred to me that he might wish to send one or more of his children here to experience this piece of his history.

"What's Tyron's ability?" I asked, watching him curiously out of the side of my eye.

Despite my family's strange status, I hadn't met a great many energy mages. They were too few in number and too far-flung in residence.

"He can give energy." She winked at me. "Like me."

I gave her a small smile, neither of us acknowledging aloud that her abilities were a little more unique than that. She had inherited from both her mother and her father, something that should have been impossible. But perhaps it was another facet of her father's unique lineage.

Another bell sounded, followed immediately by the scraping of many chair legs and the increased sound of voices.

"Now would be a good time for that missing guide." I looked around, hoping Dellion might reappear.

I spotted her as she left the dining hall in company with Jareth and sighed. Clearly she had washed her hands of her responsibility toward me.

Bryony stood, looking unperturbed. "We start the morning with combat classes outside, so I can get us there, at least. It's inside where I still get turned around."

We hurried after the flow of white robes, all moving out into the entranceway and down the steps into the Academy grounds. Despite our two kingdoms no longer being at war, I knew combat classes were also still part of training at the Ardannian Academy. Lucien loved them and often reported back on his various bouts. But my parents claimed the classes were reduced in scope from what they had been in their day, when every mage was required to spend two years at the front lines directly after graduation. I supposed the same was likely true here in Kallorway.

Large squares of dirt next to the Academy gardens had been sectioned off into training yards, delineated from the rest of the grounds by short fences that were easily stepped over. Several of them were filled with white robes, but I recognized enough of the first year faces now that it was easy to pick out the one assigned to us.

A dour-faced man waited for us, his face vaguely familiar from my arrival the day before. He introduced himself as Instructor Mitchell, addressing his comments to the whole group. He didn't ask for any of our names, although he did bow twice, once toward where Darius and Jareth stood together and once toward me.

"We will begin with basic exercises to assess your differing capabilities," he said. "If you didn't bring a weapon with you to class, you may collect one from over there." He pointed to where a row of swords lay on a length of leather near one of the fences.

I frowned. It hadn't occurred to me to bring a sword to class on the first day. In Ardann basic exercises meant hand-to-hand sparring that then graduated up to wooden poles and only to bladed weapons once everyone was at a sufficient standard. Apparently in Kallorway, trainees were expected to arrive already experienced in swordplay.

Royce saw my expression and smirked at me, exaggerating his movements as he drew the elegant weapon at his hip. I turned my back on him and hurried over to the laid-out swords. I grimaced when I got a good look at them. They were serviceable but not of high quality.

Glancing over my shoulder, I saw that all the Kallorwegians bar one had come with their own weapons. I should have noticed they all had sword belts buckled over their robes.

Bryony and Tyron had both joined me, however, along with a short boy with brown skin and a focused expression. Wardell, the boy who had so disgusted Ashlyn at breakfast, murmured what sounded like an encouragement to the other boy as he moved toward the fence. From their features, they looked as if they could be related, although everything in this boy's manner suggested he was as serious as Wardell seemed flippant.

"You didn't bring a sword either?" Bryony asked him brightly, earning a startled expression. "Never mind. I'm Bryony, by the way."

The boy looked cautiously from her to me before answering. "I'm Armand."

"Are you related to Wardell?" Bryony asked, apparently having noticed the same similarities as I had.

The boy hesitated again before nodding. "We're cousins."

He snatched a weapon from the ground, rushing back to the others before anyone could make any further attempts to engage him in conversation.

"A friendly lot, these Kallorwegians," Tyron said with a wry grin. He bowed in my direction. "I'm Tyron, Your Highness. I imagine Bryony has already told you about me. She's friendly enough to make up for all the rest of them."

Bryony grinned unrepentantly while I chuckled.

"That's always been her way. It's a pleasure to meet you, Tyron of the Sekali."

"And you, Princess." He leaned over and chose his weapon, taking more care in his selection than Armand had done.

I wished I had arrived a few days early as it seemed most of my year had done. It would have been helpful to get the chance to explore the Academy and get to know my year mates before classes started. But commitments had kept me in Corrin until the last possible moment, and I hadn't wanted to press for an earlier departure when I knew how reluctant my parents were to see me go so far away.

I forced myself to turn my focus to the weapon options available, choosing the one that looked best balanced. It didn't fit my hand particularly well and was a little longer than I would have preferred, but it would do well enough for a training day.

Instructor Mitchell called for us to pair up, and I hadn't even had the chance to move when Royce appeared in front of me. He gave a mocking bow.

"Would you do me the honor, Your Highness?"

CHAPTER 7

I had intended to partner with Bryony, but I could see both Darius and Jareth watching me, the younger prince's expression openly curious, while his older brother remained guarded. I sighed. I might as well get this over with sooner rather than later.

"Certainly," I replied, keeping my voice light.

"You may free bout while I move among you and assess your capabilities," Instructor Mitchell said. "But I would remind you that this is merely a training exercise. We don't need any injuries on our first day."

He sounded bored by the whole process, and I suppressed an urge to shake him. He showed none of the care an instructor should have for a group of new trainees of unknown and differing skill levels.

I only had time for a single concerned look at Bryony, however, before swinging my sword into guard position.

As soon as my blade was up, Royce called a start to the bout and went on the attack. I skipped back, neatly parrying his lunge while leaving him room to attack again.

My lack of counterattack invigorated him, and he pushed

forward even harder. I let him attack and then attack again. He ignored the instructor's direction to moderate himself, weighting his attacks with full force, and striking for vulnerable points.

His forward momentum drove me halfway across the yard until my back was nearly at the fence. Once I was confident I had his measure, however, I lunged forward in a swift strike.

Buoyed by his earlier assumptions and my initial passive response, Royce was entirely unprepared for my move. My blade danced along his, twisting his weapon neatly aside. As soon as the tip of my sword hit his neck, I paused, not so much as scratching him, my control perfect.

"Yield?" I asked, not even out of breath.

His eyes bulged, but he gasped out, "Yield," and I lowered my weapon.

I stepped back with a friendly smile, letting none of my anger show. I couldn't afford to antagonize him, despite the provocation. He was reasonably skilled with a sword but had demonstrated none of the precise control I had done. If I had been unable to defend his blows, he would not have had the ability to stop without harming me as I had done for him.

"Thank you," I said, tinging my voice with unnatural sweetness, "for taking Instructor Mitchell's words to heart. It has been several days since I have had the opportunity for a true *practice*."

Royce stared at me, a single bead of sweat running down the side of his face.

"I apologize for my cousin's enthusiasm," said a new voice at our side.

I turned to see Darius regarding Royce with an expression that filled my veins with ice. My opponent's face whitened.

"We, too, have had to travel to the Academy," the prince continued, "and have been some days without serious practice. It is easy to get carried away." Nothing in his voice or manner suggested he had ever been carried away by anything in his life.

"I have no need for your apology, Prince Darius," I said lightly. "We are all friends here, are we not?"

He turned, the same controlled danger of his expression showing in every line of his body. He regarded me for a long moment.

"Indeed, Princess Verene. And it would be well for us all to remember that Kallorway and Ardann are not so very different."

His dark gaze turned back to Royce, who was no doubt heartily regretting his foolish assumption that a royal of Ardann might be sent to the Academy without adequate training in combat.

Royce bowed, more deeply than he had ever done before, and mumbled something that might have been an apology before hurrying away. Darius watched him go and then returned to his brother's side, ignoring the fact that every bout around us had stopped, and the other trainees were all watching him warily.

All except one.

Bryony sidled up to me. "Hee!" she whispered in my ear. "That was fun to watch. I wouldn't be Royce right now for anything."

I let myself relax, grinning at her. "Would you ever want to be Royce?"

She rolled her eyes. "Of course not. Now pair with me for the rest of the lesson. Just promise you won't cut me to ribbons."

I laughed. "You can't fool me. You're forgetting we fought every day the last time you came to Corrin. You're a better fighter than your mother. I'm the one who should be worried about being carved up."

She winked at me. "I promise to go easy, then. I'm sure I would die of fright if the crown prince ever looked at me like he just looked at Royce."

I shook my head as I took up my position across from her. "I'm not sure anything frightens you, Bree. And sometimes that frightens me. There are some things we should all be afraid of."

And I was starting to wonder if the crown prince of

Kallorway was one of them. Because while I would rather die than show it, I never wanted Prince Darius to look at me like that, either.

~

I managed to find my way back to my suite to wash before lunch without a guide. Bryony accompanied me, claiming she wanted to see how royalty lived. I was relieved to feel the power still cloaking my door, although Bryony made no comment on it. Of course, as an energy mage, she was unable to sense power at all, although she could instead sense the energy in every person.

Sensing energy was a great advantage in tracking and warfare, but I preferred my own ability to feel power. It was the only characteristic I shared with power mages, and it allowed me to feel in some small part like I belonged in their world.

I had her place her hand on the door and spoke her name, giving her access to my rooms. No doubt she would barge in on me at some point, and I'd prefer she not trigger my defenses when she did.

Inside the suite, she poked around while I cleaned up and changed my clothes. My assigned servant had clearly been back because my wardrobe was now full of clean and pressed garments.

"Well, what do you think?" I asked Bryony, when I re-emerged into the sitting room.

"It's more utilitarian than I expected," she admitted. "Not so different from my accommodation, except that I only have one large room. I guess I shouldn't be surprised given how long Duke Francis has been in charge. He doesn't seem the type for excessive luxuries."

"I suppose your father knew him when he worked here back during the war years," I said.

She nodded. "Father says the duke hasn't changed at all since he first arrived. He just gets a little grayer every year."

"The Kallorwegian court has seen plenty of upheaval in the decades he's run this Academy," I said. "It's fortunate for the kingdom he's managed to keep their training ground outside of the conflict."

Bryony yawned. "Now you sound like my father. Leave the lecturing to our instructors, if you please. My stomach is rumbling, and I don't want to miss lunch."

As if on cue, another bell sounded, and she pushed me forcibly from the room, although I noticed she dropped the contact as soon as we were in the public space of the corridor. It still brought a smile to my face, though. I hadn't realized how much I was dreading four years of being treated by everyone I saw with either cold formality or thinly veiled malice.

There was no sign of Royce at the meal. Either he was hiding after his humiliation, or he knew well enough to stay away from Darius for a while after the public rebuke. Either way, I couldn't regret his absence.

Tyron sat with us, his manner just as open and friendly as it had been in the training yard. Bryony had told me she paired with him for her first bout and ruled him competent with his borrowed sword, if uninspired. It was a very Bryony sort of description, and I rather dreaded how she might describe my swordplay if ever asked.

Tyron certainly seemed unflustered at being surrounded by strangers in an unfamiliar environment, and I welcomed his presence with us. Perhaps I would end up with more than one friend, after all.

We were served soup and roast meat with platters of vegetables and large fluffy rolls, the food just as good as the duke had promised. They were less complex dishes than we had been served the night before, but I found the simpler fare more satisfying after the exertions of the morning.

While I ate, I took the opportunity to more closely examine the rest of my year mates. Dellion, who had made no further effort to complete her assigned duties as guide, now sat with another tall girl, the two speaking little. I had yet to meet the second girl, but her manner gave no indication of where her loyalties might lie. She looked neither pleased nor displeased to be in company with the queen's niece.

At the other end of the table, I was surprised to see that Darius and Jareth sat with Wardell and Armand. Jareth chatted with the two cousins, leaving his brother free to make only the occasional contribution to the conversation.

Tyron grinned when he saw me watching the group. "Don't worry. Their Highnesses will make their way around to us eventually."

I frowned at him. "What do you mean?"

"Prince Jareth has only just arrived, but Prince Darius has been here for a couple of days already, and he distributes his royal attention equally among his year mates."

Bryony nodded. "Just watch. At the evening meal they'll sit with Frida and Ashlyn. I suppose it will be our turn tomorrow morning."

I raised an eyebrow. "That sounds very…methodical."

"I'm told the Kallorwegian court requires a careful hand," Tyron said.

I took another mouthful, chewing slowly. It fit with what I already knew of Darius—which was very little, precisely because of this sort of behavior. Reportedly, he maintained a careful balance of neutrality between the factions of his father and his mother, making it almost impossible to guess his true allegiances or intentions, let alone his feelings toward Ardann. I should be glad of it, though. It was the reason my aunt had suddenly found me so useful.

I glanced from Darius and Jareth to my table companions. Two energy mages from the Sekali Empire and a princess of

Ardann. How did we fit into the careful dance of the Kallorwegian princes? Did they resent our presence for complicating their
already difficult lives?

If they did, it would make my own task even more difficult. I
sighed softly and took another mouthful. First I needed to
survive my first day. The rest would have to come later.

Yet another bell drove us from our meals back into the
corridors. We shadowed the two girls Bryony had named as
Frida and Ashlyn, hoping they would lead us to our next class.
Their heads remained bent close together, their words too quiet
for us to hear, though we walked close behind. From the
contemptuous glances Ashlyn kept throwing at Wardell and
Armand ahead of them, I wondered if the cousins were the
topic of the whispered conversation. The girls certainly knew
each other as well as the two boys. And all four of them seemed
uninterested in the foreigners in their midst, despite my royal
status.

At least the Kallorwegians seemed to know where they were
going, leading us across the entranceway and down a wide
corridor on the opposite side. Doors lined it, and I remembered
Dellion had told me the ground level contained only the dining
hall and classrooms. We must be going in the right direction,
then.

Armand stopped at one of the doors, holding it open for his
cousin, but letting it swing shut in the face of Frida. Clearly
whatever faction these two pairs hailed from, they were on
opposing sides. I was fairly certain now that one of the boys was
the nephew of the Head of the Creators—who aligned himself on
the Mage Council with General Haddon—and one of the girls
was the daughter of the Head of the Wind Workers—who usually
voted with the king.

Frida rolled her eyes at her companion before opening the
door for herself, holding it open for her friend to precede her.
When she saw us close behind, she hesitated, glancing first at

69

something inside the room and then at me. With a slightly pained smile, she held the door wide, allowing all three of us to enter.

"Thank you," I said, and she nodded before scampering off to take a seat at a double desk with Ashlyn.

It wasn't just Royce and Dellion, then. The rest of our year appeared equally loath to associate with me, although apparently they weren't willing to publicly offend me, either. Or perhaps Frida was afraid of following in Royce's footsteps and receiving a reprimand from Darius.

The room behind the door held six double desks, exactly the number needed for our small year, which surprised me. With so few of us, I had expected to see a large number of empty seats. The front row of three desks were already taken, and I would have slid into the closest seat to the door, except that Bryony strode further into the room, taking the closer seat on the middle table instead.

I followed behind, raising a single eyebrow at her as I took the further seat at the same desk, placing me across an aisle from Darius and Jareth. Bryony just gave me a smug grin.

Wardell and Armand had taken the seats in front of the princes, while Frida and Ashlyn had taken the ones at the other end of the row. Between them, and in front of us, sat Dellion and the girl she had joined at lunch. But since they were both sitting straight, their attention trained on the front of the room, I got the impression they were together more out of a mutual desire to avoid Royce than any friendship.

Unfortunately that left Tyron to sit across the aisle from Bryony with a spare seat beside him. And, sure enough, a moment later the door opened again, and our missing year mate appeared, slipping into the seat beside Tyron.

Bryony flashed the other energy mage a sympathetic glance only to look quickly forward when the man at the front of the room cleared his throat loudly. When he saw he had all of our attention, he smiled broadly, clapping his hands together in enthusiasm.

"Ah, I see we are all here. Welcome, welcome to your first day at the Academy. I always love the first day." He beamed around at us all, but only Bryony beamed back. Everyone else looked somewhere between bemused and unresponsive. Feeling sorry for the effusive instructor, I smiled and received a broad grin in response.

"And, of course, a special welcome goes to the royal guest in our midst." He bowed in my direction. "Welcome to Kallorway, Princess Verene."

My smile fell away instantly, replaced with a chill that crept up my spine. For the second time that day, I reminded myself they were common enough words, likely to be repeated by anyone. But my earlier ease had disappeared, my spine straightening and my muscles tightening at the lingering thought that it had taken someone of skill to compose on my sitting room wall. And who would be better at composing than the Academy composition instructor?

"I am Instructor Alvin," he continued, appearing not to notice my change of manner, "and I will be your composition instructor during your studies at the Academy. Of course I must spread my time across the year levels, but I always like to spend the first day with the first years."

He actually rubbed his hands together, his smile growing even broader. "And this year is one of especial interest as we have two energy mages among us. Welcome Bryony and Tyron. I am most excited to delve more deeply into your abilities as well as to see the beneficial effect your presence will have on the compositions of your fellow trainees. I predict this year will surpass our usual expectations by great margins."

Everyone in the front row twisted to look back at our desk and the one next to us. I could almost see the calculation in their eyes as they reconsidered their earlier attitudes toward Bryony

71

and Tyron. The two trainees from the Empire might be outsiders, but they were valuable outsiders.

Darius, however, didn't even glance our way. No doubt he had long since considered every possible ramification of both their presence and mine.

Instructor Alvin launched into a lecture on the basic theory behind written compositions, and I let my mind wander. Not only was the information irrelevant to me, but my parents had already covered it in their wide-ranging efforts to test me since my birthday. I was interested to see my year mates actually composing, but apparently we weren't to advance to such levels on the first day.

Against my will, my eyes were drawn constantly to my left where Darius sat such a short distance away. If I was bored after the lessons my parents had given me, I could only imagine how uninteresting he found the lecture. He had turned sixteen more than two years ago and must have received extensive private tutoring, despite the official stance against such activities. All mages were supposed to receive their education at the Academy, but royals were well-known not to follow that stricture.

But as I had already come to expect, I could read nothing on his face. And his eyes never strayed sideways to me. He had rebuked Royce on my behalf, but there was no indication to suggest it had been because of any great interest in me or Ardann. Wishing to avoid a diplomatic incident was one thing, but it was a long way from wanting to open up or forge a close alliance.

I glanced past the crown prince to his younger brother. Jareth wouldn't have had Darius's two years of training, but it was evident he knew the basics the instructor was enthusiastically discussing. Unlike Darius, his face was more open, and he examined his year mates with interest. Perhaps I would have more success focusing my efforts on him.

But something in me rebelled at the idea, my eyes sliding back to Darius against my will. I had seen the leashed power and authority inside him, and the effect it had on others, and I couldn't forget it. He might appear cold and detached, but there was no doubt he was a true leader, the kind with the strength to hold a kingdom together by willpower alone.

And despite the utter lack of encouragement, determination rose up inside me in response to him. I had come all this way and left everything I ever knew, and I had done it to succeed, not to back away when I encountered opposition. Darius was the force to be reckoned with in Kallorway—I could sense it. My aunt wanted me to learn his mind, but I wanted more than that. He was the key to Kallorwegian politics and the ally Ardann needed. I just had to work out how to convince him of that.

CHAPTER 8

When the bell finally rang, releasing us from the tedium, I hoped the day might be over. But when I filed out of the door, the trainees ahead of me were turning toward another classroom rather than the stairs. I followed behind, wondering what else we would be studying.

I entered the new room expecting to see the same arrangement of desks but was instead greeted with mostly empty space. A single large desk stood at the head of the room with a junior instructor behind it. I looked questioningly at Bryony, but she just shrugged her shoulders.

"Welcome first years," the instructor said. "Please approach one at a time and indicate your chosen discipline. I will then direct you to the appropriate room."

I blinked at her, my mind trying to make sense of her words. No one else looked confused, although no one rushed forward eagerly either. Duke Francis had said something about discipline studies and choosing a discipline in his visit over the summer, and I had rushed to assure him that I was as ready to study and learn as any other trainee, even if I couldn't complete the actual compositions. As a princess, I would never have joined a discipline after the Academy anyway, and learning more about how they functioned could still have use when navigating the court.

But perhaps I had been too quick with my reassurances. It now looked like I had conveyed the impression of knowledge-ability and subsequently missed an important element of differ-ence between how our Academies operated. Ardannian trainees didn't pick a discipline in first year.

Still no one moved forward. I glanced at Darius, wondering if he would take the lead, but he hung back near the edges of the room. Perhaps he didn't want to influence everyone else's choices.

Finally, with a shrug, Armand stepped forward and spoke to the instructor in an undertone. If he had been hoping to keep his selection private, he needn't have bothered. The instructor replied at full volume, her tone displaying no particular interest in his choice.

"Very well. The creators receive their instruction in room seven. You may proceed there now."

She turned her attention to a sheet of parchment in front of her, writing what looked like Armand's name onto one of the lists there. After an awkward moment of hesitation, Armand moved toward the door, giving Wardell a nod on his way past.

"We're supposed to choose a discipline?" I asked Bryony, still trying to grasp what was happening. "Right now? Surely not permanently, though?"

Dellion, who stood on Bryony's other side, broke off her thoughtful contemplation of Prince Darius to raise both eyebrows at me.

"But of course permanently. We have to indicate our chosen discipline so we can begin our studies. Is that not how it's done in Ardann?"

"No, not exactly," I said. "We don't make our final choice of discipline until after graduation."

"After graduation?" She regarded me with faint surprise.

"Don't tell me you do no discipline-specific studies at your Academy? How inefficient."

I forced down my instinctive reaction and considered her words. I was here to understand how these Kallorwegians thought, and I couldn't do that if I grew defensive over every element of difference.

"We leave the more intensive discipline-specific training to the disciplines themselves," I said. "I suppose it is inefficient, in some ways. I imagine when you all graduate and join your discipline, you'll be much more capable members from the beginning. I can see the appeal of that."

She started to turn away, but I kept going.

"On the other hand, it's a big decision to make on your first day at the Academy—without any experience of composing, let alone experience with any of the disciplines. In Ardann, trainees focus on basic compositions for the first year and then from second year onward have the chance to study across a range of disciplines of their choice. It allows us to find where we're best suited. I can see value in both approaches."

"A diplomatic response." Dellion sounded amused. "Although your arena training must be a shambles if that is your way."

She glanced a final time at the unmoving Darius before shrugging and crossing the room to the instructor, taking the place of Wardell who was now heading for the door. I frowned after her. What did advanced combat lessons in the arena have to do with anything?

"I'm surprised Ardann has so many mages they can afford to use their resources so flippantly," said a quiet voice behind me.

I turned slightly to find Darius had stepped forward. My pulse, which had spiked at the unexpected sound of his voice, now took off at an alarming pace. I looked at him measuringly, trying to hide my irrational reaction.

"No, indeed," I said. "Ardann may have more unsealed mages than Kallorway, but we're no Sekali Empire. What we cannot afford is to have our disciplines full of mages ill-suited to their choice. Or to have senior mages expend valuable time training new members of their discipline only to have them step away from their commitment. We would rather take the time up front to test the interest and disposition of trainees to ensure they end up where their talents best place them. And there is value in a broad foundation. None of the disciplines stand entirely alone."

Darius regarded me, his expression unreadable. "Well, you are in Kallorway now, Princess, and we do things differently here. So which discipline do you intend to study?"

I opened my mouth only to close it again. I had assumed, when I thought about it at all, that I would spread my study evenly across the various disciplines in order to increase my understanding of how all the elements of our kingdom functioned.

I shot a slightly panicked look at Bryony. I wasn't ready to commit myself to four years of intensive study in a single discipline—especially when I would never have the chance to actually engage in the work of that discipline.

My mind raced through the options, grateful that at least the disciplines themselves were the same here as at home. The University and the Academy weren't options for study but instead attracted the academic-minded or instruction-inclined from across various areas of specialization. Which left eight remaining disciplines: law enforcement, the seekers, the healers, the growers, the wind workers, the creators, the Armed Forces, and the Royal Guard.

I knew something of all of them, of course. Along with the University and Academy heads, the heads of those eight disciplines formed the all-important Mage Council, responsible for advising the monarch and helping form Ardann's laws. My family studied the members of the Mage Council with as much focus as others studied important texts. Managing the ten powerful dukes and duchesses—or generals in the case of the

Armed Forces and the Royal Guard—was one of the core elements of maintaining stability in a kingdom.

But that even-handed focus didn't help me now. I had no idea how to prioritize one discipline over the others.

"She'll study energy compositions with me, of course," Bryony said, slipping her arm through mine.

I threw her a grateful, albeit confused, look, and she came to my rescue again with a further explanation.

"When we arrived, Father asked about their intentions for us energy mages and discipline studies. He wanted to be sure my time would be well-spent here, since four years is a long commitment."

"We may get energy mages only rarely in Kallorway," Darius said, "but you are not the first."

Bryony continued to smile, not in the least deflated by his comment. "I'm glad Tyron showed up because it will be much nicer to have two of us to study and experiment together. We're to spend some time on specific study relating to our energy compositions and the rest of the time moving between the different discipline classes. They want us to learn how we can best work together with the different strains of power mages."

My eyes widened slightly. That sounded perfect for my purposes. I nodded decisively and turned back to Darius.

"Yes, I intend to study energy compositions with Bryony."

He gave me a hooded look I couldn't read. "Do you indeed? How...interesting."

I tried to guess what he could mean but could make little sense of it. The choice seemed a natural one in my circumstances, especially when it allowed me to remain with my one ally at the Academy.

"Perhaps we will learn the—" Darius cut himself off and shook his head, glancing quickly around the room which had emptied somewhat while we talked but was not completely cleared.

I frowned at him, trying to restrain my curiosity, but he merely shook his head again, and moved back toward his brother. Jareth raised an eyebrow at him, looking past him at the two of us and saying something in a quiet murmur.

"What was that about?" Bryony asked.

"I have no idea," I whispered back. "Crown Prince Darius is not at all easy to read."

"An important skill in his position, I'm sure."

I nodded slowly, still watching the two princes as they finally moved up to the instructor behind the desk. Jareth made no attempt to modulate his voice as he chose the discipline of the royal guards. Darius spoke more quietly when he selected law enforcement, but in the near empty room his words were still audible.

So the crown prince wished to learn more about the laws of the kingdom and how they were enforced. Because he approved of them? Or because he wished to see them changed? I watched him leave the room with his brother, a crease between my brows.

"That makes sense." Bryony nodded approvingly. "Darius will rule the kingdom, and his brother will keep him safe."

"Is that the role of the second child after the heir?" I asked, not entirely able to keep the despondence from my voice. "How unfortunate for Lucien. I suppose Stellan will have to step up."

Bryony grimaced and gave my arm a supportive squeeze. "Lucien and Stellan are lucky to have you," she said loyally.

The instructor still waited at the desk, her pen poised above her piece of parchment. We moved close enough that I could read the binding composition at the top of the page which allowed it to be used as regular paper. Any words she wrote on it would be safe from unleashing power.

Her eyes moved between the three of us, settling on me. "You wish to study with the energy mages, Princess Verene?"

I nodded.

"Very well." She wrote my name down along with Bryony's and Tyron's.

I couldn't imagine it mattered much to anyone what I studied. Not given my limitations. But I was still glad not to encounter any opposition to my choice.

"You'll be in room eleven."

I told myself I was imagining the faint look of pity on the woman's face. What was wrong with room eleven?

Tyron led the way back out of the room, turning further down the corridor and stopping at one of the doors at the far end. It had a small number eleven burned into the wood.

He smiled back over his shoulder at Bryony and me. "Ready, ladies?"

Bryony rolled her eyes and pushed past him. "I've been waiting for this for years."

Inside, we found a single instructor waiting for us. She had a thin, sharp face, and her expression darkened at the sight of us. I had a sudden inkling as to why the previous instructor had looked sorry for us.

"Three of you." Her tone was flat. "So I'm to have the pleasure of instructing you, Princess of Ardann."

Her voice and face indicated it was anything but a pleasure, but I could take no exception to anything in her actual words. I settled for giving her a regal nod.

She turned her gaze on Bryony and Tyron.

"No, I'm not an energy mage," she said, in response to a question no one had asked. "But no, that doesn't mean you're the experts here. I'm the senior discipline instructor at the Academy, and I've been here a long time. I've personally tutored all of our previous energy mage graduates. They may have been few in number, but they achieved levels of proficiency you are far from possessing in your current unschooled state."

Tyron pressed his lips together and glanced sideways at Bryony. They both looked taken aback at her combative approach, but neither spoke. She might not be pleasant, but if she spoke truthfully, she had knowledge to share. And, at the end of the day, that was the only thing that mattered.

"You may call me Instructor Amalia," she added. "Or Senior Instructor." She paused to look balefully between us all, but again no one spoke. "We will begin by finding out just how little you all know."

An indeterminate length of time later, the beautiful sound of a bell set us free. After the grueling session of verbal testing, my brain rejoiced at the sound. Thanks to my parents, I wasn't completely ignorant, but I couldn't equal the knowledge of Bryony or Tyron who had grown up among energy mages.

I was only glad I had put in the work at home to become proficient with a sword. At least there was one out of three lessons where I wouldn't be the most useless in the class.

But my words to Royce about my lack of recent training had been true. It was a number of days since I had last practiced in earnest, and my body was aching from the combat lesson almost as much as my mind reeled from the intensity of the day. I could only be glad our new discipline instructor hadn't given us any assignments to occupy our first evening. It was an unexpected reprieve given her obvious belief that we were ignorant children in much need of instruction.

When I bid Bryony goodnight and retreated to my private sitting room, I stripped off my white robe and sank onto one of the sofas with a sigh. Rubbing my head, I reviewed the day. In retrospect, it had been something of a failure.

As much as I wanted to learn more about composing and energy mages in general, I couldn't lose sight of my purpose here. It didn't matter how much knowledge I gained; I would never be able to compose. So while I didn't want to disgrace my family or Ardann by performing terribly in my classes, I couldn't let learning become my main focus.

My aunt wanted to understand the allegiances of my year

mates, but that was only a step toward her eventual goal. The time had come for Ardann to forge deeper ties with Kallorway and begin to truly heal the damage of the long war. But when it came to the well-being of Ardann, Aunt Lucienne was cautious. She wouldn't commit the kingdom to any sort of alliance until she knew who and what would best serve our interests. She was hungry for information to inform her next move—especially information on the future king—but I wanted to deliver more than that.

I was determined to forge real ties with Kallorway and win allies for Ardann. But all I had learned so far was that my year mates appeared to perpetuate the divisions that crippled the Kallorwegian court, and that neither faction seemed interested in a connection with Ardann. Hardly encouraging news to suggest my time here would be worth the sacrifice.

Somehow I had to find a way to connect with the other trainees. And with one trainee in particular. I had to discover what kind of ruler Darius intended to be and convince him that Ardann and Kallorway were better off together.

A scraping sound, loud in the stillness, jerked me from my thoughts. I sat upright, staring at the left wall of my sitting room where the noise had originated. The tapestry that hung there fluttered and moved before being thrust completely aside by an opening door which had been hidden behind it.

CHAPTER 9

I leaped to my feet, my hand thrusting instinctively toward one of my hidden pockets as I had been trained. But my fingers hadn't even closed on one of my father's shielding compositions before I recognized the figure who strode through the door.

Prince Darius.

My hand stilled, and I slowly lowered it again without retrieving a shield. He carried neither parchment nor weapon, and I had no reason to suppose his intent was to attack me. Using one of my compositions would both deplete my stores and potentially offend him. At home I had been trained to respond to even a hint of danger, but I had to think differently now.

The prince came fully into the room, stooping to pick something up from behind the other sofa. When he straightened, he held a stray downy feather.

"I heard some among us were overly enthusiastic in their welcome." He regarded me with a closed expression.

I shrugged, hiding my spark of interest in this evidence that he knew of the incident in my suite. Did the servants keep him apprised of events within the Academy, then? Or had his information come through Duke Francis? I was here to learn about my own generation, but if I could discover something about the attitude of the commonborns toward their future king, that would be worthwhile.

"I only wish they had given some thought to the extra work they caused the poor servants," I said. "And now that I have arrived, my door is shielded, of course."

He glanced at my main door, although he didn't have to look to feel the power coating it. I, however, focused on the open door behind him, frowning at the disrupted tapestry and the glimpse of another sitting room through the opening.

"But I would have appreciated being told about a hidden entrance into my receiving room." I let my displeasure sound in my voice for once.

Darius turned his attention back to me, raising his eyebrows in a look of faint surprise. "Were you not informed? The Academy doesn't usually host so many royal trainees at once. These suites are more commonly used for visiting guests of high rank. Many of them are connected."

I refrained from giving an anxious look around the room. "Don't tell me there are other hidden entries into my suite!"

"No, indeed. These are the two suites used by my parents on their occasional visits. They connect to each other but not any others."

I raised an eyebrow. The king's and queen's suites. It couldn't be coincidence that Darius and I had been given them instead of Darius and his brother. A seed of hope sprouted. Had Darius himself been responsible for the room placements? Did the crown prince have more interest in Ardann than he was publicly willing to acknowledge?

During our one true conversation so far, Darius had cut himself off. Had it been because we weren't alone? Had he ended our interaction intending to continue it later in private? Perhaps he had organized from the beginning for us to have a way to speak alone—freely, royal to royal. That suggested he might have some interest in building ties, after all.

"Well, you can be sure I'll be shielding that door as well after this." Thankfully Layna had been generous in the number of compositions she had provided.

He gave me a half-bow. "Naturally."

Of course, I should have noticed the power of his own door shield lurking behind the tapestry. I could feel it now. But I had grown up in a palace full of compositions. I didn't pay attention to power felt through a wall.

"I will make certain to knock next time," he added.

"Be sure you do." I eyed him, remembering the strange abruptness of the servant who had shown me to my room.

She had barely given me any information, fleeing before I had the chance to ask questions. And yet she had later seemed genuinely surprised by the chaos wreaked by my unknown harasser. Had I now discovered what she had been avoiding telling me? It had surely been her role to inform me of this door so that I could secure it as I did my main door.

As soon as the thought formed, it hardened into certainty. Of course I should have been informed of all entrances to my suite and given the opportunity to preserve my privacy, as Darius had taken steps to preserve his. Ordinarily my servant would certainly have done so. Unless someone with enough influence wanted me kept in ignorance. Someone who might have wanted the opportunity to catch me off guard. There could be only one person. The only one who could access the door in question—the crown prince of Kallorway.

How much sway did Darius hold here in what was supposed to be the neutral domain of Duke Francis?

The prince looked me up and down slowly, a puzzled look slipping onto his face. I let him finish his perusal, meeting his gaze defiantly.

"It was a…surprise when I heard you wished to study at our Academy," he said at last.

"It is my aunt who wishes me to study here." I couldn't help the truthful reply slipping out.

After all his coldness, I didn't want him thinking I had been eager to spend four years in his cold, formal kingdom. And it might do good to remind him that while I was merely a junior princess, barely in the line of succession, I came as a representative of my family.

"That also surprised me," he admitted, saying the words almost reluctantly.

I raised an eyebrow. "Do you not think she values rebuilding Ardann's relationship with Kallorway? It's been more than twenty years since the war ended. It is time for a new beginning."

"The war is not forgotten here," he said.

"Yes, that's the problem." A caustic note slipped into my voice. He seemed determined to be difficult. "But might I remind you that Kallorway were the aggressors, not Ardann."

For the first time since I had met him, he looked uncomfortable, although the expression quickly passed.

"That is also not forgotten, although my grandfather, the old king, is long dead."

"Your father was not uninvolved," I murmured.

He looked at me sharply before shuttering his gaze again. "That is also not forgotten."

I sighed. This conversation was going nowhere helpful.

"It's true that they would never have sent my brother, Lucien," I said. "But I am not so valuable that I cannot be used in the cause of peace. Ardann would see our kingdoms grow close and prosper together."

"Would you now?" he asked, drawing the words out in a way that made me want to snap out a biting retort. I held it in.

"Yes, we would." I hesitated.

He must know of my limitations. My family had been open

with Duke Francis, and I had no doubt the royal family of Kallorway had been informed of the situation long before that.

"I serve my family where I am most able," I added, after a moment.

His eyes narrowed, and he took two steps toward me, closing the space between us.

"Do you? I've been wondering about that."

I frowned. "Wondering what?"

Did this have something to do with the words he'd cut off earlier when he heard my choice of discipline?

"Wondering how exactly you intend to serve your family in Kallorway."

"Exactly as I just described. I am here as an ambassador. That's why your father and the duke permitted my enrollment."

"Yes, my father permitting it was perhaps the most surprising of all. I think he was delighted to have Ardann admit that the mighty Spoken Mage had a daughter with no power at all."

I blinked, a tingling feeling rushing down from my scalp. I should be used to the snide comments and veiled insults by now, but the words hit hard delivered in such a bald way. Darius had given me no reason to expect such frankness from him.

He didn't seem to note my distress, however. Instead he prowled even further forward, until almost no space remained between us at all. The hidden danger in his eyes was back, every line of his body suggesting restrained power. It took everything in me not to pull away.

"But as for me," he said, "I don't believe a word of it."

I gasped, jerking back as if slapped.

But he made no move to back off, and I refused to step away and cede him ground. Not here in my own sitting room.

When I said nothing, he continued. "For centuries, we have sought every possible way to circumvent the limitations of power. But it cannot be done. Power—and its lack—is a birthright. And yet you want me to believe that Prince Lucas—

the product of generations of royal strength—and the Spoken Mage—the strongest mage to ever live—produced a child without any power at all? Such a thing is beyond belief. My father's desire for it to be true blinds him."

Sudden fury drove away my earlier shock. I rose onto the balls of my feet, leaning in toward him.

"Do you think I haven't spent sleepless nights thinking that very thing? Do you think every member of my aunt's court hasn't whispered such things in the corridors? Do you think I *want* to be powerless? But you cannot make something true just by thinking it should be so. Not even you, Crown Prince Darius."

I punctuated my final three words with a finger stabbing into his chest. But still he didn't budge, a solid rock against the tide of my anger.

"But you can hide the truth," he said, his voice turning silky, but no less dangerous. "You grew up in a court so you must have learned that reality on your mother's lap, just as I did. So don't think you can play games with me."

"My life is not a game," I snapped.

"Is it not?" He sounded genuinely surprised. "Then you would be the first royal able to say so." He leaned in, our faces barely a breath away now, the intensity of his presence robbing me of air. "But I think you know that perfectly well. I think you know that acting weak is the oldest deception of all."

"I am not weak," I said, hating how breathless the words came out.

A slow smile crossed his face, although it held nothing of amusement.

"It never occurred to me you were, Verene. Just don't make the mistake of thinking I am."

He pulled away, his sudden absence as great a shock as his closeness had been. Giving a formal bow, he wished me goodnight and strode back through the door to his own sitting room.

I watched the tapestry fall gently back into place, still strug-

gling to gain my breath. I had thought emotion—any emotion—
would create more fertile ground than the prince's apparent icy
indifference. But he had just pulled back the veil and let me see
what lurked beneath, and I was no longer so sure. Because Darius
didn't hate me, he saw me as a threat. And something told me he
was ruthless when dealing with threats.

And yet, when I climbed into bed, it wasn't fear of failure that
filled my mind. Instead I kept remembering that initial glint I saw
in his eyes when I first arrived. I had later concluded them far too
dark for such a thing. But now that I had seen them up close,
burning with the intensity he usually kept hidden away, I realized
they weren't dark at all but a rich, deep brown. They were the
sort of eyes that might hide far more than just a glint.

CHAPTER 10

*B*y the next morning, I had made a decision. I wouldn't shield the door behind the tapestry as I had originally intended. Instead I released a second shield to protect my bedroom door. If I was to succeed here, then I had to keep my one connection to Darius open—regardless of how he currently felt about me.

With his sitting room on the other side of the hidden door, I need have no fear anyone but the crown prince would ever use the one entrance I had left open.

The next morning I once again encountered Dellion in the corridor outside our rooms. However, this time she only nodded at me, continuing on her way to breakfast without speaking. Her grandfather had been the one to negotiate peace with Ardann, but he had never forgiven us for installing Cassius on the throne. The general did not view Ardann with a friendly eye, and it seemed neither did his granddaughter.

I trailed behind, glancing hopefully up the stairs when we reached them for any sign of Bryony. I didn't find her until we reached the dining hall, however, where she already sat with Tyron on one side. I hesitated at the sight of them, remembering their prediction of the day before. Sure enough, both princes sat across from them. Darius looked up and saw me, nothing in his face giving away that we had shared an intense conversation the night before.

My back straightened, and I marched across the hall, slipping into the remaining seat beside Bryony. I would not be scared away by Darius, whatever suspicions of me I now knew he harbored. I had four years here, and eventually he would have to see that I was being truthful about myself.

"Good morning, Princess," Jareth said, as if trying to make up for his brother's coldness with his own cheerfulness. "I trust you're finding your accommodations to your liking."

"I will admit there have been some surprises." I carefully refrained from looking at Darius. "But overall they have been very comfortable, thank you."

He smiled. "Surprises of the good variety, I hope."

I considered his words. "That remains to be seen."

A small movement made my eyes fly sideways, just in time to see Darius looking quickly away from me. A small smile tugged at the corner of my lips. The crown prince would soon discover I wasn't so easily intimidated.

"I see you brought your sword this morning." Bryony grinned at me.

I smiled back. "It will be a relief to fight with a well-balanced blade again."

Jareth raised his eyebrows. "You showed no sign of discomfort yesterday."

I shrugged. "I'm not sure royals are allowed to show signs of discomfort. Or are things so different in Kallorway?"

Jareth laughed and gave a mocking glance at his brother beside him. "Not so different, I assure you."

Darius rolled his eyes at Jareth but otherwise didn't respond to his obvious prodding. The exchanges of the brothers continued to fascinate me, as they had done my first evening at the Academy. Darius seemed to let his guard down for his brother and no one else. The two were clearly close beyond the normal sibling friendship I shared with my own brothers, and something about their bond unnerved me. Perhaps it was because Darius was so closed off and hard to read, but I struggled to accept Jareth's apparent open friendliness.

When the bell rang for the end of the meal, we all stood together, but Darius and Jareth soon drifted away from the rest of us. Bryony had also arrived with a sword belt strapped around her waist this morning, but I noticed Tyron still lacked one.

I grimaced at him sympathetically. "You didn't bring a blade from home?"

He shook his head. "I didn't realize we needed to supply our own weapon. I've learned a great deal about this place in the week I have been here, but I knew very little when I set out from the Empire."

"What led you here?" I asked. "Why come so far? Does your family have any ties with Kallorway?"

Tyron shook his head. "Not until now. I am to be the one to change that for us all."

When I gave him an inquiring look, he continued. "When my family sought refuge in the Empire with the other energy mages, they were placed among one of the clans of sealed mages. Those clans do not train their young people as the other clans or the southern kingdoms do."

I nodded. "Of course. I've heard about that. I suppose it makes sense that their only focus would be on increasing their skill and stamina in preparation for their sealing ceremony. I've heard the more commonborns they can seal, the more honor they bring to their family. And they don't train for a full four years either, do they?"

"Yes, that's right," he said. "And energy mages cannot perform sealing ceremonies—you need power for that—so there was never any question of my joining them. I always knew I would have to travel to find proper training. And by traveling just a little farther, I may win future value and position for my family."

I nodded. It wasn't so different really from my own reasoning for being here.

I spoke on impulse. "I brought a secondary blade with me which you would be welcome to use. Its reach is probably a little shorter than your preference, but it's better quality than the ones we used yesterday."

Tyron hesitated, looking to Bryony, as if to check if it was safe to take my offer at face value.

"I can vouch for any blade of Verene's," she said. "But I think you would be far better in the long run in sending for one of your own. It would be a pity to go a whole year with a blade not fit for your size."

Tyron nodded. "Perhaps I might borrow yours, Princess, just until I can secure one for myself?"

I nodded. "I'll bring it down with me tomorrow."

We stepped over the short fence into the training yard where Instructor Mitchell looked just as dour-faced as he had the day before. When warm-ups were completed, I looked around for a partner, but everyone seemed busily occupied not looking in my direction.

I sighed and turned to Bryony. Apparently after Royce's performance the day before, I was to be further shunned.

"Don't worry," Bryony said cheerfully. "You can't blame them for not wanting to face your blade. They know they'll be beaten."

I smiled, my spirits lifting, as they always did in the face of my friend's good humor.

"Instead I'll have to accustom myself to being the one beaten," I said. "Since it appears you're to be my permanent sparring partner."

"I'm sure Tyron will give you a chance to beat him from time to time when the defeat gets too much for you," Bryony said with a cheeky twinkle in his direction.

He grinned back at us. "I'm sure I could accustom myself to facing off against Princess Verene. I might even learn something."

He showed equal willingness later in the lesson, when Bryony suggested switching partners, and I was grateful for his easy-going attitude. But when we actually fought, I felt guilty for spending our entire bout thinking of the label Bryony had given his fighting style—uninspired. He was technically proficient to a reasonable degree, but he didn't have the extra flair of creativity needed to win against an equally skilled opponent. And he wasn't as skilled as either Bryony or me to begin with.

When he fought with Bryony, I finally found myself facing a new partner. Jareth bowed with a flourish before proving himself more skilled than me, although only just. He forced me to yield with appropriate restraint, and I gave him a nod as I mopped my brow.

"An excellent match. It's good to know I'll have more of a challenge here than just Bryony."

Jareth grinned lazily. "I'm more than happy to beat you any time you'd like, Princess."

"Verene, please," I said. "We are both royalty and now also year mates. If we can't dispense with the formality with each other, then with whom?"

I could feel eyes on me, but I refused to turn and look at Darius. He had been the first to drop my title, back in my sitting room, and if he thought to complain, I would remind him of it. Although somehow I didn't think he wanted that conversation becoming public knowledge.

Jareth, however, did look over my shoulder, his smile growing more sincere. The subtle change in his expression made me shift uneasily. He put on an engaging manner so easily, but seeing him respond to his brother showed how superficial it was when directed toward others. But it was too late to take back the invitation to drop formality between us.

"Certainly, Verene," he said when his attention returned to me. "I look forward to our next bout."

I gave him a half-bow, and he stepped past me. I finally allowed myself to turn and watch Darius greet him with murmured words too low for me to catch. Jareth looked back at me over his shoulder, smiling when he saw me watching them, before moving away with his brother.

What lurked beneath Jareth's smiles? And what had his brother thought of our bout?

The afternoon proceeded much as the previous day's, with everyone returning to the same seats in composition. I learned one thing in the class, however. The girl who sat beside Dellion was called Isabelle.

I was certain she had never been mentioned in any of the briefings I had received before I came and could only conclude her family rarely appeared at court. The impression was borne out by her apparent lack of friends or connections among our year mates. Some Kallorwegian mages chose to distance themselves from the power games at Kallmon, and it appeared her parents were among their number.

It was perhaps unfortunate for her that we were such a small year group, or she might have had companions from a similar background. But then I had heard many of the recent year groups at the Kallorwegian Academy had been small—a result, I supposed, of the massive social upheaval going on in the kingdom in the years between the end of the war and our births. Apparently many of the upcoming years were a great deal larger.

The days fell into a pattern, and somehow the first two weeks passed. Instructor Mitchell still had us spending our time on free bouts in combat, merely prowling up and down the yard, issuing advice as he saw fit. Instructor Alvin was still lecturing, and I could feel the impatience levels rising among the other trainees. My year mates wanted to compose. After all, they had been waiting sixteen years to finally be free to do so.

Instructor Amalia also lectured, although she did so with none of Alvin's good-natured cheer. I still found her lessons fascinating, however, since she jumped straight to an intermediate level, often engaging Bryony and Tyron in discussion.

She ignored me completely, unless wishing to test me on some minutiae of their conversation. But I appreciated the reprieve and was happy to listen. The subject matter was interesting enough to ensure I was always paying close enough attention not to be caught out by her occasional questions.

Bryony and Tyron both had the most common energy mage ability—the ability to gift others their energy. But Amalia had previously had a trainee with the ability to take energy, and all three of us were interested in her explanations of that process. When the energy mages descended from the mountains to rejoin the power mages, the Sekali Emperor had scattered them throughout his people. And since their abilities ran in families, many of the second-generation energy mages had been given little opportunity to interact with those of differing abilities.

"When you give energy," she explained to Bryony and Tyron, "it is a free gift, and the one who receives it keeps it until they have used it themselves, as they would use their own energy. You are left to restore the lost energy in the way you would restore any energy you expended—through rest."

"Can those who take energy not keep it?" Bryony asked. "That seems less than useful."

"Energy taken by force wishes to return to its rightful owner," Amalia said. "Of course I haven't experienced it for myself, but I'm told it pulls against the thief, straining with greater and greater strength, until at last it breaks free and returns."

"Unless it has no owner to return to," Tyron said quietly.

Amalia looked at him with narrowed eyes before nodding decisively. "It is an ability that lends itself to aggression. If the energy mage drains all of another person's energy, then that person dies, and their energy dissipates."

Bryony grimaced. "I've always been glad I don't have that ability."

Amalia gave her a disapproving look. "Every ability has its uses for good or ill—it depends on the creativity of its possessor to find the potential for practical use."

"As long as the energy mage shows restraint, I can see the value of such a gift," I said slowly. "There are situations where a person's life might be saved if they could be effectively rendered unconscious for a time. It's a better alternative than being forced to kill them."

For once Amalia gave me an approving look. I didn't meet her eyes, however, scared of what I might see there. Did she know why I found it so much easier than Bryony to see the potential value in any ability? I didn't have the luxury of rejoicing over a superior gifting.

"That's still aggressive, though." Bryony wrinkled her nose. "I wouldn't want an ability that predisposed me to a life of subterfuge and warfare. I can see how such a mage might make a valuable part of an intelligencer team, for instance, but what if they don't want that life?"

Amalia looked disappointed in her. "You should use your tongue less and your ears more, Bryony. I already answered your question. Creativity is needed."

"And what creative solution did your trainee find?" I asked her. "Or did he embrace a life of violence?"

"He chose a middle path, as so many of us do. He joined the Armed Forces after he graduated, but he is often sent on assignment to the healers. He assists with complicated procedures and recoveries where the patient must be kept asleep."

"Doesn't a patient need their energy to heal?" I asked.

"They need some of it certainly. But you have clearly never tried to care for a sick child who refuses to acknowledge they are sick. Sometimes stillness is most important and, in some cases, unconsciousness is needed. His services will certainly do as well as any pain relief composition, if such supplies are scarce."

"And then their energy returns to them," I said, remembering the first part of the lesson.

Amalia nodded. "Once the procedure is completed, or the patient has been lulled into a true sleep, he will release their energy back to them. So in the end they have lost none of their own energy. During his time with me, he became an expert on that release. Rather than waiting until the energy was violently wrested from him, springing back to the owner in a rush, he could release it at a controlled rate that would not wake them if he had succeeded in putting them into a natural sleep."

She looked at Bryony. "Such a thing would not work with a guard who had been rendered unconscious at their post, but the body and mind of an injured or ill patient needs sleep. They long for it, even as they fight it. Once they have been eased into sleep, they will remain there, unless woken by the shock of all their energy returning in a violent rush. With a controlled return of energy, a sleeping patient will wake to find themselves brimming with strength."

I looked at Amalia with increased respect. She might not have a pleasant manner, but if she had helped her past trainee achieve such control, then she was dedicated to her task of instruction. Had she and her trainee been the ones to discover this use of his ability?

In the mountains, the Tarxi had been without healers as we knew them. They had no doubt made use of the same type of skills employed by our commonborn healing assistants, but there was only so much that could be achieved through herbs and splints and the like. Their only advantage over commonborns had been their ability to gift extra energy to those fighting for life.

And to balance this one advantage, they had been denied the increases in knowledge constantly made by the healing disciplines. Our healers used compositions to further understand the intricacies of the human body, their discoveries recorded and built on by future healers. In the mountains, the energy mages had been cut off from all of that, as we had been cut off from their abilities. Amalia's old trainee was a perfect example of what we could learn and achieve together, and he might never have found such a use for his abilities without the knowledge and skill of power mage healers.

I carefully refrained from looking at Bryony. Once the energy mages had counted healers of their own among their number. But when our distant ancestors had banded together across both kingdoms and the Empire and expelled the energy mages from their midst, one bloodline had been deemed too valuable to lose. A mage who could heal anything, even to the point of death, was someone a king had reason to keep close.

The Kallorwegian kings had hidden the presence of these energy healers and kept them here in their kingdom. Their identity had been a closely guarded secret, their family kept close to the throne in case of need. Until one day, even the Kallorwegian kings had forgotten their true nature, and only one member of the family remained. Bryony's father, Declan.

When we were young, Bryony had confided to me that she inherited the abilities of both her parents. But she had sworn me to secrecy, and I had never told a soul. My friend could give her energy in the usual way, a gift she could then replenish, as Amalia had described. But what our instructor didn't know was that Bryony could also make a permanent gift of part of her energy—forever diminishing her own maximum level of energy and increasing that of the person who received it. Once that portion of energy was bound into her composition, she could never replenish it again. But that energy did far more than bolster the recipient. It could work miraculous feats of healing, beyond even those regular healers could achieve with power compositions.

There was a reason their service had been so highly prized by the Kallorwegian kings of old—but there was also a reason Declan had ended up as the last of his line. They could give the most precious of gifts, but it came at a great price to themselves. Some of his ancestors had lived to old age—although always weaker and more tired than those around them—but some were forced, or tempted through compassion, into giving everything they had. And so Declan had sworn his daughter to the same secrecy he had always employed. The knowledge of their ability would only endanger them.

When I did finally look at Bryony, I could see the shadow of the knowledge in her eyes. She would never follow in the footsteps of Amalia's last student and work in a healing clinic. The temptation would be too great. And if she gave in to it, intervening with her hidden power rather than just assisting with her open one, she would not live to have a future of her own. It was a heavy burden to bear.

Would I take such a burden in exchange for having an ability—any ability? Even as I asked myself the question, I already knew the answer. I would. To know that I could keep those I loved safe would be worth it. Not to mention my usefulness to the crown.

But how would I feel about passing on that ability to any future child of mine? That was a question less easily answered. After all, in all the experiments my parents had conducted with me after my birthday, testing me for every type of known ability, I had only once seen relief on their faces when I failed.

CHAPTER 11

We had a rest day once a week, but unlike Ardann's Academy in Corrin, we were too remote here to make excursions appealing. Bryony informed me the local village had grown since her father's day, but it still wasn't large. Trade came through now, from Ardann, and it was no longer dangerously near a border war, but there were bigger towns and cities to attract the majority of the travelers.

Wardell and Armand sometimes liked to go hiking in the surrounding countryside, and I had been surprised to see Dellion join them on a couple of occasions. Whenever I saw the three of them together, it reinforced the impression that my fellow trainees followed the political leanings of their families. There was certainly no natural liking on Dellion's side to draw her to either of the two boys, their shared allegiance being the only explanation for their association.

Tyron had indicated an interest in seeing more of the area, and Wardell had invited him along as well at the next opportunity. But Bryony refused to join her fellow energy mage, despite my assurances that she didn't need to stay behind on my account.

"Loyalty has nothing to do with it." She scrunched her nose.

"Would you want to spend an entire day with Wardell and Armand?"

I chuckled. "I can't say that I would, when you put it like that. Although it might be nice to get out from behind these walls occasionally."

I gave a slightly longing look at the distant sky, but I knew such activity was barred to me. Captain Vincent had sought me out on the first rest day to inform me that I was to consider myself Academy-bound.

"The duke has given his personal assurances about your safety to your family," he had said, "and it is my duty to carry out his promise. But I cannot guarantee your safety if you're wandering around unaccompanied, and neither can I spare sufficient guards to escort you."

It had been easier to accept the stricture when I realized the Kallorwegian princes appeared equally bound by it. And I couldn't blame the captain for wanting to keep us all under his eye.

So, instead of hiking, Bryony dragged me out to the empty training yards every rest day for our own training session. I complained the whole way, but it never deterred her. The girl was quicksilver with a sword and loved her time spent with the blade in her hand.

I practiced the craft more out of duty than love, but I was willing to support Bryony in her passion. Without her, my days at the Academy would have been too lonely to contemplate.

But while I enjoyed my time with Bryony, it wasn't moving my true goal any closer to reality. Royce avoided me like I was death-touched, Dellion looked down her haughty nose in my direction, despite her lack of true rank, and most of the others simply avoided me. Sometimes I thought almost longingly of the unexpected message in my room on my first day. At least then someone had seemed to care I was here.

And most distant of all was Darius. He was the one who

mattered most, but no amount of staring at it had made my tapestry flutter again with any movement of the door behind it.

I still hadn't fought with anyone outside of Bryony, Tyron, and Jareth in combat, but I had taken a few moments to observe everyone. Obviously all the Kallorwegian trainees had known something of what to expect at the Academy because they all clearly possessed some prior training. And it was increasingly obvious they found our undirected bouts unsatisfying.

Increasingly I heard mentions of the arena spoken in tones of discontent. Lucien had come home from the Academy over the summer full of stories about the battles he had won, but he had already finished second year. My heart sank at the idea that we might start in the arena in first year here. Combat was the one class where I wasn't an oddity and could participate as an equal. But once training moved to the arena—the vast shielded dome where trainees fought each other with a combination of compositions and swords—I would once again be relegated to the role of observer.

When I caught a reference to it in a conversation between Frida and Ashlyn during combat class, I turned to join them, catching them both by surprise.

"Do you know when we're to start in the arena?" I asked them. "I know the higher year levels have already been taking turns in there."

The two girls exchanged a look before Frida replied in a friendlier tone than I was expecting.

"No, we don't, that's what we were just discussing. Surely it will be soon! What's the point of being sixteen and at the Academy if they just keep us sparring like we've all been doing at home for years?"

"You wouldn't prefer to gain more proficiency at composing first?" I asked, trying to sound nonchalant.

Ashlyn shrugged. "Arena battles will help us improve."

"There's no motivation quite as potent as knowing your arena day is coming up," Frida said. "We'll have to start simply, of course, but that doesn't matter. We'll all be in the same situation."

Ashlyn grimaced. "Well, most of us. Honestly, my only hesitation is that they might call me to bout against Prince Darius."

Frida hissed at her, her eyes widening significantly, and Ashlyn gave a startled glance over my shoulder. Whatever she saw there made her mumble something unintelligible and pull Frida away.

I closed my eyes for a moment and took a deep breath before turning around.

"Darius," I said, "what a pleasant surprise." I eyed the naked sword in his hand. "Don't tell me you've come for a bout?"

He shrugged. "If you wish."

"It is the purpose of the class, is it not?"

He moved to take up a position opposite me, looking suddenly taller than I remembered. "So you're interested in combat in the arena? Does that mean you intend to participate?"

Anger flashed through me. "Of course not. My family didn't provide me with enough compositions to use them in training."

A caustic look came over his face, but he replied only by raising his blade and calling a beginning to the match. His first attack came swift and sure, and I barely managed to block it.

Jareth still occasionally fought me, and I had plenty of experience against Bryony, but Darius was more skilled than his brother and had a far longer reach than my petite friend. He drove me back with an unceasing onslaught of attacks, and it was all I could do to defend myself. I skipped backward across the yard, but unlike with Royce, it wasn't a strategic move.

I could sense the fence behind me and knew I needed to make an attack of my own, however desperate. Before I could lunge, however, Darius did so. Backed against the fence, I didn't have room for a proper defense. Trapping my blade out of the way, the prince pressed against me, body to body.

If the rest of the class were still in the yard, I was no longer aware of them. My entire world had narrowed to the harshness of our mingled breaths, the heat emanating from his taut body, and the deep brown of his eyes. It was only the second time I had been close enough to see their richness, and they had lost none of their captivating power.

"What is your ability, Verene?" he asked, his voice low and intimate despite being rough from his jagged breaths.

I blinked, thrown totally off balance by his unexpected question—as he had no doubt intended. The earlier anger filled me again, and I leaned into him instead of away, raising my face defiantly toward his.

"To do this to you, Darius. To disrupt your ordered world." My whispered words sent a shudder rippling through his straining muscles. "Is it not enough?"

He pulled away abruptly, letting both our blades drop. For a single moment, he stood still, his eyes locked with mine, and then he turned and strode away.

I watched him go, struggling to get my breathing back under control. There was no doubt who had the greater skill with a blade, and yet I felt I had achieved my first win against the inscrutable prince. I just wished I knew what his next move might be.

"Attention trainees," Instructor Mitchell called, reminding me that I still stood in the middle of combat class. "Tomorrow we will meet in the arena instead of in this yard. Consider yourselves forewarned, and come prepared."

My brief moment of strange elation drained away. It was beginning.

CHAPTER 12

*B*ryony jumped on me as soon as we left the training yard. "*What* was that?"

I winced. "So you noticed that?"

"Noticed?" She gave our immediate vicinity a quick sweep with her eyes before leaning close and dropping her voice lower. "Of course I noticed it! Everyone noticed!"

I sighed and tried to imagine how it would have looked to an outsider. I couldn't imagine it was a scene that would have endeared me to anyone else in our year.

"Well?" Bryony demanded when I didn't say anything.

I shrugged. "Prince Darius is definitely the most skilled in our class. Hardly surprising, I suppose, given his rank and age advantage. Even you couldn't beat him, Bree."

My words nearly achieved their purpose, a competitive gleam sparking in Bryony's eyes. But a moment later she narrowed them, giving me a fierce look.

"Don't think you can distract me that easily. I will bout with the prince one day, and we shall see what happens. But somehow I don't think it will go quite like your fight did."

I sighed again, also dropping my voice to a whisper. "The

lovely crown prince thinks I'm hiding my true abilities. He doesn't believe I'm as powerless as I claim."

Bryony's eyes widened. "What?!" She quickly lowered her voice. "But that's outrageous!"

"Of course it is. But it doesn't matter how many times I assure him of the truth, why would he believe me? He doesn't know how much I wish his suspicions were true." I rubbed at my temples. "I have to admit I can see his perspective. My parents spent months testing me after my birthday because it seemed so impossible I could really be powerless. Can I blame him for not taking our word for it?"

Bryony frowned. "Perhaps. But then your situation is so widely known. Would Queen Lucienne really let such a story spread if it wasn't true? I thought you power mages were all obsessed with strength and all that."

I crinkled my brow, considering the matter. Would we have allowed such a rumor if it were untrue?

"I think that's actually the problem," I said after a moment. "Far too many of us are obsessed with strength and power. That's how we ended up in a thirty-year war in the first place. And since Darius is a product of that war, he can't be blamed for thinking we might do anything to extend our control and influence."

Bryony still looked unconvinced. "But what does he suspect you of doing here?"

I shrugged. "I suppose that would all depend on what my ability is, wouldn't it? And that, at least, is fairly unpredictable... given my mother's unique situation."

I gave Bryony a significant look, and she made a wry face. Our families were the only two who knew the depths of my mother's strange origins.

"But how do you convince someone that you truly *don't* have power?" she asked. "It would be a simple situation in reverse, but..."

"He started by asking if I meant to fight in the arena." I

grimaced. "I suspect allowing myself to be repeatedly pummeled without defense might be the only option open to me."

Bryony stared at me. "You can't try to match a power mage in the arena when they're armed with compositions and you have nothing but a sword."

"If the gain was worth it, you know I would, Bree. And it's only combat practice anyway. The trainees won't be allowed to take it too far. Plus Raelynn told me she is always stationed in the arena during training to patch us up as necessary."

Bryony looked mutinous. "If your aunt was worth so much sacrifice, then she'd see your value without needing the sacrifice from you in the first place."

I shook my head. "You know it's not that simple. I'm not just doing this for my aunt. I do it for my whole family, and for my kingdom. And for myself." My voice turned plaintive. "Is it so wrong to want to be useful?"

Bryony flung both arms around my neck and gave me a tight squeeze. "Of course it's not. It's admirable." She pulled back and flashed me a smile. "Perhaps I'm just jealous because you've always been far more selfless than me."

I rolled my eyes, giving her a light shove. "You're ridiculous."

"But lovable," she said with a twinkle.

I chuckled. "But lovable."

I didn't feel like laughing when I walked into the arena the next morning, however. I had my usual protective compositions with me, as I always did, but they were to be used in dire need only. If I meant to go through with my plan and volunteer for a bout, then I would have to take whatever my opponent threw at me without running for the safety of a shield.

At least most of my year mates still lacked the capability for compositions of any strength or complexity. They were still mastering the basics and were far from even building up their stamina, let alone crafting serious workings.

As I had predicted, Raelynn was there. She sat alone a short distance around the curved arena seating from where our year was gathering. When she waved at me with a cheery smile, I waved back, hoping she couldn't see my nerves.

"You don't have to do this," Bryony whispered as we sat down. "Mitchell may not even let you."

That was definitely a possibility I'd considered. There was little advantage to him in letting me onto the arena floor when I would never be able to hold my own there. It would have been one thing if I was just a weaker trainee, in need of guidance and practice, but no amount of experience would ever enable me to match anyone here. And my royal status only further complicated the situation. In Ardann, my brother was expected to take his beatings—if fairly earned—just like anyone else. But the rules might be different for foreign royals who carried the risk of creating a diplomatic incident.

Darius eyed me coolly as he passed me on the stairs, climbing to a higher row of seating. His face was impassive, but I thought I could read a challenge in his eyes. I straightened my back. I would find a way to convince Mitchell to give me a chance.

But to my surprise, after the expected lecture about refraining from any lethal compositions, no names were called for a bout. Instead, Mitchell instructed us to break into our disciplines.

Tyron climbed up from two rows down to join Bryony and me, shrugging in response to our bemused expressions.

"Don't ask me what's going on," he said. "No one mentioned anything about arena battles in the days before classes started."

No one else looked confused, however. Instead, a buzz of excitement rippled through the group as they broke into small clumps.

Frida and Ashlyn stood together, having both chosen to study as growers. I had discovered Ashlyn was the one whose mother was Head of the Wind Workers and had felt a momentary spark of interest at her choice of discipline. Did it represent a divergence from the choices and opinions of her parents? But then wind workers and growers often worked closely together, overseeing the kingdom's crops, so perhaps it was an approved choice.

Isabelle, Dellion's desk mate, stood alone, the sole first year to be studying wind working. But with such a small year, she wasn't the only one who did so. Royce was alone in having chosen the Armed Forces, and Darius was the only one studying law enforcement. It seemed his ploy of waiting to nominate his discipline until last had successfully prevented anyone from using his choice as guidance.

Dellion and Jareth stood together, however, Dellion looking happy with her discipline mate. And Wardell and Armand remained clumped together as they usually were. It turned out the uncle who was Head of the Creators was a shared one between the two cousins, so their mutual choice made sense.

Mitchell surveyed the groupings with an even more critical eye, frowning at each of the trainees who stood alone.

"Royce, you must work with Prince Darius in the arena. The armed forces and law enforcement disciplines share enough similarities that the two of you should manage to find common ground. As for you, Isabelle..." He narrowed his eyes, considering.

"I would rather remain alone," she said quickly, flashing him a smile. "It will give me room to work."

He raised an eyebrow. "Very well, you may attempt it. However, I may have to make future adjustments."

Dellion had made a comment on our first day connecting our discipline studies with combat in the arena, but I still didn't understand what was happening. The pairs of trainees around us, however, already had their heads together, whispering to each other in what looked like strategy sessions.

"For the first battle," Mitchell said, "it will be the Royal Guard against the growers and wind worker. Creators and law enforcement alliance, you will observe and be ready with a critique of both teams' performance."

My eyes widened. So we were to skip individual bouts and go straight to team battles. And the teams were formed based on disciplines. Dellion's earlier bemusement now made sense.

"What of us?" I called down to Mitchell. "Are we to observe as well, or do you mean to let us participate?"

For the first time I saw a gleam of true interest in Mitchell's eye. "Would you like to enter the arena, Your Highness?"

"Certainly," I replied. "I am a trainee."

"In that case, Princess Verene, you may work with the Royal Guard, and Bryony and Tyron, you may work with the growers and wind worker."

Bryony let out a wordless whoop of excitement and clambered down the tiered seating. I followed at a more sedate pace, although I couldn't keep the grin from my face. I didn't know what was about to happen, but I suspected it would be a great deal more interesting than the two options I had been contemplating when I walked into the arena.

I expected Dellion to greet me with distaste, but she was all business, fully focused on our bout. When I saw Bryony and Tyron being welcomed by our opponents, I grinned at my two companions.

"I hope you're not too disappointed to have me instead of Bryony and Tyron. You can take it as a compliment to your strength if nothing else."

It was certainly clear Mitchell considered Jareth and Dellion the stronger team, and I couldn't blame him. I was too buoyed up by the unexpected turn of events to mind being assigned as a handicap.

"Don't underrate yourself." Jareth smiled, the expression just missing his eyes as usual. "I've fought you, remember. I daresay you'll prove yourself useful."

I grinned back at him. "I certainly intend to try."

"They won't have learned much yet," Dellion said. "But I assume we'll be contending with some sort of fast-growing vines."

"And some sort of water. Or wind," I added. "Isabelle is so quiet I don't have her measure yet. Is she strong? How long has she been sixteen?"

Jareth frowned in thought. "Dellion, do you remember? I'm fairly sure she turned sixteen last winter. Her family doesn't spend much time at court."

Dellion watched the other girl with narrowed eyes. "I'd be willing to bet she's more competent than she lets on in composition class. So we'd better be prepared. Jareth, I assume you brought some decent shields. Enough for all of us?"

I almost bounced on my toes, full of energy. With allies who came equipped with compositions, this would be similar to the training my parents insisted I undertake with the Royal Guard at home.

"What do you want me to do?" I asked.

Mitchell appeared beside us. "We will begin in one minute. Remember that each trainee is only permitted to work compositions of their own making."

He moved away to the other team, and I deflated somewhat.

"Sorry," I told Jareth and Dellion. "That will limit my usefulness."

"I can still work a shield to cover you." Jareth led us toward the middle of the arena. "After that, you'll need to make use of that sword of yours to keep them on their toes."

I drew my blade, exchanging a conspiratorial grin with the prince. "That I can definitely do."

There was no more time for discussion as Mitchell called the beginning of the battle. Jareth immediately ripped three separate compositions, flicking his fingers in the direction of Dellion and me. Such profligate use of his compositions spoke volumes about his strength and easily demonstrated why our instructor had made the teams so uneven in size.

Power sprang to life around me, and I felt an edge of tension I hadn't even recognized melt away. The sensation of being surrounded by power was second nature, the result of a life spent hedged around with other people's compositions. I hadn't even noticed how much being without it had left me feeling vulnerable.

I launched across the open arena floor, the dry dirt puffing up at my flying footsteps. I hadn't had the chance to ask what sort of compositions my teammates had learned so far in their Royal Guard studies, but I would leave that side of things to them. My role was to make it as hard as possible for our opponents to retrieve and tear their own compositions.

I aimed myself at Isabelle, but before I could reach her, Bryony jumped in front of me, her blade raised. I let my momentum carry me forward into an attack, wanting to test what sort of shield she had, if any.

My sword met no resistance, confirming what my senses were already telling me—she was unshielded. She blocked me easily with her blade, however, launching a counterattack that I barely managed to avoid.

I grimaced as I danced out of her reach. Apparently my own shield was only against power, not physical attacks. I was still grateful for its presence, since I didn't know what I could expect from Bryony's power mage teammates, but it would do nothing to protect me from the physical blows of an opponent's sword.

Bryony lunged forward again, and this time I was the one to counterattack. But it had been a feint, and her blade leaped free, skirting mine and driving straight for my heart.

I hadn't expected such an aggressive move, and I fumbled my defense. Before her sword could actually touch me, however, it encountered an invisible barrier and skitted away. Apparently Jareth had built in some protection against physical attacks after all, but only deadly blows. It was a wise move that would prevent the power in the shield from being drained too fast.

"Bryony!" I gasped. "You could have killed me."

She just laughed, entirely unconcerned. "Of course I couldn't have! I saw the prince tear you a shield."

"But you didn't know what type of shield!"

She scoffed. "What good would a shield be if it didn't protect you from a deathblow?"

I wouldn't have chosen to bet my life on such an assumption, but it did make sense that a royal prince would be schooled in the complexities of shielding before being sent far from home, even to the Academy.

I was about to launch another attack, ready to be reckless now I understood the limitations of my shield, but a rush of power streaked past me. Bryony faltered, her grin turning to a frown before she toppled sideways into the dirt.

"Thanks!" I called without turning to see which of my teammates had launched the attack.

Stepping past Bryony, I tried to locate my other opponents. Tyron had already been felled by what looked like a similar composition to the one used against Bryony. I shook my head. Their teammates had left them unshielded and so had wasted them. I doubted any of the teams would make that mistake again.

A battering of power rushed directly for me, but my shield turned it aside. I didn't know how many such hits the shield could take, but for now I could still feel it burning around me.

I spotted Isabelle a short distance to one side, her eyes latched on Jareth some way still behind me. She reached for a composition.

I charged, calling a battle cry, but her hands moved too quickly for me to stop her. Her focus had changed, however, and the wind that sprang up around her whooshed in my direction, smashing against me and driving me backward. For a moment it was all I could do to stay on my feet as I lost ground. I just hoped Jareth was making use of the reprieve I had given him.

The wind softened enough for me to regain my balance, but a loud yelp distracted me once again from Isabelle. Spinning, I saw Dellion struggling with a number of thick vines that had sprung up from the dirt at her feet and were winding their way around her legs, torso, and arms. She fought to keep them off, her blade lost at her feet.

Water dripped off her, and the ground around her was more mud than dirt, suggesting the growers had received some help from their wind worker to enable the vines to grow so quickly and effectively. I dove for my teammate, sliding through the mud to land at her feet. Swinging my sword, I used it like a common knife, hacking at the base of the vines where they sprang from the earth.

They gave easily before the edge of my blade, and I yanked at them with my other hand, pulling them off Dellion. She barely glanced at me as she shook her arms free and plunged her hands inside her robe.

"Shield down!" screamed Jareth's voice somewhere to our side. "Isabelle!"

Dellion didn't hesitate, ripping one of the parchments she had received and sending the power rushing toward the temporarily unshielded trainee wind worker.

Isabelle's arms and legs clamped to her side, and she teetered for a moment before crashing sideways into the dirt. I scrambled to my feet, ignoring the mud that now coated my white robe, and looked wildly around for Frida and Ashlyn.

It took me a moment to realize both girls lay on the ground, similarly restrained by invisible bonds.

"Match," called our instructor's voice from the side of the arena. "Victory belongs to Team Royal Guard."

"Woooo!!!" I pumped both arms into the air in triumph, still caught in the overwhelming rush of energy from the fight.

Dellion actually grinned at me, apparently also swept up in the moment.

"Thanks for the rescue, Princess."

I grinned back at her as Mitchell stepped into the arena. He ripped a parchment, releasing all of our bound opponents. The five of them slowly climbed to their feet, wincing and rubbing at bruised spots from their falls.

I offered a hand to Bryony, who had been lying near me, but she wrinkled her nose at my grubby state and refused the help.

"I'm afraid the vanquished don't choose the terms," I said solemnly and swept my arms around her in an enormous hug, laughing as she squealed in protest.

"Now *there's* my favorite cousin," she said, giving in and laughing with me.

When I gave her a quizzical look, she shrugged. "Sometimes you get so caught up in proving to everyone you're not useless, that I think *you* forget you're not."

I turned up my nose. "Useless? I don't know what you're talking about. *I'm* not the one on the losing team."

Bryony chuckled. "My point precisely."

We joined the end of the small line of trainees trooping back to the seats. Mitchell indicated we should join our year mates, offering no words of congratulations or praise. Not that I had expected any from someone as perpetually sour as he seemed to be. As I walked up the steps between the seats, my eyes caught on Darius. He was watching me, something hard to read in his eyes, and I was suddenly conscious of my dirty state.

"Observers, what weaknesses did you see in the approaches of the two teams?" Mitchell asked. "What would you have done differently? Bear in mind the ability level of the participants."

Darius spoke first. "Team Growers hadn't provided themselves with sufficient shields. A lack of strength in a shield can be at least partially balanced by volume of shielding compositions. As it was, not only were they unable to sufficiently protect themselves, but they wasted the extra resource of the energy mages. As evidenced by the contributions of Princess Verene to the opposing team, Bryony and Tyron could have turned the tide of battle if they hadn't been incapacitated so early."

I nodded. I had thought the same thing during the conflict. Darius's eyes flicked to me, and for a moment we were locked in agreement instead of conflict. It was a strange sensation.

The conversation flowed on, with praise given to Ashlyn and Isabelle for working together to unleash the vines on Dellion. They hadn't threatened her physical safety in any way, and so had evaded her shields. But with her arms occupied, she had been incapacitated as surely as with the power bindings my teammates had used against our opponents.

"The winning team were fortunate to have one of the princes on their side," Armand said. "He provided a disproportionate amount of power to their team effort."

Jareth grinned, not in the least abashed. When I looked down the row of seating at him, he actually winked at me, startling out a reluctant laugh. I could understand his attitude, though. As royalty, we weren't raised to think life was fair—instead we knew from the youngest age that we enjoyed both disproportionate privilege and disproportionate responsibility and pressure. I had many times wished I might exchange my position for that of any unremarkable mage in the kingdom, but I would never apologize for using what power I had been granted.

"It is true that Prince Jareth was a substantial factor in their victory," Mitchell said. "But that doesn't mean he could have won on his own. Something that is well-worth bearing in mind."

He swept a hard look over us all. "And although I weighted the teams to bear in mind his extra strength, you must consider that outside the Academy, life will not be so even-handed. If you ever find your life in danger, you are not guaranteed to be facing an opponent of equal strength. Never let that be an excuse for failure."

I suppressed a grimace. It was an easy thing to say from a position of strength. But some situations left no possibility of victory for the weaker party, however creatively they approached the situation. The conversation was still fascinating, though, and I listened to all the opinions with interest.

From the stories I had heard from my parents and then Lucien, the arena bouts in Ardann had a distinct armed forces focus. It had made sense in a time of war, when the Academy was preparing its trainees for compulsory conscription and time at the front lines. But now?

Having trainees battle with a focus on their disciplines made sense to me. It both strengthened their discipline training—forcing them to put their knowledge and learning under pressure and driving them to increase their skills—and it encouraged them to learn to defend themselves with their greatest strengths.

I would talk to Lucien over the summer. Perhaps it was time the Ardannian Academy tried some new approaches to combat training.

When we were finally freed to return to the main building, I found myself descending from the seats beside Frida and Ashlyn. While I had enjoyed the brief camaraderie with Dellion, I feared the match would have the opposite effect with the two growers.

Frida grinned at me, however. "Good job taking down Ashlyn's vines. One day I'll learn how to make them grow with a resistance to blades."

I smiled back, encouraged to see that the shared conflict in the arena had broken down some barriers, regardless of teams.

"That would be a useful composition for battle," I said. "Just don't ever let any of the vines proliferate in the wild. Can you imagine the complaints of the farmers?"

A startled laugh behind me made me glance back at Isabelle.

"I can imagine it all too well," she said, when she saw me looking. "My family live on the north coast, and our estate is largely made up of farming land."

"I'll be sure to build an incapacity to reproduce into the composition," Frida assured us, her team's defeat appearing not to have dented her confidence in her future capability.

Bryony, ahead of all of us, gave me a significant look over her shoulder. *See,* her eyes seemed to say, *look how they're accepting you now. Not useless at all.*

CHAPTER 13

*D*ellion quickly returned to her usual superior attitude, but Frida and Ashlyn began to occasionally sit with Bryony, Tyron, and me at meals. Bryony took to needling Tyron about being constantly surrounded by girls, but the easy-going energy mage just grinned and said all the energy mage boys would be wanting to come to the Kallorwegian Academy if they knew what it was like.

As first years, we only spent one morning a week in the arena, and I now actually looked forward to it. Mitchell changed the teams each week, never telling us in advance who it would be, and so I soon had a chance to fight alongside Frida and Ashlyn. My favorite weeks were when Bryony and I were assigned to the same team, but it rarely happened since we were both more skilled with our swords than Tyron.

Forcing us together into teams did more to break down the barriers between me and my Kallorwegian year mates than anything else had done. For those few hours in the arena, rank and home were mostly forgotten, our focus on our battle teams. And though much of the constraint returned when we left, I finally felt like I was making progress.

The lightness in my heart did much to counteract the growing chill in the air. But it didn't stop me from grumbling to Bryony when she continued to drag me out to the training grounds every rest day morning.

I much preferred the afternoons when I was free to find refuge in the cozy warmth of my favorite place in the Academy. Hugh's domain—the great library—was located on the floor below mine along with the offices of all our instructors. The room had surprised me at first, being quite unlike the grand double-story libraries of the palace and Academy at home. But I had quickly grown to love it.

The single-story room was deceptive in size, stretching out far further than it first appeared. I could roam through it again and again, always discovering new nooks and corners where puffy armchairs or softly lit desks invited me to stop and linger.

Instead of grand arching windows, it had hidden ones that gave you the sense you were peeping out at the real world from some secret pocket of enchantment. The gray stone of the walls might not hold the grandeur of white marble, but they made the space friendly in a way I hadn't expected.

And the endless shelves held the one thing that most truly felt like home. Words. Books and scrolls and more books. Libraries like this were a wonder and a treasure in our world where every page had to first be bound by a mage and made safe for ordinary writing. The books stored here represented centuries of effort.

But I noticed a number of shelves whose burdens had a new, shiny look most of the others lacked. When I ran my fingers along them, I wondered how many had been transcribed by sealed commonborns. Or even written by them. I knew a number of the commonborn University graduates in Ardann had written books. We had books now about topics that had never been written about before—like the lives of the commonborns themselves.

My mother was the one who had usually taken me to the

library at home, stealing me away whenever we could spare some precious moments together. From my youngest years she had impressed on me the power and value of words.

"This is a gift, Verene," she would say to me. "A gift I grew up without and that countless others will never experience. Words have power. Our voices have power—and I don't just mean mine. Never forget how fortunate you are to have access to so much knowledge and wisdom. Treasure it and remember that there are many different types of power."

Looking back, I occasionally wondered if she had sensed my lack of ability from the very beginning with the inexplicable intuition of motherhood.

Here in the library in distant Kallorway, I could pretend she was just around the next shelf. And I reminded myself I had come to this foreign place to honor her words. I had been given a gift, even if I did not have an ability, and I had a responsibility to use it for my people.

Hugh, the library head, always had a kind word and a smile for me, and often his wife Raelynn was with him. I asked her about the energy trainee Amalia had told us about, and she was full of information about his training. Apparently she had been closely involved— something I should have predicted, given the topic of their studies.

"If you would ever like to know more about healing, I'm always available," she told me with a smile. "I'm always happy to impart my knowledge more broadly than just my healing trainees."

My initial question about Raelynn's status at the Academy had been answered by the discovery of how they handled discipline training. She did serve as healer when needed, but she was also an instructor, teaching those who had selected the healing discipline.

The older couple remained my favorite of the instructors, despite my suspicions that they pitied me for being all alone here.

Somehow pity was easier to take from someone who had spent most of their life locked away in a remote Academy—and who looked and acted like they could be my grandparent.

I was named in honor of one of my real grandmothers—now the queen mother—and everyone said I had a strong physical resemblance to her. But she had never been the grandmotherly sort.

I was fairly sure she loved me—in her own way. But for someone who had dedicated her life to her role as queen and to building the strength of Ardann, it couldn't be much of an honor to have your namesake turn out to be the family failure. I sometimes imagined what it would be like to come back from Kallorway having secured some treaty or alliance. Perhaps then she could be truly proud of me.

And now that we had started in the arena, I finally felt as if I were making small steps of progress. My year mates were letting down their barriers, and I was seeing a side of them that didn't slavishly follow in the steps of their parents' loyalties. Maybe with enough time, they would finally let me see whatever truths lurked beneath the surface.

I didn't allow myself to be too swept away by hope, though. Darius never let his guard down even in arena battles, completing his assigned task with skill but never letting his emotions overwhelm him.

Thoughts of the prince had me in an especially sour mood one freezing rest day morning, as Bryony dragged me outside as usual.

"It's going to be too cold to do this soon," I told her darkly. "If it's not too cold now."

"Nonsense! We'll warm up as soon as we get into the bout."

"At the very least we're going to have to start later in the morning," I pleaded.

"Ha! I'm not so easily fooled. Once you get ensconced in that warm, cozy library, I'll have no hope of dragging you out here. First thing in the morning is…"

Her voice trailed away as we reached our year's training yard.

"Is a time we should all be in bed?" I supplied, coming to a stop beside her.

"Does the yard look strange to you?" she asked, ignoring my comment.

I frowned at it. "Strange how?"

"I don't know, it just looks…different."

I scanned the square of dirt. The ground looked hard from the frost, but that had become normal for our morning sessions.

"Do you want to go back inside?" I asked hopefully.

Bryony gave me an unimpressed look. "Don't think you're getting out of it that easily."

I assumed my best innocent expression. "If you think something's wrong, though…"

"I didn't say wrong, just different. Come on."

We both stepped into the yard, and with a further inaudible grumble, I stripped off the jacket I was wearing, letting it fall to the ground. Bryony had already drawn her sword, so I drew mine as well, settling into the familiar position ready for a bout.

Bryony jumped straight to the attack, and I let her carry the momentum, giving myself a few moments to adjust. I skipped backward and then backward again, mentally preparing for a counterattack. As I stepped back the third time, however, my heel sank into the ground. I fell, my leg twisting as I did so. I screamed as an audible crack reached my ears along with stabbing pain.

Agony radiated up from my ankle. For a moment I closed my eyes and did nothing but fight it. When I had regained a modicum of control, I opened them again to find Bryony had abandoned her sword and dropped to the ground beside me.

"Verene! What happened?"

She helped me sit up, but when she reached for my ankle, I grabbed her wrist and shook my head.

"No, don't touch it. I'm not sure how bad it is, but I don't want you making it worse."

Bryony bit her lip. "Is it broken then?"

I swallowed, part of my attention still taken up by holding back the pain. "Yes."

Her head whipped from side to side, but there was no one else in sight. No one else was foolish enough to be out here this early on a rest day—especially not now the weather had turned.

"But what happened? I've never seen you fall like that."

"There was a hole." Pain made my voice grim. "My heel hit it, and I twisted my ankle as I fell."

"What do you mean a hole?" She looked from me to the ground. "We're in the training yard, not out in some warren-studded field."

"And yet, there was a hole." I took a deep breath through my nose, bracing against a fresh wave of pain. "You did say something looked off."

Bryony scooted around me, examining the ground near my foot. I craned my neck to watch her but had to give up when the movement sent a shooting pain up my leg.

"You're right, there's a hole." She looked over at me, anger in her eyes now. "It's not a big one, but it's deep enough to be a danger."

"I don't know why I didn't see it." I winced. "I should have been paying more attention."

Bryony shook her head. "No, this was concealed."

My head shot up, my eyes meeting hers. "Concealed?"

"It looks as if whatever—whoever—made this hole filled it with loose dirt so it wouldn't be immediately obvious."

Our eyes darted across the rest of the yard in unison. What we saw made me frown and Bryony jump to her feet. She took several steps and leaned down to examine something on the ground.

"It's another one." She threw a loaded look back at me. "Just the same." She scanned the yard again. "It looks like they're all over the yard."

"That must have been what you saw when we arrived," I said. "All the patches are darker because they don't have the frost. Your mind registered that it looked different, even if you didn't realize why."

Bryony crossed back over to me, her voice dropping in volume although we were still alone. "No frost."

I nodded. "Which means someone did this recently. This morning."

Bryony frowned at our surroundings which remained stubbornly empty.

"We need to get you inside and to the healer. I could help you back to the Academy." The doubt was audible in her voice.

I managed a laugh that sounded more like a groan. "Thanks for the thought, but I'm fairly certain there's no possibility of you carrying me anywhere. You'll have to go get help. Let Raelynn know what's happened. This should be an easy fix for her."

Bryony hesitated. "You'll be all right out here on your own?"

I pushed at her, the gesture ineffective from my awkward position on the ground. "Go! The sooner you leave, the sooner you can bring Raelynn back with a sweet, sweet pain relief composition."

Bryony winced but still hesitated.

"Go!" I gave her a stern look. "There's no reason to think whoever did this is still lurking around. And I'm not unprotected you know." I patted the front of my robe significantly.

Reluctantly she nodded. Leaving her weapon discarded where it had fallen, she raced away toward the main Academy building, stepping carefully until she had exited the training yard.

CHAPTER 14

s soon as she disappeared from sight, I closed my eyes, bracing myself against my hands and letting my head flop forward. After a moment, I opened them again, however, searching my surroundings. Despite the quiet around me, it was too easy to imagine enemies drawing close when my eyes were closed.

With every minute that passed, the temptation to draw on my own supply of compositions grew. But I resisted the urge. As terrible as the stabbing, throbbing fire in my ankle felt, I knew far worse pain was possible. It would be foolish to use my reserves when Raelynn would be here soon.

Please, let her be here soon.

After what felt like hours, but was likely only minutes, running steps made me twist around, biting back a yelp at the pain that lanced up from my ankle. Bryony was in view, running back toward me with something gripped tightly in her hand.

She leaped the small fence, only slowing her pace so she could watch her footing more closely. As soon as she reached me, she ripped the parchment she held, flicking her fingers in my direction. A cool mist enveloped me, sinking through my skin and bringing numbing relief.

I gave a long, relieved sigh, and some of the tension left Bryony's face.

"Raelynn's coming behind," she said. "But I ran ahead with her pain relief composition."

"Thank you," I said. "You are a beautiful person deserving of much praise."

Her face lightened even further. "I'll remind you of that next time you complain it's too cold to be out here practicing."

I groaned. "Beauty is overrated."

A puffing made us both look up to see Raelynn hurrying toward us, her breath frosting in the air in front of her.

"Your Highness!" she cried as she reached our yard. "Apologies for taking so long."

I shook my head. "No, thank you for coming so promptly. I'm feeling fine now, thanks to the composition you sent with Bryony, but I admit I'm eager to be back inside in the warmth."

Raelynn shuddered. "Yes, indeed. It's far too cold for anyone to be out here, let alone an injured patient."

"Well, I'm sure I won't be a patient much longer. Not once you've had a chance to patch me up." I smiled at her, but she wagged a reproving finger at me.

"You may be young, but you'll still need some recovery time. Healings are draining, you should know that."

She continued to murmur to herself about the recklessness of youth as she eased herself down onto the ground beside me. She carried a small leather case which she set down and began to rummage through.

I caught flashes of colored leather as she pushed around the pouches inside, looking for the one she wanted. The familiar sight was soothing. Healers at home carried cases just like it.

She found what she was looking for, producing a rolled scrap of parchment and tearing it. Her voice turned soothing and gentle as she switched from a grandmotherly role to a healer.

"This is a composition to diagnose injuries such as breaks and sprains."

I could neither feel nor see anything, but she clucked her tongue several times, her eyes fixed on my ankle.

"Is it working?" Bryony asked.

"Of course." Raelynn turned back to her case. "I don't bother to compose the diagnosis workings so that anyone else can see them. It just makes the patients anxious, since they don't know how to interpret the visible signs it produces. In this case, you have a break, Your Highness, but a fairly clean one. Healing it will be a simple matter, I'm happy to say."

I nodded, watching as she rummaged through her case once again. This time, the parchment she retrieved was larger, filled with more words than the diagnosis one had been.

Raelynn smiled at me. "This will have you back on your feet in just a moment, Princess."

She tore the composition and flicked her fingers at my ankle yet again. A strange, grinding feeling made me wince, although I could feel no actual pain. But it was all too easy to imagine how it would have felt without the earlier pain relief composition.

But in a moment the sensation was gone. Cautiously I extended and then flexed my ankle, my instincts fighting against my brain's assertion that the injury was gone. My foot responded easily with no sign of any issue.

Bryony popped back up at my side, making me realize she had disappeared. I gave her a questioning look as she helped lever me to my feet.

"I checked the other yards," she told me in an undertone. "There's no sign of holes in any of them."

I nodded, my jaw clenched tight. I wasn't surprised at the news, but it was unwelcome all the same. Only two people ever practiced in our yard on a rest day, and I couldn't imagine anyone had a reason to target Bryony.

I tested my ankle gingerly, but it easily took my weight, and soon Bryony and I were both assisting Raelynn to haul herself back to standing.

"Thank you, girls," she said, patting both of our arms.

It was the first friendly physical contact I had received from anyone but Bryony, and it was surprisingly pleasant to know someone had forgotten about my royal status, if only for a moment.

We walked back to the Academy building together, moving at the healer's slower pace. My fingers and toes were going numb, and I was much more tired than I had been when I exited the building earlier that morning, but otherwise I felt remarkably well. Physically, at least.

When we reached the entrance, I slowed.

"Would you mind not mentioning this to anyone?" I asked Raelynn.

She clucked at me. "There's no shame in twisting an ankle, my dear. Even for a princess."

Bryony gave me a loaded look behind her back.

"Even so," I said, letting my posture grow slightly more rigid and my voice a little more imperious, "I would appreciate if you didn't mention it."

"Ah, well, there's nothing like the pride of youth," she said with a chuckle. "I'll have to tell the duke, of course. I couldn't go healing a royal on Academy grounds without keeping him informed! And Hugh was with me when Bryony here came bursting in so dramatically. But I can't imagine I'll have any cause to go spreading it further than that."

I unbent. "Thank you. I appreciate it."

I didn't know what to make of the accident yet, but I wanted the chance to think on it further before deciding who we should tell—if anyone.

Once inside the entryway, I managed to thank Raelynn a final time before Bryony hauled me toward the stairs. She towed me all the way to my suite, closing the door behind us.

"What. Was. That." She stared at me. "Did someone just sabotage our training yard? What should we do? Surely we have to tell…someone."

"Who do you suggest?" I stripped off my robe and dropped onto one of the sofas.

She paced up and down, waving her arms in the air. "I don't know! Duke Francis? Instructor Mitchell? Is there a replacement groundskeeper since my father left?"

"Groundskeeper?" I laughed. "Yes, let's go and pour out our troubles to some poor groundskeeper."

She spun around, putting her arms on her hips. "Well, we can't just leave those holes there." She frowned. "Can we?"

I rubbed my head. "Maybe? I confess I'm curious to see what becomes of them. Will the perpetrator sneak back and remove them all before class tomorrow morning?"

"Remove them all? Oh! You mean with a composition. Yes, I suppose they may well want to remove the evidence of their crimes."

"That's assuming whoever it was knew that we go out there to practice on a rest day. Perhaps they intended the holes for our class."

Bryony raised an eyebrow at me.

"I'm just considering all options," I said.

She threw her hands in the air. "Next you're going to say I was their target!"

"I'll admit it's unlikely. Unless you got any ominous messages when you arrived? I suppose you are a foreigner as well as an energy mage. Your people were driven away for being different once before."

"Ominous messages?" Bryony narrowed her eyes. "What's that supposed to mean?" When I didn't immediately respond, she sucked in a breath. "Verene, you tell me what's going on right now!"

Reluctantly I told her about the state of my room when I first arrived. Her eyes grew rounder and rounder through the story.

"Why didn't you tell anyone?" she exploded when I finished.

"For the same reason I'm not sure I want to tell anyone now. I'm not sure who to tell. Not when I don't know who's behind it."

She deflated, collapsing onto the other sofa. "Surely you don't think Duke Francis could be behind it?"

I shrugged. "I think anything's possible at this point. I'm a foreign princess, and my family and kingdom are strong. You would expect our year mates to be seizing such an unusual opportunity to make connections with my aunt through me. And yet, instead, everyone has gone out of their way to show their utter disinterest. It is quite clear that neither side of Kallorwegian politics wants me here. And apparently someone is willing to take stronger measures to send that message. But who? I don't intend to be driven away, and without knowing their identity or their motivation, I can't know if exposing them will help or harm my purpose here."

"You and proving yourself! I couldn't care less about your purpose here. It's not worth getting killed over."

"No, of course not." I shook my head at her. "No one said anything about dying. Someone's trying to send me a message, not kill me. Both incidents so far could be written off as pranks."

"Breaking your ankle is a *prank*?"

"With a supply of healing compositions in my pocket and an experienced healer close at hand? The claim could certainly be made. And in the case of today, it would be easy enough for the perpetrator to argue that they didn't know about our habit of using the yard on a rest day. They could say it was a prank intended to be discovered by our year before any bouts had begun. I wouldn't have injured myself so badly if I had just been walking when my foot went into that hole."

Bryony sighed. "I suppose you're right. And I'm sure you also don't want word of any of this getting back to your parents. Because goodness knows, it would be a disaster if they pulled you out before you've made your aunt proud."

I ignored the sour note in her voice. "Since when are you so eager to see me gone? Should I be asking what you were doing this morning before we went outside together?"

Bryony laughed. "If I ever tire of your company, you can be sure I'll let you know in a much more direct fashion."

"I'm sure you will." I threw my arm over my eyes and groaned. "I know it's not even lunch yet, but I think I'm going back to bed. I'm exhausted."

Her voice turned instantly sympathetic. "Of course you are after an ordeal like that and then a healing. I shouldn't keep you up jabbering."

I lowered my arm. "About telling someone…"

"I'll keep the secret…for now. I'll admit I also have some curiosity to see if the holes are gone tomorrow. But if you find a…a dead rat, or something, nailed to your door next, I do hope you'll tell me, at least."

I chuckled. "I promise to inform you of any dead rodents that happen to cross my path. Now go and enjoy your rest day."

CHAPTER 15

*W*hen my arrival at the Academy had been followed by so many weeks without incident, I had ceased to regard everyone around me with suspicion. But the sentiment had returned now with a vengeance.

When Wardell and Armand returned from their rest day expedition, I had to restrain myself from asking them what time they had left and who had seen them go. And when Frida and Ashlyn joined us in the dining hall, I suddenly started questioning their recent friendliness. If the instigator of these *pranks* had intended to make it difficult for me to forge connections with others at the Academy, then they were finally starting to succeed.

I took two naps during the remainder of the rest day, but still woke the next morning feeling unnaturally tired. I didn't intend to miss combat, however, and hurried out of the building with the rest of my year. On arrival at our regular training yard, both Bryony and I carefully examined the ground, but there was no sign of any disturbance. Our eyes met, but we said nothing.

The job had been done so perfectly that there was now no question in my mind the culprit must be a power mage. But I had never really doubted that. A sealed commonborn might have written the message on my wall, but why would they do so unless at the instigation of someone powerful enough to compel either their obedience or loyalty? It would be far too great a risk for no discernible reward.

No, it must be someone closely involved in the politics of the Kallorwegian court. And with the use of compositions, they wouldn't even have needed to come near the training yard. They could have completed the necessary workings from the window of their room, even, meaning their chance of getting caught in the act was almost non-existent.

Unfortunately, it could be almost any of the mages at the Academy. I had even toyed with the idea that it might be Darius himself. I knew without a doubt that he had access to my rooms at least.

But nothing about the nature of it fit with what I had seen of the crown prince. Somehow I suspected that when he sent a message, the receiver was left in no doubt of either its meaning or its source.

I was pulled from my dark musings by Ashlyn appearing before me and suggesting we bout. It was the first time she had done so, and I hated the spike of suspicion that shot through me at the new behavior. I agreed, determined not to let this latest incident mar all my previous efforts, and we completed a competent, if unexciting, match.

When we finished, she hesitated.

"It's starting to get cold," she said, sounding slightly awkward. "It will be Midwinter before we know it, I'm sure."

My suspicions rose again at her strange manner, although the exhaustion pulled at me, making my brain foggy.

"Yes, I suppose it will," I said. "Although it's still a while off yet."

"Of course." She nodded. "I suppose you won't be traveling home, given we only get a few days off class. I wanted to invite you—and Bryony and Tyron as well, of course—to return to my home to celebrate with me and my family. My parents are planning a large Midwinter party and would be honored by your presence."

Oh. My mind had been so focused on my accident, that even the mention of Midwinter hadn't alerted me to the purpose of her conversation. Now her invitation threw me off guard.

I hadn't thought our growing friendliness had crossed the line into actual friendship, and spending the holidays with a large crowd of strangers sounded less than appealing. But I didn't want to reject her overture now that one had finally appeared.

"Thank you," I said. "I can't speak for the others, but I would be happy to accept your invitation."

"Excellent!" A smile spread across her face. "I've invited Frida as well, so hopefully there will be a small crowd of us." She gave me a small bow and hurried away.

I watched her go, fighting the feeling that I had forgotten something important. I hated how successfully the events of the day before had set me off balance.

Ashlyn's mother was Head of the Wind Workers and usually voted with the king. Was the invitation a sign that the king's faction was warming to the idea of an increased connection with Ardann? And did that mean the general's faction was behind my accident?

After so many weeks of peace, my unknown harasser had returned just as a growing friendliness appeared between me and Ashlyn. Was that coincidence? Or was I being overly paranoid? It was possible the invitation was truly just a friendly gesture from a year mate.

Spinning, I nearly collided with Wardell. He grunted something and hurried away while I rubbed at my temple. Maybe I wasn't recovered enough to be in class after all.

Looking up, my eyes met Darius's. His face looked even more closed off than usual, and I gave a quiet groan. The day had barely started, and I was already more than ready to crawl back into bed.

Turning away from the prince, I hurried over to Mitchell. In a low voice I told him I felt unwell and needed to withdraw for the rest of the lesson. His expression didn't suggest much belief, but he didn't contradict me either—whether because he didn't care enough to do so or because of my royal status I didn't know.

I whispered to Bryony that I needed a bit more rest after all and fled back toward the Academy, telling myself that it was a strategic retreat and nothing more.

After another long nap, I woke finally feeling full of energy again. It occurred to me that Mitchell might have been expecting me to go to Raelynn, but there didn't seem any point in doing so now. At least if he questioned her later, she could confirm that I had indeed suffered a recent medical incident and needed rest. I just hoped she didn't say any more than that.

Someone—Bryony or my assigned servant—had brought in a tray of food and left it in my sitting room. I devoured it hungrily as I considered my options. I had been woken by a bell, and from the look of the light outside, it had been the bell between composition and discipline classes. Which meant there was no point trying to rejoin the rest of the trainees at this point.

Instead I decided to write a letter to my family. I had a small stack already waiting and would send them home the next time a royal messenger arrived with a collection of their missives to me. It would have been nice to hear their familiar voices, but communication compositions required enormous power to reach across entire kingdoms and wouldn't last long enough for a decent conversation anyway. My father was one of the few with the strength needed to create such a working, but I had only let him exhaust himself once to write me a single one for use in the direst emergency. And then only because both my parents had insisted.

The letter required some thought as I wanted to be truthful but not alarming or negative. I ended up focusing on our arena battles and my various wins and losses, and by the time I had finished, it was past the start of the evening meal.

I was still full from my late lunch, however, so I didn't regret missing it. I settled in for a quiet evening with my favorite book, in the mood for a little comfort and familiarity. I half-expected Bryony to come bursting in at some point, determined to check on me, but when the knock came, it wasn't from the direction of my main door.

For a moment I looked around in confusion before it came again, and I realized it was emanating from behind the tapestry. At least the prince had been true to his word and was warning me of his approach this time.

Warily I pulled back the tapestry and opened the door. He didn't wait for a verbal invitation to enter, brushing past me and stalking into the room. I spun around to face him, leaving the door propped open behind me.

"If you've come to check on my well-being, I'm fully recovered," I told him.

He checked at my words, the thundercloud on his face letting in a hint of confusion.

"You really were ill?"

"Exhausted due to recovery from a healing, actually—but that is much the same thing. Despite your insistence on believing otherwise, I have never told anyone here anything other than the truth." I glowered at him and muttered to myself, "Although if I ever said I was pleased to meet you, then that would have to be chalked up to a mistake at the very least."

Something flickered in his eyes, and for a startling moment I actually thought he might laugh—or at least smile. But the moment passed.

"Then I suppose you are just a meddling fool," he snapped.

I sighed and took a seat on one of the sofas, arranging my skirts neatly around me.

"Although I do believe myself now recovered, I'm not sure I have the energy for all these…dramatics, Prince Darius. Please do sit down."

He stared at me, his face growing darker and darker until I was sure he would explode. But instead he dropped abruptly down onto the other sofa. It was strange to see him so out of control of his emotions.

"Very well, if that is how you want to play it."

I suppressed a smile. Something had changed in our one bout in the training yard, and I didn't intend to let him have full control of our interactions from now on.

"I'm afraid I still have no idea what you're talking about. What have I done to so overset you?"

His usual rigid control slammed down over his face, and I watched the effect curiously. I had once thought it demonstrated ice and indifference, but it might be a sign of quite the opposite. What powerful emotions was he concealing behind it? I should probably be flattered. I couldn't imagine there were many people who ever got the chance to see behind that royal mask.

Almost against my will, I felt a swell of fellow feeling for him. I had learned to create my own mask—as every member of my family had—and I used it to protect myself. I rarely let anyone see how my lack of ability pained me.

But what must it be like for Darius? How much greater were the burdens he bore behind his mask? How much greater were the stakes?

I tamped down on the curiosity. Apparently I was enough of an equal that the crown prince occasionally let loose his true feelings. But I couldn't make the mistake of forgetting that his revealed emotions were universally negative toward me. We weren't friends, and his burdens weren't my responsibility.

He drew several deep breaths, examining my face as carefully as I examined his.

"I apologize," he said formally. "Sometimes I forget just how far removed you are from my court. Perhaps it is possible you did act in innocence."

Do *you forget?* I asked silently. *Or does some part of you always remember how distant I am from your normal life and your court? Is that why you sometimes let your guard down with me?*

I let a smile twitch across my face. "I don't know that I can promise all my actions have been *innocent,* but I can certainly claim ignorance as to how any of them might have upset you."

"You accepted a Midwinter invitation from Ashlyn."

"That's what upset you? But why?"

"Ashlyn's mother is the Head of the Wind Workers. She is extremely influential at court and is closely aligned with my father."

I arched an eyebrow. "And that's a problem?"

"Of course it's a problem." He almost growled the words. "And to make it worse, you accepted it in front of not only me but Wardell—whose uncle is the Head of the Creators and aligned with my grandfather. In the hours you've spent hiding in your room, I've already had communications from both my mother and my grandfather."

I barely kept my mouth from popping open. "But I only received the invitation this morning! Are you telling me the message has already passed from Wardell to his family and from them to your mother and grandfather? And the queen and General Haddon considered the issue of enough import to use communication compositions to complain to you? All because I agreed to spend Midwinter at Ashlyn's home?"

Darius shook his head, his impatience clear. "Not because you agreed to spend Midwinter with Ashlyn. You agreed to attend a large Midwinter celebration hosted by one of my father's greatest supporters—no doubt with your retinue of energy mages trailing behind. Apparently my father has suggested he may now attend himself."

I swallowed. After a lifetime of court politics, I could read a great many of the unspoken nuances behind his words.

I had guessed correctly that Ashlyn's invitation had come from her family rather than her, but I had obviously missed some underlying subtlety. Perhaps one relating to why I had been previously ignored for so long.

How much of this had to do with what Darius referred to as my *retinue*? I hadn't realized that in the general perception the energy mages were allied behind me. But I could see how such an impression had arisen.

Energy mages were scarce in Kallorway. Having two choose to attend their Academy this year must have been something of a coup. But their apparent allegiance to me put that decision in a different light. And, at least in the case of Bryony, it was true that her attendance had been because of my own.

As long as the energy mages remained in the Empire, they stood apart from the politics between the two southern kingdoms. But I could see why Kallorway might be starting to grow concerned as some of their number drifted south—almost exclusively into Ardann. My kingdom already had my family to bolster their strength, and I could only imagine how the threat of us increasing our power might overset whatever delicate balances had been achieved in the Kallorwegian court.

In Ardann, the crown always hosted a Midwinter event at the palace, and invitations were a sign of honor and prestige. I had heard it was the same in Kallorway. For the king himself not to attend the event—choosing instead to honor a private ball which would no doubt include only his supporters...

The various ramifications ran through my mind at a headlong pace. No wonder the queen was furious.

"I'm sorry," I said. "I was caught off guard by Ashlyn's invitation and didn't think it through." I shook my head. "I should have known better."

A strange look crossed Darius's face. It was almost like a softening, as if my apology had been unexpected enough to catch him off guard.

"I don't know why I came here." He surged to his feet. "The damage is done, and it will be left to me to try to fix it—as always."

He strode across the room, nearly making it through the open doorway before I managed to intercept him. I did so with a hand on his arm, and the touch made him freeze, his eyes dropping to where my fingers curled over his forearm.

For a moment we stood locked in place, and I could feel the tension in his muscles beneath my touch. Then I remembered who he was and dropped my hand. He released his breath.

"Wait," I said. "This was my mistake. Let me fix it."

He laughed, a harsh and mocking sound. "How could you fix it?"

"Give me a chance," I said. "Just one day, if you like."

He hesitated, his gaze on my face.

I put my chin up. "I am a princess, remember. I grew up in a court, just like you."

He barked out another laugh that held no hint of humor. "Just like me? I think not, Verene. What do you know of pressure with your pretty, united court and your strong queen? The court in Corrin is child's play compared to the court in Kallmon—thanks to your family."

I bristled. "Thanks to my family? Thanks to your father and his father before him, you mean. They are the ones who brought war to the south for thirty long years."

"Indeed," Darius said, the ice back in his voice. "And we are never to be allowed to forget it."

I raised a haughty eyebrow. "Never? No one has sealed your

power, Crown Prince, or that of our year mates. A new generation is coming."

"Yes." The word came out low and fierce. "And I am never to be allowed to forget that either. I repeat that you know nothing of pressure, Princess."

I fought back the sympathy that rose in me, anger and frustration helping push it back down.

"You think I know nothing of pressure? What do you know of my life? You think it's hard to have too much strength compared to those around you? Imagine what it's like to have none! Imagine, if you can, what it is like to have the greatest mage who ever lived as your mother, and to know every day of your life that you are nothing but a disappointment. There are many types of pressure, Prince."

I deflated, as if pricked by a pin, my swirling emotions draining away and leaving ice of my own in their wake.

"But then, of course, you don't believe I am powerless, do you? And so you could never understand."

He looked at me in silence for a moment, too many emotions chasing through his eyes for me to identify them. How had we come to be standing so close again? When had I lost control of this meeting?

Because I didn't feel in control anymore. My racing pulse was far too aware of the coiled energy bound within him and the intensity of his gaze as it seemed to weigh me. Why did I care so much if he found me wanting?

"Give me one day," I said. "I can fix this."

"Very well, Verene." His words were barely above a whisper. "I will give you a day and no more."

And then he was gone.

CHAPTER 16

I slept badly that night, something I determinedly blamed on my nap during the day, ignoring the frequency with which a certain pair of brown eyes intruded on my restless nighttime thoughts. I had given myself a day to find a way around the problems I had created, and I was determined not to fail.

For once I was up well before the morning bell. I had decided on my first course of action, but only when I emerged from my suite did it occur to me that I didn't actually know where to go to pursue it. Where did the instructors eat their meals?

I hesitated only for a moment, though. I didn't want to be caught by any of my year mates—and most especially Darius—before I had at least worked out a plan of action. If I wanted to speak to the library head, I would have to start in the library—the only place I had seen him since the day of my arrival.

I descended a single floor and hurried to the library. The doors did not yet stand open, but when I tried them, they were unlocked. I had never been here at this time of the morning before, and I found it utterly still and quiet.

I let myself stand inside the room for a moment, breathing in the smell of the books and the peaceful solitude. My troubles seemed to shrink a little beside the immense weight of history and wisdom that resided between the pages around me. I was not the first person to make a mistake, and I would not be the last, and yet the kingdoms rolled on.

"Princess Verene! This is an unexpected surprise." The librarian's voice sent a jolt of urgency back through me again.

"Oh good, you're here," I said. "I wasn't sure where to find you at this hour."

Hugh smiled. "I'm a creature of habit, I'm afraid. I can usually be found here. My poor wife has given up on luring me out and has resigned herself to joining me."

As if on cue, Raelynn emerged beside him.

"Your Highness! It's lovely to see you back on your feet. I heard you took yesterday to rest which was most wise." She must have seen a flash of alarm on my face because she chuckled. "You may rest easy, Your Highness. I did not reveal your secrets to anyone."

She and her husband exchanged an amused look, still clearly thinking I was motivated by some sort of youthful pride. But my concerns over the sabotage of the training yard had been overtaken by more urgent considerations, and I paid their amusement no mind.

"Are you here for something related to your healing?" Hugh asked.

I shook my head. "Is there perhaps somewhere we could sit? I have some questions, and I'm afraid the answers may not be short." I hesitated. "Assuming you have time for a conversation now?"

"I run a library," he said with a wide smile. "I am always happy to help those who come seeking knowledge and wisdom."

He gestured for me to follow him, leading me into a back corner where he opened a door and ushered me into an office. Raelynn followed behind us, curiosity on her face.

Large windows lit the spacious room, revealing nothing but ordered cleanliness. I couldn't help suspecting Raelynn was the cause of such tidiness—Hugh seemed too much the picture of the absentminded librarian to care about such things. I had been expecting his office to be littered with piles of books and abandoned scrolls.

Instead of going to the vast desk that dominated the room, he led us to a corner that held a small sofa and a puffy armchair. I took the chair while the two of them squeezed onto the sofa and looked at me with expectant faces.

I drew a deep breath. "While I believe I have some understanding of the factions that divide the Kallorwegian court, it has been made clear to me that there are subtleties I am yet to grasp."

They exchanged a knowing look, and I hurried to add, "As an outsider, I cannot hope to grasp the intricacies of these matters in the same way my year mates do. I wish only to understand what is obvious to those who grew up in this world."

I could see in their faces that they, too, had heard of my misstep. But I ruthlessly suppressed the embarrassment. I had decided they were my best hope of getting clear answers, and I didn't intend to back down.

"Acknowledging our own weaknesses is half the battle," Hugh said.

"And seeking help goes a long way toward the other half," his wife added. "We will help you, if we can."

"Of course." Hugh nodded. "You are young, despite your rank, while we are old. We came to this Academy with the duke, too many years ago for me to have any desire to count them. We have seen much in that time, though we watch from afar."

"Ah, but every mage, from the least to the greatest, attends the Academy," I said. "So you do not merely view from afar. You have had the chance to observe those of power and influence while they were still young and less guarded." I smiled. "And foolish, like me."

"I am sorry to say that some never outgrow their foolishness." Hugh gave a weary sigh.

"And some are never as young as they should be." Raelynn sounded sad.

Was she thinking of the same guarded face that filled my mind at her words?

"I think, to properly answer your question, I have to go back to a time long before you were born," Hugh said. "I know that in Ardann, all is governed by your system of families—the great families and the minor families. It was always a little different here."

I nodded. That much I knew, but I didn't interrupt him. I would listen to everything he thought important enough to tell. It was the only way to be sure I didn't miss hearing something of value that I didn't yet know.

"Family is important to us, of course, as are the strengths of various bloodlines, but we don't keep track of sprawling extended families in the same way you do. Perhaps it has something to do with the way we approach training here at the Academy, but the loyalties of most mages have always aligned with their disciplines."

I nodded. It explained why Wardell and Armand, cousins, had both chosen the discipline of their uncle. And it even explained why Frida and Ashlyn had aligned their choices, although I still wondered about them not selecting the wind workers.

"It makes sense that with such a system there would be pressure from families to choose certain disciplines. I have to confess I've been curious about Ashlyn not choosing to follow in her mother's footsteps as Head of the Wind Workers."

"I cannot speak to what pressures young Ashlyn may or may not experience at home," Hugh said. "But times are not what they once were."

"The war," I said.

He nodded. "The war. At first many were lured with the

promise of the riches and power that would flow once King Osborne had crowned himself emperor of the south. But Ardann proved less easy to conquer than many had hoped. And while the wealthiest and most powerful of the families were able to guard their children from conscription, not all were so fortunate. Factions formed, and over time, the fault lines of the court grew deeper."

This part of their history was familiar to me—it was these fractures my family had exploited when they allowed a sealed Cassius to ascend the throne.

"The old king is long dead," Hugh said, "but King Cassius stands in his stead. And many still stand behind him. The crown still has power—and will one day grow strong again. And those who look to the crown see old General Haddon as a traitor to the kingdom. He was the one who struck the treaty that led to the mass sealings, and he was the one who chose those sealed."

"And Frida's and Ashlyn's families support the king," I said slowly. "Which would suggest their parents are sealed. But surely Ashlyn's mother cannot be if she leads the wind workers." I frowned. "I'm sure none of the discipline heads are sealed."

Hugh chuckled. "If only it were so simple. It has been twenty years and more since the end of the war. Times change, and allegiances shift."

"Ashlyn's family were canny enough to keep away from the politics of the war," Raelynn said. "They focused mainly on their business as merchants before the peace was signed and the sealings were conducted."

"But they were swift to pounce afterward, and her mother rose to prominence quickly," Hugh said, with a significant look at his wife. She nodded her agreement.

"And what of the two of you?" I asked, unable to be sure of their own allegiance given the slightly derogatory way they spoke of both the general and the king.

"We follow the duke," Raelynn said firmly. "As we always have."

"The duke believes the Academy is a place of learning not of politics," Hugh said, a note of pride in his voice. "We maintain true neutrality that doesn't shift when it sees the way ripe for advancement."

"And I'm sure the Academy prospers for his stance," I said. "It's an honorable one."

"Isabelle comes from another such family," Raelynn said, a note of affection in her voice. "Although in their case I think it's more disinterest than principle. They live in the remote north east, far from the capital. I believe her choice of the wind workers is motivated by nothing but her own interests and inclination."

Much of Isabelle's aloof manner made sense in the light of that information. She not only had few connections at the Academy, but she likely had little desire to cultivate them. She had said her family owned farming land near the coast—her skills as a future wind worker would be of value to them.

"So Dellion, Wardell, and Armand all come from families that favor the queen and her father, the general," I said, mostly to myself. "While Frida, Ashlyn, and Royce are aligned with the king. And the disciplines play a lesser role than they once did." Perhaps I had been placing too much significance on my year mates' connections to various discipline heads.

"I don't know that I would say that," Hugh said slowly. "It is more that now the greater factor is whether you side with the king or the general. The disciplines still take the lead in those matters. It is why I imagine Ashlyn was free to choose the growers. They are allied with the wind workers behind the king."

I nodded. It was only natural the growers and wind workers would have stuck together. The two disciplines had always worked closely in their efforts to secure the kingdom's crops. I could imagine their support was a vital element of the king's grasp on power. How had he secured it? Perhaps with displays of favor such as the proposed attendance at their Midwinter celebrations.

I frowned, nibbling at my lower lip. Offending the wind workers—and potentially through them the growers and the king himself—by withdrawing my acceptance of Ashlyn's invitation didn't seem likely to win me any thanks from Darius.

"What is Darius's role in all of this?" I murmured.

"Poor boy." Raelynn clucked sympathetically, startling me out of my thoughts. I hadn't even realized I spoke aloud.

"The king promises those who follow him that when the prince is trained and mature enough, he will step aside and let his son take the throne," Hugh said, confirming what we had heard in Ardann. "No one can question the power of Prince Darius, and those who follow the crown expect great favor under his strengthened regime."

I found it hard to imagine King Cassius willingly stepping aside from his only remaining power and authority.

"Strangely," Raelynn said, a wry note in her voice, "he hasn't seemed overly eager to see his eldest son complete his training."

I swallowed a snort. I clearly wasn't the only one skeptical of Cassius's intentions. And it aligned with one of the rumors we had heard at home in Corrin about the prince's delayed start at the Academy. The Kallorwegian king was a great deal more interested in a son who promised strength than a son who possessed such strength.

"So the prince is aligned with his father." I spoke slowly, trying to understand how such a reality matched his anger at my actions.

"The *prince* shows no such partiality," Hugh said. "He does not refute support for those who support the king—both the current and future one—but he shows equal favor for his father and his mother. Most consider it only natural for any child."

"And each side believes his true preference lies with them," Raelynn said.

"His mother certainly retains enough support that she could prove a challenge to him if he chose to openly support his father," Hugh said.

Raelynn's face twisted in disgust. "Never mind the queen. It is their grandfather who worries the princes, you mark my words. The man has grown hard during so many years questing after power. You would think he would be content to see one of his blood sit the throne, but he wants utter loyalty. If you ask me, the prince is worried about a sinister end if he lets his support for his father show too strongly before he has secured the full might of the throne."

"Raelynn, hush!" Hugh said, warning in his voice.

She looked indignant but subsided with a wary glance at me.

"I am appreciative of your sharing with me so openly," I said. "You may be sure that I won't cause either of you trouble. I'm sure everyone will assume that any information I have comes from my own family."

Hugh nodded gravely. "We thank you for your circumspection. Raelynn allows herself to get carried away at times, but we bear no ill will toward anyone at court."

"No, of course not," I said with equal gravity.

Hiding one's true feelings was a necessary part of maintaining decades of neutrality, and I had no intention of causing the kind couple any difficulties.

A distant bell sounded, its ringing muffled inside the office. I stood.

"With that in mind, I had best be on my way to breakfast. Thank you again for assisting me."

"After so many years of teaching, you get to have a sense for people," Raelynn said. "And you're a good girl, I can tell—for all you're Ardannian." She glanced at her husband. "We would live to see Kallorway at true peace with our neighbors once again, if at all possible. Perhaps you are the means to achieving such an end."

"It is my most earnest desire," I said. "It will not be Ardann that stands in the way of such peace."

"See," Raelynn whispered to her husband as he held the door open for me. "I told you she was a good girl."

He looked at his wife and then me, his eyes grave. When he spoke, his voice was quiet and hesitant.

"You must understand, Princess Verene, that the Kallorwegian court has stood for many years in careful balance. There are certainly some who still carry hatred for Ardann, but there are more who fear the consequences of upsetting that balance."

For a moment he looked as if he meant to continue, but then a sound from the corridor outside the library made him pause and give his head a small shake. I waited for a moment, but he said nothing more.

"Thank you, Hugh," I said in a quiet tone. "I understand."

I hurried out of the library and down the hall, my mind whirling. I could understand his reluctance to say anything about Ardann, and I appreciated that he had been willing to comment on the matter at all.

What he had said made sense. If Ardann were to make a formal treaty, it wouldn't be with the captain of the Royal Guard or even the queen. If we made an alliance, it would have to be with the crown, and such a thing could wreak havoc on the existing balance of power. The initial careful disinterest of my year mates made more sense now, but what did it mean that the Head of the Wind Workers was making overtures? Had the king and his faction decided the potential gain of such an alliance outweighed the risk of antagonizing their opponents in their own court? Or had the general had some way of blocking them that they had now managed to circumvent?

For every answer there were more questions. And I still needed to find a way to extricate myself from the Midwinter party without offending anyone of significance.

I moved slowly toward the central stairs, trying to think of an acceptable solution. Several people passed me, bowing or curt-sying briefly, and I nodded at each of them. Most were servants, but the last to pass my way, heading downstairs, wore a gold robe.

Only after I had acknowledged his silent greeting and he had passed on, did my mind fully grasp that it was Captain Vincent. I paused, about to step out onto the staircase. Captain Vincent. He was responsible for the safety of those at the Academy, and Layna had assured me he showed every sign of taking his task seriously. Why had it not occurred to me to tell him of the sabotage to the training yard?

My mouth opened to call after him, but I closed it again before any sound emerged. What exactly had Layna told me? That he was young for the seniority of his position and newly appointed to his post by the king himself. Given Ashlyn's invite that should make him safe, but I couldn't be sure. There was too much that I still didn't know.

No, I couldn't risk telling him. Not until I had more information.

But his presence, and the thought of the potential danger that lurked for me here in Kallorway, triggered a thought in my mind that grew into a fully formed plan. It was so obvious, in fact, that I didn't know why I hadn't thought of it before. Hugh had emphasized balance, and this was the perfect way to achieve just that.

CHAPTER 17

Instead of heading downstairs, I turned up, climbing to my own floor. But I didn't turn right toward my suite. Instead I hurried down the opposite corridor, entering the open door that led to the waiting room outside Duke Francis's office. The next door through into his office also stood open, and he looked up from his desk at my entry.

"Your Highness, please come in."

I entered, and he indicated for me to close the door behind me.

"I trust you have recovered from your unfortunate injury."

"Yes, thank you. Raelynn was most skilled in her healing." I moved forward to stand before his desk. "I come on another matter."

He laid his pen down, giving me his full attention.

"Certainly, Princess Verene. How may I help you?"

I folded my hands in front of me and spoke in my primmest voice. "I wish to ascertain whether the strictures you have put in place about my not leaving the Academy grounds on rest days extend to the holiday festivities as well."

"Ah." He sat back, surveying me carefully.

"Naturally," I said, still in the blandest of voices, "as your guest here, I shouldn't wish to embark on any course of action that might cause you alarm." I widened my eyes slightly. If Duke Francis was as dedicated to neutrality as everyone claimed, then he would be my ally in this.

"Ah, yes, indeed. I see." He regarded me for another moment. "That is most considerate of you, Princess Verene. And I can assure you that if you were to leave the Academy grounds over Midwinter, it would indeed be a matter of some concern to me."

"It had come to my attention that perhaps it might," I said. "And your promises to my parents must, of course, be given the ultimate consideration." I paused. "However, it causes me some distress to think that I might miss the opportunity of celebrating with my new year mates. With that in mind, I would like to ask you a favor."

The duke sat up straight, a gleam of interest in his eye. "You find me most curious to hear what it might be."

"I wonder if you would permit me to host a Midwinter Ball here at the Academy. Naturally I should wish to include all of the trainees and instructors in the invitation, and not just my own year mates."

"I see." The duke steepled his hands together, looking as if he meant to speak, but I continued on.

"But I should not wish any of my fellow trainees to be separated from their families for the festivities, if it can be avoided, so I would propose that the families of the trainees also be invited. I think," I said with a small smile, "that such a thing would be unexceptionable. And—naturally—I should insist upon bearing the expense of such an event."

"Naturally." The duke sounded amused.

My family had told me before I left home that I wasn't to consider funds an issue, but this was the first time I had encountered any reason to spend their gold. I could now understand why they had thought I might find such an opportunity. I just hoped they would approve of my decision.

"I understand," the duke said, "that in Ardann, socialization among year mates is considered an important element of the Academy experience."

"It certainly is," I said. "And I am greatly desirous of forming such close bonds with my Kallorwegian year mates."

Duke Francis nodded slowly. "I do not see how anyone could take issue with a princess of Ardann hosting a cultural event to celebrate Midwinter with her fellow trainees and their families. Such a thing is—as you say—unexceptionable. And naturally you could not hold it anywhere but here at the Academy."

"Thank you," I said. "I am most grateful for your assistance. I'm afraid I'm not familiar with all the trainees here, let alone their families, so I was hoping you might be willing to send out the invitations."

The duke nodded again, briskly this time. "I shall see to it personally. And I shall put you in contact with Zora. She is the head servant here and will oversee the practical details for the ball."

His attention returned to the parchment in front of him, and I took the gesture as a dismissal. Hurrying from the room, I wondered if there was still time to make breakfast. But a rumble in my stomach was drowned out by the bell. I was too late.

I headed straight for the external doors, already thinking longingly of my lunch. Bryony pounced on me in the entrance way, though.

"There you are! I was about to dash up to your suite. Here, I grabbed this for you." She thrust a sweet roll at me which I accepted eagerly as we continued on to class. "Are you feeling better?"

I nodded, my mouth too full to answer with words.

"Good. I was worried when I didn't see you at breakfast."

"So-wwy," I said around my mouthful.

"No more trouble from your ankle?" she asked in a low voice.

I swallowed hurriedly. "No, nothing like that. Just the exhaustion."

Movement behind us caught my eye, and I realized Darius was close behind. He was looking at me with a question in his eyes, the slightest crease between his brows.

"This morning I was busy taking care of something else," I said to Bryony, my voice unnaturally loud. "But it's all been arranged now."

Bryony threw a confused look over her shoulder, her bemusement only deepening at sight of the prince.

"Well, that's good…I guess."

"Are we in the arena today?" I asked, forcing myself not to look backward again.

"I think so. It seems to amuse Mitchell to move the days around."

"I think it's part of the training," I said. "We always have to be prepared and all that."

Bryony yawned, clapping her hand over her mouth. "Well, my sword and I are always prepared, that's for sure."

But when we sat in the arena seating, facing Mitchell, he surprised us yet again.

"Today we will be experimenting a little differently from usual. All trainees will participate in the battle, but there is to be no use of power compositions."

"No compositions?" Royce looked unimpressed. "So we're to battle like commonborns?"

Mitchell gave him a superior look. "I didn't say no compositions."

"Yes, you di—"

"Energy compositions!" Bryony cried over the top of Royce's protest. She clapped her hands in excitement.

Our instructor nodded. "Soon you will begin experimenting in your discipline classes with the impact of extra energy on your ability to compose. But it is a rare situation where you will have the luxury or capacity to compose in the middle of a battle. That does not, however, mean that extra energy is without value. As you have all experienced, battle itself is physically exhausting, and it is all too easy to make a fatal mistake if forced into combat when your energy reserves are low."

"Sounds like a pretty useless exercise to me," Royce muttered. "How often will we have an energy mage available in the middle of battle—and how much good would a little extra energy do anyway?"

But he hadn't pitched his voice low enough, and Mitchell heard him. Directing a quelling glare at Royce, the instructor responded to his murmured complaints.

"Do not forget that the activities you undertake here at the Academy are training. They will not always correlate exactly with real world situations. But you may rest assured that every exercise has been selected by those more knowledgeable than yourself with the purpose of training some aspect of your ability. You are not the first mage to underestimate the importance of energy—and some of them have not lived to tell the tale. If you do not wish to join them in the grave, then I suggest you show your instructors and the exercises they set a little more respect."

He regarded Royce with narrowed eyes, letting a moment of taut silence stretch out before continuing. "And, as for the matter of having an energy mage available..." He raised an eyebrow. "I can only recommend you start treating your year mates with a little more respect as well. You may find it greatly assists in that particular endeavor."

Royce flushed and glanced sideways toward Bryony and Tyron. Mitchell, however, was already continuing, his attention now on the whole class.

"You will soon find yourself assigned exercises in composition that may seem repetitive but which are designed to increase your stamina. You must think of this battle in much the same way. The point is not the actual fighting, nor even victory. The purpose is to make you more aware of your own energy and of how quickly it can become drained. The more you grow your awareness of your own energy levels and reserves, the more capable you will become of both physically exerting yourself and composing without pushing your limits too far. As you know, there are few dangers to a mage as great as the danger of pouring too much power into a composition. If you fail to sufficiently monitor your energy, then you are at far greater risk of such an end."

"So how will the battle work?" Tyron asked.

"You will captain one team and Bryony another," Mitchell said. "I hope you have both come equipped with sufficient compositions."

Bryony nodded eagerly. "We've hardly had any opportunities to use them yet."

"You may pick your teams one at a time, starting with you, Tyron."

"Prince Darius," Tyron said without hesitation.

"Prince Jareth," Bryony countered swiftly.

"Princess Verene," Tyron said, catching me by surprise.

I blinked at him while Bryony gave me a regretful look and named Dellion as her next teammate. I had assumed I would be picked last, forgetting for a moment that no one was permitted to use power compositions. I sat a little straighter, a smile spreading across my face. We were being judged purely on our skill and strength with a sword, and I had suddenly become a valuable team member.

The whole class was soon divided up, and we were instructed to gather in our teams on the arena floor. Only when we were actually standing together did I realize that it would be my first time fighting alongside Darius.

As well as the crown prince and me, Tyron had selected Wardell, Ashlyn, and Isabelle. As we clumped together, he handed out a roll of parchment to each of us. I unfurled mine and read a basic energy composition to give whoever worked the composition a boost of energy. It looked familiar because I had attempted it myself under my parents' direction.

"What's our strategy?" Darius asked.

Tyron shrugged. "I'm only captain because I'm the one with the compositions. I suspect I would do better to leave the strategizing to you."

Darius accepted the transfer of leadership without surprise or comment.

"We're evenly matched without high ground or the ability to make any. Nor do we have any shelter or element of surprise."

Wardell cracked his knuckles with a surprising amount of anticipation on his face. "So a good old-fashioned brawl, then."

Ashlyn rolled her eyes and said something under her breath to Isabelle, who chuckled. Wardell just grinned and winked at them both.

Darius ignored his small army, apparently deep in thought. He was clearly taking the exercise far more seriously than any of the others. I eyed our opposing team who were huddled around Bryony and Jareth.

"We need to go for Frida, Armand, and Royce," I said.

Darius caught my intention quickly. "If we can remove any of their players—even the weakest members—we'll gain superiority of numbers."

"They'll try to stop us, of course," I said. "But we have to try evasion rather than engaging them. Once we let Bryony, Jareth, or Dellion corner us into a fight, we'll risk them employing the same strategy against us."

"So you're saying evade and avoid." Wardell shook out first his neck and then both his legs. "I can do that."

Mitchell approached, ordering us all to hold out our swords. He ripped a number of compositions, pointing at each blade in succession.

"You will now find that your edges are temporarily blunted," he said. "We can't risk twelve sharpened blades flying around in a battle without shields of any kind."

"Will you be calling the fatal blows?" Darius asked.

Mitchell nodded. "If I call your name, you should return immediately to the arena seating."

Apparently he had already completed the exercise with the other team because we were directed to take our places on opposite sides of the arena. As soon as he declared the bout begun, all six of us tore the compositions in our hands.

The force that hit me was far greater than I expected, my whole body contracting violently at the unexpected foreign substance pouring into it. But a moment later any discomfort was overwhelmed by a wave of buoyancy. So much energy filled me that I felt as if I could lift off the ground entirely and float into the sky. Everything around me looked sharper, and the air in my nose and mouth was crisp and clear. How had I not noticed what a beautiful day it was?

Something else nudged at my senses, but before I could get a grasp on it, Darius yelled, "Go!"

My feet responded before my mind could even repeat the command. I ran for our enemies with my teammates spreading out on either side as we sprinted forward.

Bryony called a command of her own, and the six of them broke into two groups of three, standing back to back in two small circles, blades facing out. She stood in one group and Jareth in the other.

I eyed the arrangements. It was a sensible strategy in the face of our direct attack and would make our task of separating out the weaker fighters more difficult. I eyed the group that included Bryony, Royce, and Armand. That was their weak link.

Catching Darius's eye, I inclined my head in their direction, and he angled his run to bear down on them, me only steps behind.

"To me!" he called, and the rest of our team converged on us as well.

Seeing their huddle completely ignored, Jareth broke away from his position, Dellion and Frida following his lead. They moved fast, faster than I had seen any of them move before, but we were going at an equal speed.

They tried to fall on us from behind, but when Dellion lunged at Wardell, he merely danced out of her reach, making a mocking face as he evaded her attack. She snarled and lunged again, while he continued to retreat. Soon he was fleeing halfway across the arena, his laughs floating back to us along with her frustrated snarls.

Darius tried to lunge at Royce, but their circle spun, leaving him facing Bryony instead. The movement put Armand in front of me, however, so I pressed forward with an attack. His first defense was strong, but when I followed with another immediate counterattack, his response time was weaker than it needed to be against my heightened reflexes.

I saw my opening and lunged in with a kill strike, tempering my force so as not to bruise him too badly. Just as I committed, however, I felt two spots of power blossoming behind me.

My arm jerked in surprise, but it was too late to pull out of the move. My blunted tip hit him just above the heart, and I didn't wait for Mitchell to complete his shouted call of Armand's name before spinning around to face the threat at my rear.

I couldn't be the only one who had felt the forbidden use of power. Why hadn't our instructor already intervened? Trying to circumvent the rules was a foolish move when there was no way to hide the action from every power mage present.

"Ashlyn." The declaration of my teammate's defeat came as I was spinning around and went some way to explain how Jareth and Frida were both confronting me.

They must have dealt Ashlyn a deathblow and somehow shaken off both Isabelle and Tyron. Out of the corner of my eye, I saw Royce engaged in battle and realized that accounted for at least one of my missing team members.

Had I missed another name being called in the distraction of my battle with Armand? If so, I might need to face both opponents without assistance.

Our plan seemed to be falling apart—perhaps due to whatever compositions had been worked behind me. They must have come from either Jareth or Frida, or both.

The power still clung to them, though, so it wasn't likely to have been an attack. I frowned as I barely succeeded in beating back Jareth's first lunge. Perhaps they were shielded, then.

But it didn't feel like a shield. The power didn't surround them in a bubble. The sensation was more of a pulsing force inside each of them. Now that I was focusing more closely on them, it didn't seem like any composition I could remember feeling.

Tyron appeared from my left, distracting Frida with a wild attack. But Jareth kept his focus on me. When he attacked again, all his movements faster and more forceful than I had ever felt them in practice, I was too slow to respond. Distracted by the force that still burned inside him, I missed the flexing of muscles that would have alerted me to his attack.

His sword pushed mine neatly aside and whacked gently against my neck.

"Princess Verene." Mitchell's loud shout rang across the battle.

Jareth grinned at me and turned his attention away. I stood frozen for a moment, staring after him in confusion. Was it still the lingering sensation of forbidden power coiled inside him that made me see something sinister lurking in his eyes behind his surface smile?

Mitchell called my name again, his voice disapproving this time, and I jolted into action. Stumbling across the arena floor, I passed our instructor. Now that I was no longer distracted by the swirl of battle, I noticed a similar sensation pulsing inside him. It didn't burn as brightly as the power I had felt during the battle, but it seemed to emanate from a similar place at his core.

I looked back over my shoulder as I continued on to the seating, but Mitchell's attention had returned to the battle that still raged. Was it something to do with the exercise then? Some composition he had worked? But why? And for what purpose?

I sat next to a dejected-looking Ashlyn.

"At least you killed Armand," she said with a sigh. "I didn't manage to achieve anything before Prince Jareth defeated me."

"Never mind." I struggled to focus on her words and form a coherent response. "He's a strong fighter, and you bought the rest of us time at least."

"Not enough from the look of it."

"What?" I frowned at her, distracted by the force that I now felt pulsing inside of her as well.

She pointed back toward the battle.

For the first time, I focused my attention on the ongoing conflict. Frida and Royce were both walking toward us, shoulders slumped. That meant my team had managed to knock out all three of our enemy's weaker fighters, just as we had planned.

But we had lost Ashlyn and me in the process. Which meant the numbers were only slightly in our favor as Darius, Tyron, Isabelle, and Wardell faced off against Bryony, Jareth, and Dellion.

A moment later, Dellion finally caught Wardell, delivering a death blow that looked like it carried all her pent-up irritation at his evasive tactics. He would have a lovely bruise by tomorrow unless Raelynn took pity on him and deemed it a serious enough injury to warrant healing.

Dellion was all the way across the arena, though, so it took her precious seconds to race back toward her remaining team. In the time she took to reach them, Darius managed to score a clear hit against his brother.

Mitchell called the younger prince's name, but a moment later he was calling both Tyron and Isabelle as well. Bryony had managed to fell them both. I couldn't help a small smile of pride for my friend's skill despite the deadly blow to my team.

We now had only Darius left, and Dellion had arrived to support Bryony. The two of them circled the crown prince warily. He was the best fighter in the class, but he was outnumbered, and Bryony wasn't far behind him in skill.

The battle raged on for several more minutes, Darius holding them off with remarkable feats of swordsmanship. But eventually they managed to come at him from both sides, and Bryony delivered a killing thrust. Mitchell called Darius's name, and declared Bryony's team the victors.

She whooped and hollered, racing back across the arena to celebrate with her teammates. Darius followed behind, his head high and posture rigid. It was impossible to tell from his expression if he was proud of having fought well or resentful of his defeat.

I watched the hubbub around me with a detached air, trying to understand what I was sensing. The battle had ended, but the power still lingered. And now that everyone had gathered together, I could tell that every one of my year mates was infected with it.

Bryony eventually made her way to me, congratulating me on my one kill. I mumbled out my own praise of her efforts, too distracted to put much thought into my words. She gave me an odd look but was distracted by Tyron, sitting behind me.

She beamed at him. "That was fun."

"It was an interesting exercise." He gave a quick frown. "More distracting than I expected. It nearly caught me off guard a couple times."

She nodded. "Everyone felt so full! It was almost bursting out of them. I've never felt it with so many people before—and then with so much movement as well."

I twisted so I could see them both clearly. "Everyone felt full? What does that mean?"

Tyron gave me an odd look. "Everyone's energy, of course."

"You get used to how it feels," Bryony explained. "But it's unusual to feel someone pulsing with so much energy, let alone twelve people at once. Usually people want us to give them energy when they're desperately low, or else because they're using it immediately on a composition. It's different on a battlefield."

"It was amazing," Ashlyn said enthusiastically beside us. "I've never felt so...alive. And I could move so fast." She grimaced. "Not as fast as Prince Jareth, though."

Bryony laughed. "Yes, the advantage is greatly diminished when your enemies have it as well. But you can imagine how it might help if they don't."

Their words faded away as I stared at my friend in shock. It pulsed, she had said. And it was bursting out of them. I looked around at each of the trainees, one at a time.

It didn't feel like power, really. That's why I hadn't been able to pinpoint what composition it could possibly be. And it burned right at each person's core because it was a part of them.

Somehow, impossibly, I was sensing the energy of everyone around me.

CHAPTER 18

I stumbled my way through the rest of the day in a daze. I kept expecting the new sensation to fade, but it didn't. And it was incredibly distracting.

I was used to the sense of power that hung over so much of the Academy, but now that it was mixing with my newfound awareness of every person in my vicinity, my mind was being continually overwhelmed.

Bryony kept reassuring me about my performance in the battle, and I let her think it was the source of my abstraction. I couldn't exactly announce the truth in the middle of the dining hall—especially when I didn't understand it myself.

Power mages couldn't sense energy—except their own in the most general sense. Only energy mages could sense the energy of others. Well, energy mages and my mother, who was some sort of strange hybrid.

My brother, Stellan, a spoken energy mage, could feel it, of course. It had been the first sign of his ability. As soon as he was old enough to communicate, he had shown an awareness of the location of everyone around him—even through walls.

After I turned sixteen, I had been desperate enough to try

every known ability, but I hadn't been surprised when my parents had extensively tested me with power compositions first. I could sense power like Lucien, not energy like Stellan. It had seemed clear to me, despite my parents' hopes, that I wasn't destined to be any sort of energy mage.

And yet now, here I was—able to sense both power and energy, as my mother alone could do. As soon as I could snatch a moment to myself, I rushed to my room to try composing both a power composition and an energy one.

Nothing happened. They were just words on a page.

I paid extra attention in discipline class that afternoon as Bryony and Tyron discussed the battle with Amalia, but there was no hint as to what could have affected me in such a way. It was clear from their conversation that the compositions they had distributed had been nothing more than regular ones to gift energy, as mine had appeared to be when I read it. And yet I could think of no other catalyst for this change.

Unlike my brother and other true energy mages, my mother hadn't been born with the ability to feel energy. She said she had first sensed it after drawing someone else's energy. I hadn't crafted my own composition to interact with the energy of another, but I had worked Tyron's composition and received his energy from it. Perhaps that had been enough?

While I had worked countless power compositions in my sixteen years, supplied by either my family or my guards, I couldn't recall ever having worked an energy one before. They were in short supply in Ardann, even at court, and no one had any reason to give energy to a junior princess who couldn't use it to compose.

But for my mother, the new sensation had come alongside the expansion of her abilities. Yet my efforts to compose continued to fail. A sudden thought lanced through me as I listened to Amalia instructing Bryony and Tyron about replenishing their now-depleted supply of compositions.

My brother couldn't write energy compositions either. He had to speak them. Was it possible I was like him after all?

Under my breath, in the quietest whisper I could manage, I recited the words I had earlier written, reading them off a mental scroll. I aimed my gift of energy at Bryony, holding my breath as I completed the working. Nothing happened. I felt no drain on my energy, and Bryony didn't falter in whatever response she was making to Amalia. Given how it had felt to receive energy in the arena, I couldn't fool myself that something had happened without either of us sensing it.

With more trepidation, I tried the words for a composition to take energy, limiting myself to skimming the smallest portion. Again, nothing seemed to happen. Next I tried to shield my energy, but my renewed hope was already dwindling. Shielding was the least common energy mage ability.

At least it was easy to picture the necessary words, the intense concentration with which I had attempted the same compositions with my parents bringing them easily back to mind now.

Finally, with great nervousness, I attempted a composition like the ones Bryony's father, Declan, used. I carefully worded it as my parents had showed me, attempting to give away only the tiniest sliver of my energy. Again, nothing happened.

I let out a long breath and slumped in my seat. For a moment it had seemed like everything had changed, but it turned out nothing had changed at all.

When I felt someone walk down the corridor outside the classroom, I flinched, earning a concerned look from Bryony.

"Are you sure you're all right?" she whispered to me. "It isn't like you to take a defeat so hard. Mitchell praised your strategy, remember?"

I just shook my head, and since Amalia began speaking again, Bryony had to let it go. She continued to throw me worried looks, however, despite the sudden small lift to my own spirits.

Feeling the person go past had reminded me of the small

advantage that came with this new ability. Being able to sense the location of everyone around you was a skill that could come in useful, especially if I was to live my life at court beside my brother. Perhaps I might help foil an assassination attempt one day.

I shook off the foolishly heroic daydreams. Despite the tumult of the beginning of her reign, my aunt had ruled in peace for many years now, and I sincerely hoped Lucien would do the same. I could be waiting a long time if I hoped my moment of glory would come through such a clumsy assassination attempt as someone concealed inside a room or behind a curtain.

It was still comforting, though, to know when there were others around me. I suspected I would grow accustomed to the sensation and no longer feel the need to flinch or shield my over-crowded mind. Bryony certainly didn't give any indication of the extra sense at all.

At the evening meal, I headed off any questions from my friend by directing us to seats beside Frida and Ashlyn and launching straight into speech myself.

"I'm so sorry, Ashlyn, but it turns out I can't go home with you for Midwinter after all."

She froze, her fork halfway to her mouth, a horrified look on her face.

"I wasn't thinking when I accepted your kind invitation. It would have been lovely, but I'm forbidden from leaving the Academy grounds." I grimaced. "Even on rest days."

She put down her fork and frowned. "Forbidden to leave the grounds? Whatever for?"

"Security reasons." I sighed. "Duke Francis had to make my family all sorts of promises about my safety, and I can't ask Captain Vincent and his men to go trooping around after me wherever I go, leaving everyone else unprotected."

"Oh," she said slowly. "Of course."

"Not that I mean to suggest your home is unsafe," I said hurriedly. "But there is the travel to consider."

"Perhaps—"

I jumped in before Ashlyn could suggest her family send guards to accompany me from the Academy or some such.

"But I was so sad at the idea of missing out on celebrating Midwinter with you all that I begged the duke to allow me to host a ball here instead."

Ashlyn stared at me, whatever she had been about to say forgotten.

"A ball here?"

I nodded. "For all the trainees and instructors. And your families, of course. Duke Francis has promised to send out the invitations as soon as possible. It won't be an Academy ball, exactly, but rather an Ardannian one. I'm to share my home's festivities with you all."

"How exciting!" said Frida. "I can't think when there was last a ball here."

Ashlyn slowly smiled. "I'm sure my mother will understand needing to cancel her own plans in the circumstances. Of course we must put everyone's safety first."

I grinned, almost able to see the thoughts whirring through her brain as she surveyed the small crowd in the dining hall. It would be an exclusive invite list, but one that included some of the most powerful people in the kingdom—among them the royal family.

And no one could complain at being unfairly excluded since no politics had gone into deciding who was invited. Even the king was only receiving an invitation because his sons attended the Academy. Midwinter had always been a family celebration. And it just so happened the families involved spanned both factions of politics. Balance, as Hugh had said.

Bryony seemed just as delighted as Frida, gaping at me and asking why she hadn't known anything about the plan.

"I only asked the duke this morning," I said. "And then I was distracted by the battle in the arena before I had a chance to tell you."

She accepted this truthful explanation, joining Frida and Ashlyn in an enthusiastic discussion of gowns and accessories. I used their distraction to slip away in the most cowardly way, avoiding any private conversation with my friend.

I would tell her of my discovery, but I wasn't ready to do it tonight. I needed time to adjust to the idea myself.

When I reached the peace of my suite, I breathed a sigh of relief and sank onto one of the sofas, massaging my temples. It had been an unexpected day in many ways and felt as if it had been going for at least a week.

But as the minutes passed, my feeling of peaceful solitude slipped away. People kept walking down the corridor outside, and a bright flare of energy entered the room next to mine.

The newly arrived energy might have been easier to ignore except for two things. One, it burned with more strength than most of those I had encountered, thanks to the leftover excess from our arena battle that morning. And two, I knew it belonged to Darius.

The awareness burned in my mind, making it impossible to forget how close he was. He paced up and down his room, and I could think of nothing but how much he would hate me being able to track his movements in such a way.

Power always hung about him—shields, I assumed. Constant shielding required an excessive use of power, and few attempted it. But Darius was both important enough and strong enough to be an exception. No doubt shields had been the first compositions he had trained to create after turning sixteen.

But there was so much power everywhere in the Academy, including coating half of his room, that I no longer noticed it. This feeling was different, though. It was so new I hadn't yet learned how to push it from my mind, and it was part of him in a way his shields weren't.

And so I tracked his movements, even while I tried to force my mind away. When he came closer, though, I sat up, no longer pretending disinterest.

When he hesitated, directly behind my tapestry, I bounded to my feet and rushed across the room. Pushing aside the heavy material, I yanked open the door just as he raised his hand to knock.

As soon as I saw his face, I realized my mistake.

"You're full of surprises, Princess." The intensity of his expression belied his light tone.

I stepped aside, and he entered my sitting room.

"Perhaps I'll have to come and visit you one day," I said. "If you're going to keep dropping in on me like this."

He turned, fixing me with such a piercing stare that I dropped my eyes.

"Perhaps one day you will," he said at last, and it was impossible to tell from his tone whether or not he welcomed such an idea.

"I'm sorry about your loss today," I said. "You fought well. I should have been more help, but I was…distracted."

"I noticed."

My eyes flew back to his. How had he noticed that in the middle of the fight? Or did he mean afterward? I had been abstracted all day.

"I'm sorry," I repeated.

He brushed my words aside. "It was a good strategy, and it might have worked if things had gone differently."

I sighed. "If I hadn't been so easily defeated."

He paused, the moment stretching out into a strange awkwardness between us.

"I heard Bryony mention your ankle," he said at last. "Was that…"

"My ankle? No, it's fine. I mean, it was injured, but Raelynn healed it. I was only tired from the healing yesterday."

His brows drew together. "You injured it badly enough to need Raelynn? How did that happen?"

I mentally kicked myself for letting so much slip.

"Practicing with Bryony on the rest day. It was a clean break."

"A break?" He stepped closer, and I had to steel myself not to step back. "It was that bad? Just from a bout with Bryony?"

I bit my lip. Darius had far more experience with practice fights than Raelynn. Unlike the older healer, he knew just how unusual it was for an experienced fighter to receive such an injury from a friendly bout. Especially on even ground like a training yard.

"There was a...hole," I said reluctantly. "My foot landed in it."

He froze, his unnatural stillness making the hairs on my arms stand on end. Somehow I had said too much.

"Why weren't you practicing in the training yard?" he asked, his voice harsh.

"We were." The words were wrenched from me reluctantly.

"There are no holes in the training yard," Darius said, danger in his voice now.

I said nothing in response, our eyes locked in a silent battle of wills. I could feel a strange anger emanating from him, though, and read the implacability in his eyes. At last I sighed.

"There are no holes there now. But they were there early in the morning on the rest day. The whole yard was littered with them—concealed ones."

"Someone sabotaged our training yard?" The anger in his voice was no longer restrained, and I shivered at the sound of it, although it didn't seem to be directed at me. He looked too savage for the soft lighting and gentle elegance of my sitting room.

"On our rest day," he added.

He said no more, but he didn't need to. One thing I had never doubted was his understanding, and he had made it clear he was keeping a close watch on me. Neither of us needed to say what we both understood.

"It was a foolish prank." I shrugged, trying to defuse the moment. "There was no chance of any real damage being done— not with Raelynn on hand."

"The Kallorwegian Academy does not tolerate such wasteful pranks."

I raised an eyebrow and glanced at the patch of my wall that was still cleaner than the stones around it.

"Does it not?"

His eyes followed mine, and his frown deepened.

After a pause, he said, "At least it did not before." He looked back at me. "Who have you told about this?"

I shrugged. "No one. Bryony was there, of course, but Raelynn thinks it was just an accident."

"No one?" His eyes searched my face.

I shifted uncomfortably. "Despite my misstep yesterday— when I was suffering the unnatural exhaustion that comes after a healing—I am not usually incautious. It is obvious someone is unhappy about my presence here. But until I know who and why, I don't intend to go blundering into a situation I don't understand."

"I will find out who they are," Darius said, and the fire in his voice made me sure he would succeed, although I couldn't imagine how.

"I hope you'll tell me when you do." I kept my voice light.

He paused, looking at me as if he hadn't considered doing so. I raised a challenging eyebrow at him, and he slowly nodded.

"Of course." Another pause. "I heard about your plans for a Midwinter Ball."

"Well?" I asked coolly. "Will it do? Ashlyn didn't seem offended by my retracting my acceptance—at least not once she heard my alternative plan."

He nodded almost reluctantly. "It should work."

"Will your family come?"

"I think you have effectively tied their hands. How could they not come to spend the holiday with their two children and attend the most exclusive event of the year?"

A look of actual amusement crossed his face as if he found humor rather than offense at his parents being maneuvered in such a manner.

"I'm glad it meets with your approval," I said. "I was wondering if you would prefer to return to the capital for the break."

"Prefer the capital? When I have finally managed to break free from it? No indeed."

He spoke quickly, almost thoughtlessly, and I didn't immediately respond, unused to hearing him speak without restraint. My silence seemed to bring him back to himself, and he gave me a formal half-bow.

"But I hope you will keep that to yourself."

"Of course." I offered him a tentative smile. "I am aware of the unpleasant combination of tedium and tension that so often accompanies royal functions. It is freeing to spend so much time away from them."

"And yet, there is no true escape," he said, almost too quietly to hear. "At least, not yet."

I raised both eyebrows at that, but he wasn't looking at me. What escape was there for either of us? Royalty wasn't a birthright you could walk away from.

He shook himself slightly, the movement barely a ripple. But it seemed to signify he knew he had grown too loose in the dim privacy of my sitting room.

"You will excuse me for barging in on you once again, Princess."

He offered me another half-bow and crossed back to the

door, passing me on the way. But in the doorway, he hesitated and glanced back.

"But I didn't barge in on you, did I? How did you know I was there, Verene?"

Caught off guard by the question when I had thought him almost gone, I could think of no immediate explanation. He stepped back toward me, not needing to move far to place us close together.

"And you claim you weren't distracted by your ankle during the fight today. Something else happened. What are you not telling me?"

"I don't have to share all my secrets with you, Prince of Kallorway," I said.

He slowly raised both eyebrows. "So you admit you have secrets?"

"I thought you were convinced I do," I murmured.

"Yes, but you denied it. And now you do not. Interesting."

He leaned in closer and then closer still. One of his hands reached up and brushed back a loose strand of my hair so he could place his lips beside my ear.

"Make no mistake about it, Verene," he whispered, his breath sending ripples up and down my spine. "I intend to discover all of your secrets."

He pulled back, cold air rushing in to take his place. I blinked once, and the door was closing behind him, the tapestry dropping back into place. I shivered.

I told myself I was glad he was gone, but my room felt strangely empty without him, and the temperature seemed to have dropped several degrees.

If this was his new tactic for winning my compliance, then I was frighteningly weak to it. Because the more I saw of the true fire behind his ice, the more fascinated I became with a prince who seemed to view me as part challenge, part enemy.

CHAPTER 19

*A*s the days passed, I grew used to my new ability, just as I had predicted. I learned to largely tune it out, just as I did with the sensations of power all around me. And I also learned how to read it, noticing when those around me were tired or full of energy.

When I scolded Bryony one day for pushing herself too hard while restocking her compositions, she marched me straight back out of the dining hall. In the empty entranceway, she put her hands on her hips and demanded I finally tell her what was going on.

I confessed what had happened and endured the inevitable deluge of questions. It proved just as painful as I had anticipated to see my own progression of emotions mirrored in her face, the excitement and hope dulling as I assured her I had tried everything. When she finished by giving me a bright smile that looked slightly forced, I almost winced.

"This is still exciting," she told me. "It's quite a useful ability to have, you know. And if it's not too late for you to develop this new ability, who knows if you might still develop another?"

I shook my head firmly. "Such dreams are best left in my

childhood, Bryony. Don't encourage me. There is precedence for a delayed awakening of sensing energy. There's no precedence for someone who could not compose suddenly learning to do so."

She deflated a little.

"But don't worry," I said. "I'm quite adjusted to the whole thing now. And I'm ready to look on the positive side. Any ability is better than none, and I now have a link to both the power mages and the energy mages."

I smiled at her, but when she didn't smile back, my expression dropped into a frown. "Please don't be upset I didn't tell you immediately. I just needed some time to process it all."

"I understand. Some things are difficult to talk about." The significant look she gave me reminded me that Bryony had secrets of her own. We all had our different burdens to bear.

Eventually the weather turned cold enough that she no longer forced me outside on our rest day mornings, instead contenting herself with driving us both up and down the many flights of stairs. She was determined that if we couldn't have a proper practice, we would at least stay in shape.

Secretly I enjoyed the forced exercise. With my body pushed to its limits, my mind let go of everything that crowded inside it, entering a state of peaceful nothingness that I almost never achieved.

Bryony often led us up and down the hidden stairs frequented by the servants and along the separate corridors they used. The mages of old who had built the Academy hadn't liked the idea of the servants using the same spaces as them. But I often saw servants on the main stairs and in the wider mage corridors now, and I hoped it was a positive sign of change. Just as I hoped they didn't mind our invasion of their space.

At the very least they grew used to us, flattening themselves against the wall at the sight of our approach instead of dropping into a bow or curtsy. And from the smiles on many of their faces, I think they found our training runs more amusing than anything. Or perhaps it was rather bemusement as to why we punished ourselves in such a way by choice.

We were glad of the freedom to use the hidden spaces once Midwinter drew close. The families of the trainees poured into the Academy, and as a princess of Ardann, I couldn't allow powerful members of the Kallorwegian court to see me red-faced, puffing up and down the stairs. But I had also never been so in need of the stolen moments of peace the exercise provided.

Zora, the Academy's head servant, had turned out to be even more competent than I could have hoped. Knocking on my sitting room door one evening, not long after my conversation with the duke, she had proven herself intelligent and experienced.

After ascertaining that I understood the likely cost of an event on such a scale—and being assured that I was fully supportive of her hiring such extra help as she could find in the local towns and villages—she had softened considerably. Her efficient list of subsequent questions made it clear she had the capability for the task, and as our conversation wore on, she even began to display true interest.

I explained how we decorated in Ardann, and our traditional holiday fare, and we had a lively discussion about the similarities and differences with Kallorway. She seemed to think the cook would welcome the challenge of the new dishes, and she was full of ideas on how to procure the necessary decorations.

By the time she left my room, I had full confidence about the success of the event. And, sure enough, as Midwinter approached, decorations appeared around the Academy. They were an artful blend of the usual Kallorwegian ones and the style I was used to from home, and seeing them gave our regular classes a holiday feel.

I didn't know how Zora had procured the shiny red berries

that only grew in the foothills of the southern Grayback mountain range, located on Ardann's eastern coast, but I appreciated the sight of them woven among the more traditional deep green Kallorwegian garlands.

I did know where the floating golden lights came from, however. All the composition classes had been making them for weeks.

When Royce dared to complain, Alvin had merely asked where he left his holiday spirit. But Dellion had tossed her head and given him her best haughty look.

"You never learn, Royce. Instructor Mitchell told us to expect such tasks. How else are we to increase our stamina?"

Royce had ceased to complain after that, but the poisonous looks he shot at Dellion's back increased.

A royal messenger had finally arrived from Ardann, allowing me to send back my stack of letters, the one with the request for funds marked urgent. The promised riches arrived, the amount generous enough that I was able to tell Zora to give all the regular servants a Midwinter bonus to thank them for the extra work the event was creating. I saw a marked increase in the smiles I received on Bryony's and my morning runs after that, so I didn't regret my impulse.

The day before Midwinter, the royal party arrived. I had half-expected to be evicted from my suite for the duration of their stay, but none of the trainees were moved. Apparently suitable accommodation had been found elsewhere in the Academy.

Classes had finished the previous day, and the same group who had greeted me on my arrival were arrayed in the entranceway to welcome the king and queen. Duke Francis had sent for me, saying that since I was hosting the event, I must be sure to greet my most illustrious guests.

I stood with Darius on one side of me and Jareth on the other, conscious that it was the closest I had been to the crown prince since our last encounter in my sitting room. He gave no acknowledgment of that interaction, however, and I schooled my features into similar indifference.

Jareth seemed full of good humor, laughing over my head at his brother and making quietly mocking comments to me in an undertone as we watched members of the court drift into the entranceway to await the king's arrival.

Darius attempted several quelling looks, but his brother merely laughed them off. I couldn't help but be amused at some of his more outrageous observations, doing my best to suppress the chuckles that bubbled up. But at the same time, I wished I could take several steps away to distance myself from him.

I resented the picture we must present, especially with Darius beside us, stiff and formal. Although it was obvious they were close, the two brothers couldn't be more different. Darius was cold and closed off in public but allowed me glimpses of his true self when we were alone. Jareth, on the other hand, had a consistently friendly manner, and yet had never made the least effort to seek me out or get to know me.

A new arrival slipped up to stand just behind me, and I turned to give Bryony a grateful look. I had considered asking her to accompany me—especially given what I had learned about the significance of our friendship in the eyes of the court—but I had not done so. Bryony was not only basically family, she was also my best friend. I would not ask to use her in such a way.

But when she stepped up to join me of her own volition, I accepted the support gratefully. And when Tyron appeared a moment later to stand beside her, I was even more grateful. I had far less claim on him than I did on Bryony, but with the two of them behind me, I didn't feel so alone.

Jareth turned to greet them both with the same ease he had displayed chatting with me. But when the king and queen at last arrived, he stood as straight as Darius, his focus on his parents.

The first thing I noticed about King Cassius was that he had his son's dark eyes. The second was that he also had his son's cold face. But I had learned that Darius's ice was a mask, hiding the fire that burned beneath. Looking at the king, I had to suppress a shiver. There was no hidden gleam in his eyes—he looked as if his ice ran soul deep.

Queen Endellion came in on his arm, although she touched it with only the lightest pressure of her fingers. No one looking at them would suppose there was any love lost there. The queen's face did light up at sight of her sons, however, and she dropped the contact with her husband to hurry forward and embrace them both.

The king seemed to find the display distasteful, but he made no protest, instead greeting the duke and the various courtiers who had lined up for his attention. When he reached us, the queen stepped back, and I curtsied to them both.

"Mother, Father," Darius said, "may I present Princess Verene of Ardann, Academy trainee."

"Your Majesties." I forced a smile onto my face. "It is a pleasure to meet you both."

"And this is my grandfather, General Haddon," Darius continued, drawing my attention to the older man who had entered behind the royal couple. He was tall and imposing, despite his age, and he surveyed the entire crowd as if we were all beneath him.

"I have had a great curiosity to meet the Ardannian princess who would study in Kallorway," Queen Endellion said, her voice cool and regal. "I am most charmed."

She inclined her head toward me, the sandy hair that both her sons had inherited piled up in an elaborate arrangement that made my own simple braid seem insufficient. I let none of my insecurity show on my face, however, as I returned the gesture.

"So you are Elena's daughter." King Cassius had a note in his voice when he said my mother's name that made all my senses prick with unease. "You don't look like her—although you're short enough, I suppose."

Beside me, Darius grew impossibly stiffer. He had told me once that he considered his father's judgment clouded by his resentment toward my mother. I should have been expecting the king's disdain. But it still took all my willpower to keep my face and voice impassive.

"I'm told I look like my grandmother, Queen Verena."

The king made a noncommittal noise in his throat and moved on to greet his sons. I kept my posture rigid and my face calm, knowing we still had an audience.

When the king glanced back in my direction, I took a step to one side, more clearly revealing Bryony and Tyron behind me.

"Please allow me to introduce two of our fellow trainees, energy mages Bryony and Tyron." I indicated each of them with my hand as I said their names, and they both gave a deep bow.

The king's eyebrows lowered, and he looked from them to me. His wife stepped into the breach, expressing her pleasure at meeting them, and her hope that they might have a chance over the holiday to spend some time together.

Tyron regarded the king and queen with almost as much interest as they showed in him, but Bryony was doing a poor job of concealing her dislike. I should have foreseen her reaction and told her to stay away. She saw my mother as a beloved aunt, and she didn't have my training on keeping her emotions hidden.

But the duke stepped forward, ready to show the king and queen to their accommodation, and the moment passed. As soon as the crowd began to break up, I gripped Bryony's arm and whispered urgently in her ear.

"You're going to have to hide your feelings better than that, Bree! They aren't fellow trainees, remember. We can't afford to offend them, no matter what they say."

"I would certainly recommend keeping your true feelings hidden from my parents," Darius said in a low voice.

I jerked, my heart racing at his unexpected closeness. But by the time I had registered his presence there, he was already gone, lost in the crowd.

Bryony raised an eyebrow. "That was almost...friendly? By the prince's standards, anyway."

I shrugged. I hadn't told her about the prince's visits to my sitting room, or the charged interactions we'd had there. Friendly wasn't a word I would use to describe him, but our relationship was certainly far more complex than it looked on the surface.

I had thought I would be trapped into another formal evening meal in Duke Francis's dining room that night, but apparently the queen insisted on a private family meal. It was a natural request, since Midwinter night itself would be taken by the ball, and it neatly avoided the question of who would have been included in a larger event. The duke's room wasn't big enough for all the courtiers who had gathered to spend the holiday with their children.

The next morning I was woken by Bryony jumping on my bed.

"Go away," I mumbled. "I *was* enjoying one of the few days a year we don't have those incessant bells waking us up."

"But I have something for you." She gave several more enthusiastic bounces.

"Don't want it," I groaned, trying to bury my head under my pillow. "Just want to sleep."

The pillow was whipped away, and I groaned again. "I'm writing to Layna and requesting a new set of compositions for my door, especially keyed to keep you out."

"Ha! You know you love me." She lobbed a small wrapped item onto the sheet near my head and began to look around the room. "Now where's my present?"

"Ah, now we come to the truth of it." I sat up and pointed an accusatory finger at her. "That's why you're here at the crack of dawn."

She rolled her eyes. "It's hardly the crack of dawn." She scrambled down from the bed and flung open the curtains. "Look! I've been terribly restrained."

With a final grumble, I admitted the morning looked reasonably advanced and directed her to the wardrobe. She flung open the doors with so much enthusiasm that I couldn't help smiling.

Along with the letter from my father—at least half of which was clearly dictated by my mother—and the funds from my aunt, had come a package from my Aunt Coralie. And since my earlier collection of letters had told them all about Bryony's unexpected presence at the Academy, the package had contained not one dress but two.

I had told Bryony her gown was my Midwinter gift to her, and she would have to wait until Midwinter morning to see it. Naturally she had been dying of curiosity ever since.

My own dress was a predictable red with gold embroidery—the colors of the Ardannian royal family. But the color looked striking against my dark hair, and my aunt had chosen the design well. The skirt had enough size to give me some presence without looking ridiculous on my small frame, and the fitted bodice and elegant neckline reminded me I was a princess and not just a first year trainee.

Bryony nodded approval at the way the shaped neckline swept off both my shoulders, leaving my collarbone completely bare, but most of her attention was focused on her own dress.

With my friend, my aunt had been able to be less constrained. She had chosen a gown in a deep, warm purple that made Bryony's skin glow. Its high collar hinted at the style of robes worn by the Sekalis, but the resemblance to a robe ended there. Her arms were bare, and the fitted dress was balanced with a soft edge thanks to the folds of silken material which fell from mid-thigh to the ground. It looked restrictive to me, but Bryony was in raptures over it.

We spent a lazy morning together in my suite before the whole afternoon was absorbed by ball preparations. Two maids appeared after lunch to help us, telling me they had been sent by Zora. One of them proved excellent at arranging hair, and I sent even more silent blessings in the head servant's direction. The woman truly was a gem, and I hoped Duke Francis gave her sufficient appreciation.

We were at last declared ready and allowed to escape. Since I was officially the host of the event, we were the first to arrive, ready for me to greet the other guests. The only room large enough for a ball was the dining hall, and it had been closed since breakfast. The extra servants hired for the occasion had delivered everyone's lunches on trays to their rooms while the transformation of the hall was underway.

Despite my confidence in Zora, I still gasped when we slipped through the doors, closing them behind us. The space was utterly unrecognizable.

Soft golden globes floated in the air, creating a false ceiling that gave the room an otherworldly air. I knew they were fueled by compositions from all the trainees, and I hoped seeing them here would give my fellow students a sense of pride and ownership in the event.

The tables and chairs had all been cleared away, except for one long table against the far wall, laden with so many delicacies I feared its legs would collapse. Bryony exclaimed and ran straight for it, falling on a plate of Ardannian pastries which she declared she hadn't eaten in forever.

But I took a moment to spin in the middle of the room, taking in the garlands and red berries that decorated the walls. They sparkled in the light of the globes as if dusted with shining gold, an effect that must have been achieved by either the fourth years or perhaps an instructor. It was certainly beyond the capability of a first year.

A small platform had been set up against the left wall, and a group of musicians sat there, tuning their instruments. When they struck up a practice tune, I wondered if they had somehow been brought from the capital. It would be unusual to find so many skilled musicians in the small populations that lived near the Academy.

Zora appeared silently beside me, and I had to restrain myself from embracing the woman.

"You are a true wonder!" I told her. "How did you achieve all this?"

She gave a satisfied smile. "When you've been somewhere as long as I've been at the Academy, you learn what you need to learn. Even managing mages becomes easy after enough practice." She winked, surprising a laugh out of me.

"You are full of surprises."

"You're not quite what I expected either, Princess," she said. "But we're about to open the doors, so it's time for you to be in position."

I nodded and moved to stand next to the entrance. Two servants in formal dark green uniforms opened the double doors, securing them in place. And within moments, the first of the trainees arrived, their families in tow.

I smiled and nodded and murmured welcomes for so long that my throat grew parched and my feet sore. The room filled up, the bright gowns giving it even more of a festive air.

I received many compliments on the arrangements and the style. Everyone seemed determined to be pleased, although I knew the guests included many from both sides of court.

Tyron arrived alone, and I sent him in search of Bryony, whispering suggestions for which dishes he should try. He gave a low whistle at the state of the room, not appearing too grieved to be without his family, although I felt sad on his behalf.

I had done my own grieving that morning, softened by the presence of Bryony. I was used to a formal ball at Midwinter, but I usually spent the day leading up to it with my parents and brothers, and the day after—my father's birthday—was always spent without any formal functions at all, by my mother's decree.

I pushed the thought away. I had chosen to come here. I wouldn't allow myself to be distracted now that I had the opportunity to make the kind of impression my aunt had sent me to make.

I looked around the room of chattering, dancing people. Did the ball communicate what I wished it to? Did the members of the court look around and think to themselves, *Ardann is rich, and gracious, and inclined toward friendship*? I hoped so.

At last I saw King Cassius and Queen Endellion crossing the entranceway toward me. Once I had greeted them, I could finally be released from my post. Any more latecomers would have to join the party without ceremony.

The royal couple stopped in the doorway, Cassius coolly surveying the crowd while the queen cooed over the decorations. I curtsied to them both.

"You've done a lovely job, my dear," Endellion told me, and I accepted her thanks with a smile, as I had to, although it felt wrong to take the credit for Zora's work.

"I hope you enjoy the celebrations," I told them. "And the small taste of Ardann. It is my family's desire that all future holidays might be celebrated in such unity and amity."

Cassius turned to look at me properly for the first time, his eyes sizing up my appearance and his lips turning slightly downward. But he didn't actually protest, merely giving his wife's arm a slight tug.

"Come, let's get this over with," he said.

"Really, Cassius," she whispered before their steps took them out of hearing range.

"Never mind them, everyone else looks like they're enjoying themselves." Jareth stepped through the door behind his parents with a friendly smile.

I returned his smile, my own well-practiced by now. But a moment later my eyes caught on Darius, now standing in front of me, and my face froze.

CHAPTER 20

I had never seen him dressed formally before, and if I had thought his presence commanding in a trainee's robes, it was nothing to how he looked now.

He wore a gold circlet on his head, heavier and more elaborate than the one nestled among my own dark locks, but he didn't need it to proclaim his royal status. His clothes were a severe black, alleviated only by a purple sash across his chest, partially overlaid over a second gold one.

He gave a shallow bow while my mind scrambled to recover my previous calm.

"My apologies for my family," he said in tones low enough that only I could hear.

Was he truly embarrassed by his family's behavior, or merely concerned for the political ramifications if I reported his father's offensive attitude back to my own family? He had himself firmly under control, icy indifference the only emotion visible on his face, so I couldn't tell.

"This is a day for celebration," I said, managing to find my tongue. "Do not think of it."

He inclined his head toward me in acknowledgment of my words before turning to survey the transformed dining hall.

"Zora is to be congratulated," he said.

I blinked at him. He knew the head servant?

But of course he did. Perhaps she was the source of his information about the extra cleaning my room had needed on my arrival.

"She's done an incredible job," I said. "I'm most appreciative of her efforts."

"Are you?" His eyes weighed me in an entirely different way from his father's.

It seemed a rhetorical question, so I remained silent. Darius was intimidating and unsettling enough as a fellow trainee—I had no idea what to make of him as a crown prince among his court.

"I suppose it is left to me to ask you for a dance," he said. "At some point in the evening."

I bit my lip, for some reason more offended by his wording than his father's open disdain.

"Don't feel yourself obliged, Your Highness."

He raised an eyebrow, trapping me with an intense stare. "Is that a refusal?"

Part of me longed to say yes, but my courage failed me. Or perhaps it was merely my sense of duty reasserting itself.

"Of course not, Prince Darius. As the host of this ball, I would be honored to dance with you."

"Good." His eyes still held mine, something flashing in their depths. "Because I intend to claim one."

He stepped into the moving crowd, and I was left standing alone, reminding myself to breathe.

Thankfully Bryony emerged and pulled me toward the food table, reminding me that I'd barely touched my lunch.

"I'm not having you collapse in the middle of the ball. Especially not if you're going to dance with Prince Darius." She grinned at me wickedly. "Doesn't he look too delicious for words all dressed up like that?"

"He looks dangerous," I said.

"Mmmm." Bryony almost purred. "The delicious kind of dangerous."

"Bree!"

"What? Don't tell me you haven't noticed. That boy is far too handsome for his own good."

"Or anyone else's," I muttered, turning to select something to eat so I wouldn't have to give a real answer. I wasn't ready to admit to anyone, even Bryony, just how much I noticed everything about Prince Darius.

The food tasted as delicious as it looked, but I wasn't left to enjoy it for long. Royce was the first to ask me to dance, clearly pushed into it by his family, and I was forced to acknowledge that despite his many faults, he was elegant on a dance floor.

After that, the invitations came non-stop, many from courtiers decades older than me. I accepted as often as I could, smiling and making every effort to be charming as I answered their questions about Ardannian Midwinter customs and how I was enjoying my studies. No one was tactless enough to mention my well-known lack of power, although plenty of them were full of curious questions about my energy mage friends.

To my surprise, I even began to relax somewhat. It felt so much like a royal function at home. I might be out of place in a composition classroom, but here in a ballroom, I knew all the steps. It took little effort to turn away prying questions with a light answer and to seem congenial without promising anything. I had been practicing such skills my whole life.

With such a crowd of people, I saw little of my year mates, although I was surprised to spot Wardell and Frida dancing, as well as Armand and Isabelle. I caught sight of Jareth at one point, leading his cousin Dellion out onto the floor, which seemed a bold move considering I had seen him conversing with his father only moments before.

But when I later caught sight of him in a corner of the room laughing at something his grandfather was saying, the dance made more sense. He seemed far more at ease with the old general than he had with his father.

I had so far managed to avoid more than a brief introduction to the general, and even that interaction had been tainted by Raelynn's dire words, ringing through my mind. It was easy to see how someone might find him a forbidding figure since he spent the dance watching from the wall, his expression haughty. The smiles he had given his younger grandson were the only ones I saw him bestow the entire evening.

He certainly looked thunderously displeased when Ashlyn brought her mother, the Head of the Wind Workers, to talk to me. She was full of warmth and gracious words, and although I apologized for the disruption I had caused to her own plans, she waved my words aside without hesitation. Her manner suggested that while the king might dislike me personally, politically I was becoming a more palatable proposition.

Bryony popped up at my side from time to time, but she was as besieged with requests as I was, and usually only had time for a few words before being claimed for the next dance. On one such occasion, when I had taken a break for a much-needed drink, I was watching her disappear back into the crowd when an elderly gentleman approached me. He introduced himself as Ashlyn's grandfather and asked me to dance. Before I could give him my hand, however, a tall figure stepped from the crowd.

"I believe this dance is mine." Darius claimed my outstretched fingers.

Before I could protest, Ashlyn's grandfather bowed and stepped back. I gave him an apologetic smile, but his focus was on the prince. Was there anyone in this room who would have gainsaid Darius, no matter how outrageous his request?

He led me forward toward the middle of the floor without further words. Space cleared around us, no matter how tight the crowd, allowing us free passage. When the first strains of the song sounded, his hold on my hand shifted, his other arm encircling my waist.

I took a deep breath, placing my free hand on his shoulder and letting him draw me close. Then the music swelled, and he swept me into movement.

Murmurs surrounded us, but I let them fade away, my attention on my partner. He moved with as much elegance as he fought, firmly leading me without pushing or pulling. In fact, he gave no sign of expending any effort at all. It made the dance truly effortless for me, and yet my breath still came unaccountably fast.

"You look beautiful." His usual detached tone robbed the words of any special meaning.

But when I looked up into his face, my brow creased, I almost fumbled my step. His tone and expression might be clipped and unfeeling, but his eyes burned into me.

"Th...thank you," I faltered.

"I think you may count tonight as a victory." His gaze didn't leave mine. "I am honest enough to confess that when you asked for a day to fix the situation, I wasn't convinced you were capable. But I admit I was wrong."

"Does that happen often?" I asked, unable to keep a hint of amusement out of my voice.

"I generally don't have the luxury of making mistakes. But you seem to be an exception to all my rules."

"Am I?" The words came out more breathy than I had intended.

"Well, for one, I make a point of never dancing with young, unattached females," he said.

I raised an eyebrow. "Well that would explain why we seemed to attract so much attention at the start of the dance. But I'm a

194

foreign princess studying in Kallorway, remember. I was already breaking all the rules."

"That's what scares me."

"I'm not convinced anything scares you," I replied, although I didn't think he had intended me to hear his quiet words.

His gaze, which had momentarily dropped away, captured me again. "You utterly terrify me, Verene."

It was hard to think when he said such confusing things, not when I was pressed up against his chest and he was looking at me with eyes that seemed to be pleading for something.

"I can't imagine why," I managed to gasp out.

"Can't you?" His eyes dropped to my lips before sweeping back up to capture my gaze again. "You have secrets, Princess, and I don't like secrets. You're not part of my plan, and you could ruin everything."

Indignation pushed through the haze that had descended over my mind. "But you're full of secrets!"

A slow smile spread over his face, reaching up to his eyes and transforming him once again. With a smile like that it was too easy to forget my warning to Bryony that he was the dangerous type of attractive.

"It's only other people's secrets I dislike," he said, and I couldn't help rolling my eyes at his surprising sally.

"Naturally."

"Naturally." He repeated the word gravely, but his eyes danced with amusement.

Before I could reply, his eyes caught on something over my shoulder. The smile instantly disappeared, something hard replacing it, and his eyes no longer met mine.

The tempo of his steps changed, our movement quickening as he maneuvered me through the crowd toward the edge of the dance floor, although the song wasn't ending. As we spun, I tried to catch a glimpse of what he'd seen, but we were moving too fast for my eyes to latch on to anything.

As soon as we reached the edge of the dancers, he stopped abruptly, releasing me so fast I staggered slightly.

"What?" I asked. "What is it?"

"This was a mistake." His harsh tone grated against my raw emotions, and I had to fight to keep from visibly reacting.

But I couldn't let anyone see me shaken, not when I knew how many eyes must be on us.

"It was just a dance," I said.

"It's never just a dance."

He inclined his head slightly in my direction and turned on his heel, striding away around the edge of the dance floor. I followed his path with my eyes and saw he was heading toward his brother. But Jareth's attention was focused on something on the other side of the ballroom—something in the same direction as Darius had looked before his manner changed so completely.

I followed Jareth's gaze and saw the king standing by the refreshment table. Someone stood beside him, talking at him, but his attention was on his older son. And even at this distance, the calculating anger on his face made me shiver.

I looked around wildly and spotted the door just behind me. Making a dash for it, I escaped into the calm and cool of the entranceway. I moved along the wall until I was out of sight of the ballroom before collapsing back against it and sucking in deep, steadying breaths.

I needed to regain control of myself and do it fast. Because while I couldn't let my emotions take over in the middle of the ballroom, neither could I afford to disappear for long. Too many eyes were on me tonight.

When I had calmed enough to resume my social mask, I slipped back through the doors, trying to lose myself in the crowd. But my eyes searched the room against my will. A new song had started, and I found Darius back on the dance floor, this time with Bryony.

Despite myself, I felt a small barb lodge in my heart. So much for his rule.

I accepted the next offer I received blindly, smiling and laughing without absorbing what my partner was saying. But gradually I forced myself to resume my usual manner, doing my best to ignore the infuriating crown prince as he methodically danced with every girl in our year, one by one.

And when I was finally able to collapse into my bed, I did so with the relieved thought that I was so utterly exhausted nothing could keep me awake. Not even the confusing, changeable face that tried so hard to fill my mind.

I mostly stayed in my rooms the next day, escaping the endless string of goodbyes taking place in the entry of the Academy. When I grew too restless to stay still, I slipped downstairs to the library where I could pace up and down among the shelves. Hidden from sight, I tried to grasp at the peace the library usually brought me, but it proved elusive.

Darius had begun by saying the ball was a victory for me, but he had ended by saying it was all a mistake. And from the look on his father's face, it had certainly done nothing to soften the king toward Ardann. The faction that stood behind the crown might seem the most disposed toward me at the moment, but I would do well not to think their support certain.

And there had been nothing confusing in General Haddon's clear distaste of both the event and me. The old man had been furious about the reception I was receiving.

It was hard in all of that to see anything of victory.

No matter how many shelves I paced, I couldn't decide if I had done my goal here more harm or good. I knew I was dwelling so fiercely on the problem in order to avoid thinking about the even more complicated question of my own emotions, but the knowledge didn't deter me.

Eventually I gave up, however, and returned to my rooms. I told myself my desire to be in my own suite had nothing to do with the hope that a certain prince would appear in the hidden doorway to explain his inscrutable behavior. But from the way my eyes kept sliding to the tapestry, I wasn't listening.

There was no sign of Darius, however. All three meals had been delivered to our rooms on trays, while the servants—who had mostly been given the morning off—spent the afternoon returning the dining hall to its usual state.

Eventually the inactivity grew too much for me, and when dusk fell, I slipped out of my rooms for a run. The level of activity in the Academy—in both the main corridors and the hidden ones—soon drove me outside. The cold air burned in my lungs, but I welcomed the sensation after the stuffy day spent inside.

I pushed myself hard, falling into the focused mindset that let everything else drop away except my pounding feet, rasping breath, and burning legs. The last of the daylight faded, but the moon was bright, and I didn't slow, the activity warming me against the cold of the night.

Something, some small sound that was gone almost as soon as I caught it, brought my attention back to my surroundings. I tried to place myself. I was sure I had set out to run laps around the main Academy building, but somehow I had wandered off that path and into the gardens tended by the grower students. What had led me here? I couldn't remember now.

My steps slowed, something still jangling at the edge of my awareness, telling me something wasn't right. I remembered to reach out with my new, extra sense and realized I wasn't alone out here in the darkness. But no sooner had I identified the presence of at least one other person, than my leading foot landed on nothing but air, and I fell forward.

CHAPTER 21

*T*he hole was large enough and deep enough that my whole body catapulted into it. Thankfully the dirt was so freshly turned, my landing was softer than it should have been.

Gasping more from shock than pain, I took careful stock of the different parts of my body. Nothing felt injured.

I gazed up the sheer dirt sides of the pit. Only the stars in the sky above were visible. The irony of the situation didn't escape me. A tiny hole had broken my ankle while a fall into an enormous pit was without notable injury.

But the panic caught up to me a moment later. Who had left this here? And why? And how was I going to get out?

I pushed myself to my feet and touched the side of the hole. Dirt crumbled away at my touch. But I hadn't even attempted to climb out when something invisible hit me hard. My whole body spasmed, sending me back down into the dirt at the bottom of the pit.

The sensation reminded me a little of the feeling when Tyron's energy hit me after I worked his composition. But that working had been followed by a pleasant, buoyant feeling as his energy poured into me. Now it was the opposite. Something had latched on to my deepest self and was drawing it out.

I could feel the invisible force pouring out of me so vividly that I grasped for it with both hands, as if I could stem the flow by physical action. Scrambling to my feet, I spun wildly, but from down here there was nothing to see.

My energy—my life force—continued to be wrenched out of me, flying into the air and out of the hole that trapped me.

A shield. I needed a shield.

My trembling fingers thrust into my robe, fumbling with haste, and I found the pocket that held my most powerful shield. Pulling it out, I tore it, power springing up around me. But it did nothing to stop the draining of my energy.

Too late I realized I had wasted my shield. It was one against both physical attack and an attack with power, but this was an energy composition. I needed a shield against energy.

I was sure my father had crafted me one. But with the scarcity of energy mages—let alone energy mages who could drain energy—I hadn't placed it in one of my most accessible pockets.

I tried to remember where to find it, but my fingers were trembling from exhaustion now, my brain growing foggy as I lost more and more of my energy. If I didn't find it within the next several seconds, my life would be over.

My mind acted out of desperation, reaching out along the sensation of flowing energy, following it back to its source. I could see it in my mind's eye, my brain creating the scene my extra sense could detect. The stream of my energy ended in a bright pool which grew bigger with every moment that passed.

"No!" I screamed, the attempted shout made soft with exhaustion. The words swam across my mind in bright letters at odds with the weakness of my voice. "That energy is mine!"

As I spoke the last word, something changed. The pool bubbled and burbled, and the flow reversed course, energy flowing back toward me instead of away.

The final dregs of my energy dripped back into me, followed quickly by more. I managed a shuddering breath, wondering why my face felt wet. A moment later I noticed I was lying flat in the dirt. When had I lain down?

The flow of beautiful energy cut off abruptly. My mind reached for it, seeking the bright source, but it was veiled now, dimmed in a way that was hard to describe. *Shielded,* my mind supplied.

The energy moved away from me, going faster and faster until it left the circle of my awareness. Still I lay in the dirt. I had received back enough of my energy to save my life, but standing up felt out of my reach, let alone climbing out of the pit.

Perhaps I would lie here until morning. I wondered, idly, if I would freeze to death in that time. I seemed unable to muster the proper emotional response to that thought. Had my father provided me with a warming composition?

How nice it would be, I thought, *if I could compose one myself.*

Something niggled at the back of my mind. I couldn't compose anything. That was one of my deepest truths. And yet— wasn't that what I had just done?

What exactly had just happened?

I had spoken and declared the energy mine…and it had returned to me. Had I just done a spoken energy composition? It seemed impossible, not least because that wasn't the way energy compositions worked. It wasn't how any compositions worked. You could block someone else's composition, or combat it, but you couldn't twist it mid-working, changing its very nature.

More time passed, although I didn't know how much. Should I be doing something to warm myself up? I couldn't think what.

"Verene! Verene, are you out here?"

A hint of unfamiliar desperation colored the otherwise familiar voice. Darius sounded worried. Why was he worried?

"I'm here," I called back, my words sounding feeble after the strength of his voice. Could he even hear them? I could barely hear them myself.

A distant, frustrated growl was cut off by the sound of tearing parchment. The sound brought another thought floating to the front of my mind. Was that the sound I had heard while running? What exactly had led my feet along this precise path?

But the sensation of questing power distracted me. It butted gently against me, wrapping itself around my length and then disappearing again.

Well, that was better than the last one, I thought. *That didn't hurt at all.*

Running steps sounded somewhere in the garden, and then a face appeared at the edge of the hole.

"Verene!" Darius sounded somehow both horrified and relieved. "Are you hurt?"

"I don't think so." My brow furrowed in confusion. "I just feel so tired. So very tired."

"Hold on." He disappeared, and I frowned. I had liked the sight of his face.

Another tearing sound reached me, and this time the power that found me cupped me gently, bearing me up into the air and lifting me from the pit. It placed me on the soft dirt of the garden bed beside the lip of the hole, and Darius's face once again appeared above me.

"That was nice." I smiled up at him.

"What happened to you?" he asked, his voice grim. "What is this?"

"It appears to be a hole," I said after a moment of deep thought. "It certainly felt like a hole. But perhaps I'm wrong. My brain seems a little muddled right now."

His eyes grew alarmed.

"Don't worry," I said, suddenly desperate to smooth away the trouble on his face. "They just drained most of my energy. But I got some of it back."

"They?" The word came out like a snarl. "Who's they?"

"Well…" I gave the question an even longer moment of thought. "I suppose it must have been whoever dug the hole. They didn't introduce themselves, though." I frowned. "Very rude."

Darius groaned. "You're nonsensical."

"Am I? How strange." Once again I felt there should be an emotion connected with the thought, but I couldn't seem to locate it.

"I'm glad you came, though," I added. "I thought I might freeze to death in there overnight. I don't think I would have liked that."

"Neither would I," he said, the words a whisper.

"But how did you find me?" I asked, the question appearing in my mind out of nowhere. "Do you often walk the grounds at night? It's quite strange of you."

He bit back another strangled groan. "No, of course I don't! And neither should you be! I was looking for you."

"But the corridors were too crowded for running." My voice sounded pitiful. "There was nowhere else to go."

"And someone must have known that," he said. "Someone who was watching you, ready to follow you out here and spring their trap. We can just be grateful one of the servants saw you leave the Academy."

"Oh, do you think it was a trap?" I frowned, trying to marshal my thoughts into line. "I suppose it must have been, now that you mention it."

"You need help," Darius said. "And you're not walking anywhere."

He scooped me up, cradling me against his chest, and stood easily to his feet. I rested my head against his shoulder and sighed.

"This is nice, too," I said. "I might like it better, even."

"If you remember any of this, you're going to be horrified."

His voice held a note of amusement that I liked. I didn't hear it there often, although I couldn't remember why.

The rhythm of his steps and the comfort of his strong arms had nearly lulled me to sleep when a loud voice hailed us. I opened my eyes briefly but decided the effort was too great and closed them again.

"What's this?" asked a sharp voice. "One of my guards heard shouting, and…" An inhaled breath. "Is she hurt?"

It was Captain Vincent, my tired mind supplied, prodded by his mention of a guard.

"Thankfully not," Darius said, his voice hard and imperious. "But she needs to rest."

"What happened?" Even in the face of a prince, the captain wasn't ready to back down, and I wanted to applaud him.

If I hadn't been too tired to open my eyes.

"*Someone* was foolish enough to dig a large hole in the garden and then leave it there," Darius said. "She was running and didn't see it in the dark."

"I'll have it filled in immediately," the captain said. "And have a talk with both the grower instructor and the gardeners." His voice dropped a little. "And my men, too. It's their job to notice any threats to safety, even ones that don't come with a sharp blade attached. One of them should have seen it on patrol."

"Indeed." Darius's voice was colder than the winter air around us. "Now if you'll let me pass?"

"Of course, Your Highness." Captain Vincent stepped aside, and our progress resumed.

"Do you think he'll notice it's not an ordinary sort of hole?" I asked without opening my eyes.

"If he's half as good at his job as he's supposed to be, he will," Darius said, a dark note in his voice. "And then it will be very interesting to see what he does with that information."

"We could tell him," I suggested helpfully.

Darius's arms tightened around me slightly.

"We could. But he's new here and appointed directly by my father. I haven't had enough time to work out exactly where his allegiances lie."

"Layna liked him," I said. "But I didn't tell him about the other hole either."

"Yes," Darius said slowly. "That other hole."

"It wasn't quite so large as this one, though," I said. "So he probably didn't notice it."

A rumble in his chest might have been a suppressed chuckle. I snuggled closer to him.

"You're so warm," I said, the sleepiness returning. "I like it."

Something soft brushed against my hair, although I couldn't tell what.

"Sleep if you need to, Verene," Darius said in a softer voice than I had ever heard from him.

"I think maybe I will," I agreed.

I felt the change in the air when we stepped into the building, though, and my eyes flew open when we started up the stairs. Someone—an older trainee I didn't recognize—was coming down, and she stared at us in surprise.

I wondered if I should explain the situation to her, but I couldn't seem to form a coherent sentence in my mind. Darius, however, turned his head and gave her a single look that sent her scurrying silently out of my line of sight. I could imagine his expression even if I couldn't see it. He could be scary when he wanted to be.

We went up and up, finally turning onto a floor I had never visited before. The prince didn't slow, however, striding up to one of the doors and kicking it with his boot. When it didn't immediately open, he kicked it again.

CHAPTER 22

"I'm coming!" cried an indignant voice that cut off into a gasp as the door swung open.

I recognized that voice.

Darius carried me into the large room and laid me down gently on the bed against one wall. I turned my head and saw the astonished face of my friend.

"Bree! I've never seen your room before. Why have I never seen your room before?"

"What's wrong with her?" Bryony sounded horrified. "What happened?"

"That's what I want to know," said Darius. "But it seems she's been drained of energy. She's not talking sensibly."

"Excuse me!" I protested weakly, but they both ignored me.

"Oh! Of course! That's why you brought her here. Wait, I'll get my strongest one."

Bryony hurried over to a desk, coming back with a fresh, flat parchment. "I only composed it this afternoon."

I frowned at her. "So that's why you feel so low. That's no way to spend a holiday, Bryony."

She put the parchment into my hands.

"I wrote it for the arena, so you need to rip it yourself. Go ahead, Verene."

I frowned. "But this is yours. I didn't like it when someone took *my* energy. I don't want to take yours."

Bryony gave Darius a wide-eyed look.

"Rip it, Verene." He leaned forward, his face filling my view, his voice commanding.

I sighed. "Fine."

Mustering the energy to move my arms, I ripped the parchment slowly in two. A jolt hit me, making me twitch against the bed, and for a second unreasoning panic gripped me. But then the sweet feeling of energy poured into me, and I calmed. This wasn't like the last one.

It didn't take long for the composition to do its work. My exhaustion drained away, replaced by horror. I sat up and looked from Bryony to Darius. The sight of his face made me swallow, the blood draining from my cheeks.

"What exactly did I say?"

He grinned, his whole face softening and transforming in a way that made it hard for me to tear my eyes from him.

"I wondered if you would remember. Maybe don't try too hard to recall all of it."

I groaned and buried my face in my hands. "How about you try not to remember it as well?"

"No chance of that. I intend to savor every word."

He chuckled, and I was gripped by the memory of how his suppressed laughter had felt while he held me against him. All the blood came rushing back to my face in what must have been an embarrassing riot of color.

"Ugh, Bryony, kill me right now."

"Um, I have no idea what's going on, but it kind of looked like someone already tried that." My friend somehow managed to sound both amused and worried.

My eyes flew open, and the humor dropped instantly from

Darius's face.

"Yes," he said, his usual seriousness back in his voice. "It did look a lot like that."

Reluctantly I nodded. "I think someone did. And they nearly succeeded. I was absorbed by my run, and they must have guided me somehow." I shook my head. "I sensed something wrong but not in time to stop myself falling into that hole."

"Hole?" Bryony looked between us.

"Someone dug a giant pit in the middle of the gardens," Darius said grimly. "No doubt they did it with a composition, or it would have taken hours."

I nodded. "The sides did seem unnaturally sheer. I fell straight in, like a fool. And while I was still trying to get my bearings, they hit me with an energy composition. A draining one."

"What?" Bryony gasped. "But where would anyone at the Academy get a composition like that?"

I shrugged. "I have no idea. But they had one."

"You got a shield up in time, then?" Bryony asked.

I flushed again. "No. Although you can be sure I'll have one at hand next time. It all happened so fast, and by the time I realized I needed one, it was too late to find it."

"So how are you still alive?" She looked confused, and I couldn't blame her. I didn't have a satisfactory answer to that question myself.

"You said you got some of your energy back," Darius said, his eyes locked on my face, his words tense. "What exactly did you mean by that?"

I bit my lip, looking between him and my friend.

"And just now you said you could feel Bryony was tired. It's time for the truth at last, if you please. How did you save yourself?"

I threw up my hands. "I don't know! I don't understand it myself."

I drew a deep breath. Darius had just saved me, and I clearly wasn't going to get away without a proper explanation this time.

"When I arrived at the Academy, the only ability I had was the ability to sense power."

"And to read and write," Bryony added.

I nodded. "I was basically a sealed mage. That's it. I swear it. But when I worked Tyron's energy composition in the arena during our battle, I started sensing energy as well."

"Like an energy mage?" Darius frowned at me.

"Yes, but limited to just that sense. I think working his composition unlocked the ability somehow, but I couldn't do anything else. I tried everything—I redid all the experiments we did back in Ardann. Nothing else worked. It hadn't unleashed any other ability."

"Sensing energy wouldn't have saved you in that pit," he said.

"No," I said slowly. "That was something else. It started with the sensing, though. I followed the energy back to wherever it was going, and then I got angry and declared that it was mine. So…it turned around and came back to me."

"A verbal composition?" Darius said. "So you *are* like your mother!"

He stepped back, his face closing off, and I stood, reaching out to him, suddenly desperate to have him hear me.

"If I am, this is the first time I've ever done it."

"Oh sit down, both of you." Bryony pushed me back onto the bed, pulling forward two chairs and gesturing imperiously for Darius to sit in one. "She's telling the truth, so stop getting all high and mighty, and help us figure out what just happened out there."

Darius continued to frown, but he sank down into the chair, crossing his arms across his chest and fixing his eyes on my face.

Bryony also turned to me, her exasperation transformed to excitement.

"I can't believe it, Verene! You composed! This is amazing!"

She made a face. "Well, not the part where someone's trying to kill you, obviously. But the rest. So you composed an energy shield for yourself? That must make you an energy mage, then. A shielding one."

I shook my head. "No, it wasn't a shield. I didn't stop my attacker's composition, I just...reversed it. I started pulling the energy back to myself. But he—or she—must have activated a shield themselves because I didn't get much before the flow was cut off."

"You mean you worked a composition to drain their energy?" Bryony asked. "That's a slightly more common ability than shielding."

I shook my head again, my frustration building, although at myself more than anyone else. "No, I didn't take *their* energy, I just took control of their composition and changed it."

Darius dropped his arms from his chest, leaning forward in his chair. His words came out slowly, each one dropping from his lips separately.

"You took control of their composition. And you changed it."

"Sort of." I shifted uncomfortably. "I mean, I didn't change it completely. I just reversed it."

"That's impossible." His tone was flat, his face shuttered.

"Of course it is! Do you think I don't know that? But I'm telling you what happened."

"Spoken compositions were impossible too, thirty years ago." Bryony's voice dropped calm into the middle of our tension. "And Verene is literally the daughter of the Spoken Mage." She gave Darius a piercing look. "Do you really want to refuse to consider the possibility she might have an impossible ability? It would explain why no one could work out what it was. Who would ever think to test such a thing?"

She turned her gaze back on me. "You can feel power as well as energy. Do you think you could take control of a power composition?"

I bit my lip, trying to recall the feeling when I reached into my attacker's composition.

"I'm not sure. It wasn't like a regular composition. This one was attached to them. They were pulling my energy into themselves. I don't know if it would work with a regular sort of composition."

Bryony nodded, tapping her finger against her lip. "That makes sense. Power mages are always avoiding open compositions that connect to them after they're worked because of the danger of draining so much energy that they die. But it's different for us. We don't have the same risks."

Darius's brows drew together. "What do you mean? Are all your compositions open ones then?"

"In a way?" Bryony looked at me, but I gestured for her to go on. Unlike Darius, I had covered this in discipline class, but Bryony was the expert. "Our compositions have to be open because the whole point is for them to connect to someone's energy. But they're not draining our energy, so there's no risk to us. Those of us who give energy—like me—have that energy drained when we write the composition. Once it's worked, it connects with the person who works it, but since it's giving them stored energy, there's no concern. For those who drain energy, the composition connects with them in order to feed the energy into them, but once again, there's no risk."

She laughed wryly. "Well, no risk to the person working it. There's a great risk to the victim, of course."

"Shielding is different, though," I reminded her. "Energy mages who can compose shields write them closed just like most power compositions."

"That's true," she conceded, flashing me a look that reminded me there was another type of energy composition that was closed as well.

"But taking and giving energy are the most common," I said quickly. "And those are done as open compositions—in a way, at least. So it's possible I need a connection to the mage's energy before I can…twist it—or whatever we're calling it."

"We need to experiment!" Bryony sat up straight, glee on her face.

"But not now," Darius cut in. "It's the middle of the night. Verene needs to sleep."

"I'm fine," I said. "Now that I have Bryony's energy."

He shook his head. "Classes start again tomorrow, remember. You'll just end up exhausting all your new energy if you spend the night trying to compose."

Bryony looked disappointed, but she nodded her agreement. "And apparently someone wants you dead. So exhausting yourself doesn't seem like a good idea."

From Darius's dark look, the same thought had occurred to him.

"And if I'm likely to be attacked at any moment, I should know how to use my new ability," I muttered rebelliously, but I said it under my breath. They were right, and I knew it.

"I don't want you alone," Darius said. "Bryony, you need to move in to Verene's suite."

"What?" I glared at him. "Since when did you have the right to order me around?"

He met my gaze without flinching. "Since I pulled you almost lifeless out of a pit on the Academy grounds. You're a royal guest in my father's kingdom. I will not have you assassinated here."

I groaned. "Fine. Although I don't know what excuse you have to order Bryony around."

"He doesn't need an excuse," she said cheerfully. "I'm more than happy to move into your suite. Now you'll never be able to hide from me." She cackled gleefully and rubbed her hands together.

I rolled my eyes. "You're impossible."

"But lovable, remember," she said, repeating our usual joke. A smile edged over her face. "And apparently I'm not as impossible as you."

～

There was room enough in my large bed to fit Bryony as well, although it wasn't the most pleasant experience. She kicked in her sleep, and for someone so tiny, she managed to cover an enormous radius. But I doubted I would have slept well anyway.

My thoughts raced too much for easy rest, circling around and around. Someone had tried to kill me. I had nearly died. But I had saved myself with an undiscovered ability. I had power, just like I always dreamed. In fact, I had a new power—as impossible and unheard of as my mother's had once been. I was special. Unique.

But what was my power? If it was merely the ability to twist an energy mage's working mid-flow, then I had already discovered what seemed the only valuable use for it. And I could have achieved the same result without any ability at all if I had only succeeded in putting my hand on my energy shield composition.

It had been a spoken composition, too, which meant I couldn't store them up or give them to anyone else. In short, it didn't seem like a very *useful* power—more a curiosity than anything else.

Except it had saved my life. When someone had tried to kill me. And so the circle started again.

And laid over it all, intruding whenever I started to drift into sleep, was the memory of being carried in strong arms while I babbled incoherent nonsense. What must Darius think of me?

I wanted to crawl under my covers and never emerge again. And yet. His voice had been soft, and his hands gentle. He had even laughed. More than once. Powerful, burning, intense Darius was fascinating. But soft, smiling Darius might turn out to be more dangerous still.

When I did manage sleep, my dreams were chaotic and fragmented, slipping away as soon as I tried to grasp hold of them.

CHAPTER 23

*O*nly Bryony's cajoling got me out of bed in the morning and down to breakfast. It felt wrong to sit in the dining hall and eat as if nothing had happened but, as Bryony pointed out, what other choice did we have?

Combat class was in the usual training yard, and I paired for all my bouts with Bryony. I was far too distracted to concentrate properly and didn't want to risk fighting with anyone else.

When the bell finally rang to release us, I was ready to sprint back to the Academy. But a tall, silent figure had come to watch the end of our class, and when I left the yard, he caught my eye, indicating with an inclination of his head that he wished to speak to me.

I shot a quick glance back at the rest of the class and found both Jareth and Darius watching me. Jareth looked curious and Darius as hard to read as he usually was in public. When he made no move to join me, I shrugged and approached Captain Vincent on my own.

He gave a small bow. "I'm glad to see you looking recovered, Your Highness. I will admit to some alarm at your appearance yesterday."

"Yes." I smiled at him as brightly as I could. "I was horrified when I got back to my room and saw how covered in dirt I was."

He cleared his throat. "Indeed. One of my men filled the pit in last night. I have interviewed all of the gardeners and grounds staff, as well as the instructor for the grower class. Each assures me they know nothing of any hole. I am inclined to believe them, but I am ready to question them under truth compositions if it is your wish."

"Oh goodness, no," I said. "Especially not the poor gardeners. Surely such a big hole was created with the help of a composition."

"That is certainly my opinion, Your Highness," he said. "It is possible the instructor is protecting one of her students, but she made a suggestion that seems to me the most likely explanation. She suspects one of her trainees made an error in one of their compositions and then left the hole there, not wanting to confess to their mistake."

I nodded quickly. "That does seem more likely than someone leaving it there on purpose, doesn't it?"

"Obviously, if Your Highness wishes it, I will conduct a more thorough investigation and determine which trainee is responsible. However, since no actual injury was received, I did not like to take any such action without talking to you first."

I could see the wariness in his eyes. The trainees might only be students, but they came from powerful and influential families. And if one of them had made an error, as he imagined, they would be even less likely to own to it now that it had caused an injury to a royal.

If my lifeless body had been found at the bottom of the hole, no doubt every person in the Academy would have been pressured into submitting to a truth composition. But the incident as it stood—as far as the captain knew—did not warrant any such drastic action.

His eyes crossed to the rest of the class who were now

walking back toward the Academy. I watched as they dwelled on Darius's back.

Ah. That was the other factor causing him pause. Some sort of accident had occurred, that much was clear to him. But he had also found the crown prince alone in the grounds, at night, carrying me cradled against his chest. I flushed a little at the realization that he probably suspected he had stumbled on something far outside his purview as captain of the guard. He had many reasons to wish to leave this matter alone.

"No, indeed," I told him. "You did the right thing. As you can see, I am unharmed, and feeling foolish for stumbling into the hole in the first place. I am more than happy for you to let the matter rest there. I'm sure the growers will receive a lecture from their instructor and will not make such a foolish mistake again."

His brow lightened. "I appreciate your forbearance on the matter, Your Highness."

I smiled. "And I appreciate your not spreading my own foolishness around further, Captain."

He bowed again. "Of course, Your Highness. I will leave you to your lunch." He strode away toward the guard barracks, and I watched him go for a moment, a crease between my brows.

Darius hadn't been certain we could trust him, so I was relieved for him to let the matter drop. But at the same time, a small part of me wondered what would happen if we just gave him all the information. Perhaps he might be able to uncover the identity of my attacker.

The two princes were sitting with Bryony and Tyron when I arrived at lunch, but I could hardly discuss my conversation with Captain Vincent in front of Jareth and Tyron. Darius stood to pull out my chair, however, and I managed to whisper that the captain was abandoning any investigation.

He gave a single swift nod as I sat down before taking his place back beside his brother. Jareth watched Darius with narrowed eyes, apparently too attuned to him to miss that something was going on. But when he realized my attention was on him, he began an animated conversation with Tyron.

I continued to regard him with narrowed eyes. Maybe it was my increased suspicion levels after the attack the night before, but something about Jareth continued to make me uncomfortable. I just wished I could put my finger on what it was.

My mind worried over the question while we ate our meal, and I decided at last that I didn't trust him. Not because he had ever behaved in a threatening way toward me, but because I had never seen behind his mask. It was easy to forget he had one when it was so much more friendly and outgoing than any royal I had previously met.

But the more I considered what I had so far seen of him, the more convinced I became that it was a mask all the same. And there was something unsettling about a mask that was so very disarming. Even now, Tyron was laughing, forgetting himself so far as to clap the prince on the back.

But it was dangerous to forget yourself around royalty, especially Kallorwegian royalty. Jareth might seem the least frightening of the family, but at least Darius's presence reminded everyone they must tread carefully.

When the bell rang to send us to class, Darius managed to brush against me as we exited the dining hall.

"Tonight," he whispered. "After the evening meal."

I didn't have the opportunity to respond in any way, but he had already swept on. I wanted to roll my eyes at his imperious manner, but I had to admit, I was already counting down the hours. I wanted to get through class so we could finally experiment and work out the limits of my new ability.

All through composition class I kept thinking about the words I had spoken to twist my attacker's working. They had been unpolished, hardly what you would call a real composition. But they had carried desperation behind them. Perhaps that had helped shape them to the purpose I needed.

As I watched my year mates composing, my limitations again pressed in on me. They could all sit here and practice, but I couldn't even attempt to use my power on my own. I needed someone else to make an active working before I could try my own ability. It would slow down my capacity to experiment significantly.

In discipline class it occurred to me that the situation was even worse than that. Only Bryony could help me, and she could hardly pour out her energy endlessly while I fumbled around, attempting to intercept it. And the worst-case scenario was that my ability might be limited to preventing someone stealing my energy. We had no way to replicate that scenario at all.

By the time we stood up from the evening meal, I had reached a state of dejection. Someone wanted to kill me, and I had no way to discover their identity. After a long day of regular classes, all my bright hopes about my new discovery seemed foolish and naive. I began to doubt I could even stay in Kallorway. The earlier incidents had been one thing, but attempted murder was another altogether.

Bryony trailed behind me to my room, chattering away. She had picked up on my low mood and was trying to lift my spirits, but her efforts did little.

When we entered my sitting room, I could see that someone had been hard at work. With so many other things on my mind, I hadn't even thought about my new roommate, but Darius must have spoken to Zora.

The furniture had all been rearranged, leaving room for a sturdy single bed to be placed against one wall. It had a small side table next to it and had been surrounded by a set of tall wooden panels, sectioning it off from the rest of the room.

When I continued on through to my bedchamber to change my clothes, I discovered a second wardrobe. When I peeked inside, I saw a flash of purple silk.

"Your clothes are in there," I told Bryony when I returned to the sitting room. "It looks like they brought your whole wardrobe down. Literally."

"Excellent!" She bounced through the door to take a look.

"Are you sure you don't mind being here?" I asked her when she reappeared. "You're sacrificing all of your privacy just to help me."

"Verene." She gave me a look. "You're not asking me to help you get ready for a ball or something. Someone tried to kill you. I've been trying not to think about it all day because it's just so awful. Of course I'm going to be here." A determined look came over her face. "I'm not letting you out of my sight."

Tears filled my eyes. "Thank you, Bree. Not just for this. For being here at all. Thank you for coming to the Academy. I had no idea how much I needed you."

"It's not like it's a great sacrifice. I've learned so much already, and I'd rather be here than in some Sekali school. You're not the only one who appreciates having family in a strange place, you know."

"Of course." I mopped at my eyes. "I'm sorry. It's all just been a little…much."

"I'll bet it has." She patted the back of one of the sofas. "Why don't you sit down for a moment? We don't have to start experimenting straight away."

I sat down but immediately sprang back up, unable to sit still. "Yes, about that. We should probably wait for Darius."

"Prince Darius? Is he coming here?"

A knock sounded from behind the tapestry, and she stared around in confusion. "Where did that come from?"

I hurried over to thrust aside the material, pulling open the door behind it before Darius could knock again.

"There you are! I thought you'd never…" My words trailed away when I saw he wasn't alone, his brother standing so close their energy almost blended together in my senses. I should have been paying more attention.

Jareth raised both eyebrows, looking between me and his brother. When Darius said nothing to relieve the awkward moment, he spoke.

"Good evening, Verene. I hope you don't mind, but I could see something was going on, and I hate to be excluded."

He gave me what was no doubt meant to be a disarming smile, but I only managed a weak one in return. Stepping aside, I gestured for them both to come through into my sitting room.

Darius entered first, nodding coolly to Bryony. "I thought Jareth might have some insights to offer. He's recently completed a tour of the Empire and met a number of energy mages."

"I heard Kallorway sent a recent delegation up the Abneris," I said. "But I'd forgotten Jareth was a part of it."

Closing the door behind them both, I turned to find Bryony regarding us all with wide eyes. She sidled up to me while Jareth looked around the room with interest.

"Um, since when does your room connect to the crown prince's suite? And why did I not know about this?" She gripped my arm, lowering her voice further. "Verene, how often does he use that door?"

I shook her free, my face flushing despite my best efforts. "We've spoken on occasion. But that's it. I'm sure I told you we'd talked. He didn't believe I had no power, remember?"

"Talking and sharing a secret door between your rooms is not the same thing," she hissed before giving me a significant look and marching over to one of the sofas.

When no one else sat down, she looked around at us all.

"Well? Come on! Don't just stand there awkwardly."

I tore my eyes away from Darius and flushed again. Why did I feel so off-balance just because Darius had brought his brother?

But Darius wouldn't meet my eyes, and it suddenly occurred to me that he might be avoiding being alone with me after our unguarded interaction the night before. My flush deepened. Did he fear I was going to throw myself at him after the foolish things

I'd said? I cringed at the memories. I had snuggled into him, declaring his hold on me *nice* of all things.

Bryony cleared her throat. "I assume we're not all here to look at each other awkwardly."

I sat down hurriedly, and both princes followed, each taking one of the straight-backed wooden chairs.

"What did the captain say?" Darius asked, looking at me so calmly that I wondered if I had imagined his earlier hesitation.

"Apparently the grower instructor suggested that one of her trainees may have made an error in one of their compositions and left the hole there rather than confess to it. Captain Vincent believes it to be the most likely explanation and wanted to seek my permission to let the matter drop. I don't think he's too eager to start questioning trainees—not when I appear to be unharmed."

"And you agreed, of course," Darius said. "So he won't be looking into it further."

I nodded, carefully not looking at him. "I think he was quite pleased not to look too closely into what was going on out there."

My eyes caught on Jareth who was looking between me and his brother with a crease between his eyes.

"It wouldn't have mattered if he had," said Darius, making me forget both my awkwardness and Jareth.

"What do you mean?" I asked him.

"After I saw you both here to your suite last night, I went back to the gardens. The guards had finished filling in the hole, but I worked an investigation composition to reveal recent activity in the area."

My mouth dropped open. I knew he was studying law enforcement, but that was a highly advanced composition. The sort of composition discipline heads—the strongest mages in the kingdoms—completed personally.

"You just happened to have such a working on you?" I asked weakly.

"Since you told me about your previous accident, I made sure I did," he said evenly. "Too much time and activity had passed in the yard to use it for that incident, but I wanted to be prepared in case of another."

Just how strong was Darius, and how much private training had he received? Sitting through classes must be torturously boring for him.

"Well?" Jareth sat forward. "Don't keep us waiting. What did you find?"

I frowned at him, but I supposed it was natural for him to be as concerned as Darius about such goings on in his kingdom.

"Nothing," Darius said flatly.

Jareth sat back with a low whistle.

"Nothing?" Bryony frowned at him. "I don't understand. Isn't that one of those compositions that shows you what happened, almost as if you're watching it again?"

"Yes, it is," said Darius. "And according to my composition, there was no one there. Well, there was a giant ball of power, but no person."

"But there must have been a person," I said. "I felt them."

"They were invisible, then?" Jareth asked.

"As in, with a composition?" Bryony frowned. "Is it possible they were energy shielded instead? Would that stop them from showing up in your composition, Prince Darius?"

He frowned. "An interesting question. I will raise it with our law enforcement instructor when I get a chance. But it can't have been the case here. Or at least, if they did have their energy shielded, they were also using a whole collection of other power compositions. The area where they must have been standing was lit up like a beacon."

"The type of composition Darius used is designed to do two things," Jareth explained. "It shows what was visible during the time span it's exposing, and it also makes any power being used visible. In fact, they are often keyed to go back to the last time power was used in a particular area, or in the vicinity of a particular person."

Darius wasn't paying attention to his brother's explanation, his focus on me instead. And I could read in his face that he was waiting for me to come to the same realization he had already reached.

"So we're not talking about just one person," I said, my heart sinking. "Whoever attacked me used an energy composition to do it. But they also used a whole collection of power compositions. Which means we have a conspiracy."

CHAPTER 24

*W*e discussed it exhaustively, of course. But without further information, there was no way to come to any conclusion. Jareth then wanted an explanation of my discovery of my ability, which I gave him with the utmost reluctance and only because I could think of no reason to refuse.

"Amazing!" he said when I finished. "Have you tried it again?"

"I haven't had the chance."

"We should try it now."

Darius, who had been watching me closely, his expression inscrutable, frowned at his brother's enthusiasm.

"Verene might need longer to regain her energy levels before she starts experimenting."

It seemed he had read my reluctance, although not its cause.

"Actually she's—" Bryony began to speak, probably to tell them my energy levels were fine, so I cut her off.

"It's been a long day. Perhaps tomorrow."

Darius nodded and stood, his brother following his lead with more reluctance. Bryony stayed where she was, eyeing me strangely, but I ignored her.

Jareth was first through the door, and on impulse I reached out to stop Darius from following him.

"Why did you bring Jareth?" I asked.

Darius examined my expression, his own closed. "For the reason I told you. I thought he might be able to help. I didn't realize you were still so tired."

I felt bad for letting him believe me exhausted, but my irritation drove away the guilt.

"You shouldn't have told him without asking me first."

He frowned. "He's my brother. I tell him everything."

I arched an eyebrow, dropping my voice even lower. "Everything?"

His face didn't change, but a muscle in his arm jumped beneath my fingers.

"Everything of potential import to our kingdom."

I sighed and let my hand drop. Of course it was all about his kingdom. With Darius it was never anything else.

Jareth had stopped halfway across Darius's sitting room and was looking back at us with curious eyes. I stepped back and let Darius leave.

He stopped with his hand on the door, his eyes on me.

"Verene…"

I waited, but after a long moment he turned away, swiftly closing the door. I sighed and rubbed at both temples.

"You have plenty of energy," Bryony said from her place on one of the sofas. "So what was that really about?"

"Jareth." I turned back to her. "I didn't expect him, and I didn't feel comfortable experimenting in front of him."

"Why not?"

I shrugged. "I don't know. Or rather I don't know *him*. Not really."

"But you know Prince Darius?"

I ran a shaky hand through my hair. "Maybe not. But…I can't really say why, but I trust him."

"Well, he did rescue you," Bryony pointed out. "But are you saying you don't trust Prince Jareth?"

"I don't know. I don't want to say anything to Darius because it's just an instinct. But that family…" I shook my head. "They're not like your family or mine. Do you know some people believe that if Darius doesn't demonstrate complete loyalty to his grandfather, the general would rather see him dead than on the throne?"

"Surely not!" Bryony's eyes widened.

"And I think their father kept him from starting at the Academy because he doesn't want him to graduate and become a fully qualified mage. He doesn't want the competition for the throne."

She shook her head. "That's awful. But what does it have to do with Jareth?"

I shrugged. "Maybe nothing. But he seems to get on with his grandfather awfully well."

"You think Jareth wants to kill Darius?" Bryony sounded skeptical, and I couldn't blame her.

"No, of course not! I just mean that trusting one member of that family doesn't mean trusting another. Jareth already knows more than I would have chosen to tell him. He doesn't need to see me trying—and most likely failing—to master my ability as well."

"I'm sure you won't fail!" Bryony said, loyal as always.

"I might. Because we don't have an energy mage who can take energy for me to practice with. And for all we know, that's all my ability can do."

"We should try right now." She jumped to her feet. "I have all my compositions with me."

I nodded, but slowly. Now that I came to it, I found myself absurdly reluctant.

"I don't want to use up all your supplies," I said.

"Actually, I've thought about that." She sounded triumphant.

"Since I'll be the one working the composition, the energy will all be going to me unless you actually succeed in taking control of it. And once I've received all that extra energy, I can just sit down and write out another composition to store it again. And then we can use that new composition to make another attempt. We could practice all night and I would end up with the same number of compositions I started with."

"That actually makes sense," I said.

She put her hands on her hips. "Don't sound so surprised!"

I grimaced. "Sorry. In truth, I'm just nervous to start. What if I can't do it again? What if all this excitement is for nothing?"

Bryony gripped me by both shoulders, looking me directly in the eyes.

"You can do this, Verene. I understand why you're nervous. You've dreamed of this your whole life, so you're placing far too much pressure on yourself. But this is your moment. I'm sure of it."

I took a deep breath and nodded. It was foolishness to be so hesitant. I had chosen to come alone to Kallorway, and this was nothing by comparison.

"All right," I said. "Let's try it."

Bryony produced a composition and tore it. I could feel the energy that flowed from her hands, joining the knot of it that already pulsed at her core. I reached for it, trying to follow it like I had in the pit, but it was already gone.

She frowned at me. "Don't you need to say something?"

I groaned. "I didn't even get that far. But you're right. I'm rushing this. I need to work out what to say first."

We spent several minutes debating the wording and whether I should try to use binding words.

"I just don't think I'm going to have time," I said. "It was over so fast."

"What will you try to do with the energy?" Bryony asked.

"I guess I'll try to divert it to come to me instead. Does that sound reasonable?"

She nodded. "It seems the simplest thing to do. So why don't you just say *come to me.*"

We debated for another minute before deciding on that wording, at least for a first attempt.

But when she tore another composition, and I said the words, nothing happened.

I grimaced. "I think it's not just saying the words. I need to be connected to the flow of it as well. At least, that's how it was last time. It was as much instinct as words. But I need longer."

"Give me a minute," Bryony said. "I'm bursting with energy now. I'll write a new composition using the stored energy from both of the ones I just used. That will make a stronger working which should give you a bit more time."

I waited impatiently while she sat at my desk and scribbled across the top piece of parchment that lay there. When she finished, she looked up at me.

"Ready?"

I nodded, and she ripped it.

Once again I could feel the flow of energy, and the way it connected with her. I pictured the words we had chosen, crying, "Come to me," much more loudly than needed.

Nothing happened, and the flow finished.

I slumped back onto one of the sofas. "Can you see why I didn't want Jareth here?" I muttered, and Bryony made a sympathetic sound in her throat.

"We just need to keep trying. It's hard enough for anyone to master their ability, even when they have experienced instructors to help them. There's a reason we spend four years at an Academy, you know."

"I'd settle for any progress at all." I sighed.

"Try to think back over it again," Bryony encouraged. "What

exactly did you say, and what were you thinking? Maybe you overlaid extra meaning on the words without realizing. That's advanced composition, but you were in a desperate situation—you might have managed it."

I put my arm over my eyes and thought back. Everything had been so rushed and hazy, my exhaustion fighting with my instinctive will to live. But gradually I recaptured the moment in my mind.

I had sensed my energy flowing into the other person, and I had been so angry. They were taking my essence and stealing it away. I had declared it was mine and pictured it coming back to me—and it had come.

"I said, *that energy is mine,* or something like that. I...claimed it, I suppose."

Bryony's eyes were focused on a distant point, her mind clearly working over it from every angle.

"Perhaps you should try saying those words instead?"

I pictured doing so and grimaced. It sounded so melodramatic in the calm of my sitting room, when I was trying to claim Bryony's energy. But I was getting desperate enough to try anything.

"All right. We'll try again."

Bryony turned back to her parchment. "Just give me a minute to write it back out. It's a strange feeling being so full of energy—and not entirely pleasant. I can hardly keep still."

I waited in silence until she was ready. When she looked at me inquiringly, I held up a finger. Closing my eyes, I tried to recreate the emotions of the night before as closely as I could in the vastly different circumstances.

After a moment, I nodded. "Ready."

She ripped the composition, and I latched on to the feeling of energy flowing into her.

"That energy is mine," I said with as much conviction as I could muster.

I could feel the moment I claimed ownership over the energy, the direction of the flow twisting and snaking toward me. It hit me hard, sending me falling back against the sofa, gasping for breath.

"You did it!" Bryony threw herself at me, shrieking.

I laughed and fended her off, energy coursing through me and making me want to run victory laps around the room.

"Do we try again?" Bryony asked, jumping up and down as if she had been the one to receive an extra serve of energy.

I was about to agree when my leg started jittering. I clamped down on it and grimaced.

"We probably shouldn't."

"Why not?" she asked. "I'm sure you'll have it mastered in no time."

"I hope so," I said. "But right now, I'm filled with enough energy, I don't know how I'm ever going to sleep. I'm not sure it's a good idea for me to try to stuff any more in. And, unlike you, I can't just compose it away again. So, unless you've been hiding yet another ability and you can siphon some of this off..."

"I didn't even think of that." Bryony frowned. "It's going to make practicing difficult."

I sighed. "Not so much difficult as slow. One success a night might be my limit."

But as I climbed into bed hours later, I couldn't wipe the smile off my face. All my life I had longed for an ability—any ability—I could claim as my own. And now I had one. I might be far from mastering, or even properly understanding, it, but it was mine. I was a proper mage, and no one could claim otherwise.

As the weeks dragged on, the weather slowly warming again, it was hard to hold onto my sense of positivity. My progress felt glacially slow, given the limitations of my practice.

MELANIE CELLIER

Bryony and I had taken to rising early, practicing in the morning before breakfast so I could burn off the excess energy during the day and have some hope of sleeping at night. Tyron was the only one in the Academy who might have noticed the difference in me, but he said nothing, although I noticed him giving me the occasional strange look.

But now that my efforts were successful, we couldn't practice every day. Bryony's idea about turning the energy back into compositions to be reused only worked if I failed. Once the energy was in me, it became useless, and Bryony couldn't afford to be siphoning energy into me every day, not if she wanted to keep up with all our classes as well.

On the mornings I succeeded in taking some of her energy, I could feel the difference in combat class. I often beat Jareth and even Bryony now, although I had yet to defeat Darius. The extra energy made me fast and alert beyond my normal levels. It was noticeable enough that Mitchell even commented on my new erratic performance. Some days I performed at my old level while some days I performed with an apparent increase in skill, and he clearly couldn't account for it.

Jareth managed to corner me during a bout early on, asking when I would be ready to try my new ability, and I had to agree to both princes joining us that evening to observe me at work.

I felt so ridiculous saying the words with an audience that it took three tries for my composition to succeed, and I was once again struck by the weakness of my new ability. What good was it in the real world? Even claiming the energy out loud, so boldly and dramatically, went against every instinct of my training. It was distastefully lacking in subtlety.

Darius was encouraging, however, praising my progress and suggesting a whole range of experiments, several of which I hadn't tried. But so far, it seemed my ability was limited to diverting the energy being transferred by someone else's composition.

He started joining us every two or three evenings after that, though—thankfully without Jareth in tow. With his assistance, we tried experimenting in different ways, trying to see if my ability could be used for other things. I tried taking energy directly from someone who wasn't working a composition by claiming it as my own. But I had never felt more foolish saying the words, and it didn't work.

I could twist one of Bryony's compositions to come to me instead of her, but I couldn't initiate one of my own. And when I tried diverting the energy to Darius instead of me, that was just as much of a failure.

It didn't help me remain positive that we were making even less progress in our attempt to discover the identity of my attacker. When I confessed to Darius one evening that I was considering the need for a return to Ardann, he startled me by gripping my arm.

"You can't just run away now." His voice was low, and his eyes burned. "That would be letting them win."

I bit my lip, unable to meet his intense gaze. "I don't want to leave, but if we can't even work out their identity, isn't it irresponsible of me to stay?"

He shook his head sharply. "They've shown themselves to be cautious. They don't want to be discovered, or to leave any trace of themselves behind. You're never alone now, and they haven't tried anything in weeks."

His grip tightened. "I won't let anyone harm you, Verene. But I have to know who did this. And if you leave now, we might never discover the truth."

"Very well," I said, giving way before the fire in his voice. "I don't want to leave, turning tail before I've even completed a year."

That earned me one of his rare smiles. He opened his mouth to say something, but Bryony came out from behind the parti-

233

tions that separated off her bed, and he let my arm drop, merely wishing us both goodnight.

"That looked intense," she said, regarding me curiously.

I flushed a little, unable to deny it. My heart was still racing.

"Darius was convincing me not to run away like a coward."

"You've never been a coward, Verene," Bryony said. "And it wouldn't be cowardly to leave a place where a secret assassin is lurking in wait for you."

"What a horrifying way to phrase it!"

She snorted. "Can you deny it, though?" Her face softened. "But I'll admit I don't want you to go. It would be horridly boring here without you."

"You don't think I'm being foolish for staying?"

She considered her answer. "No, I don't think so. It would be different if you didn't have us. But I barely leave your side, and Darius watches you more than you realize."

"What do you mean?"

"He's subtle about it, I'll give him that. But I don't think his attention is ever on much else these days."

"Goodness knows he doesn't need to pay attention in class," I muttered. "I still can't believe he could do an investigation composition as if it was nothing. Those are complex and require a lot of strength. Did you ever hear my mother tell the story of when she first arrived at the Academy back home? They used one to prove her ability, and it was a big deal for the Academy Head to use it up. The Academy Head! And Darius is only eighteen."

"Then you have a powerful protector at your back," Bryony said. "And don't forget you were the one who saved yourself when you were attacked. You're not a weak, defenseless victim."

I nodded, bolstered by her words. And in the privacy of my bed at night, I could confess I had another reason for staying here beside the two people who were starting to make it feel like home.

I wanted to master my abilities. To test them to their full

limits and find a way to make them useful just like Amalia had said back at the beginning of our discipline class.

I didn't want to run home in fear, I wanted to return home in the summer triumphant, ready to announce to my family and my kingdom that I wasn't the useless royal, after all.

CHAPTER 25

Once the warming weather turned officially into spring, the instructors all began to talk about exams. My attention was so firmly on the private lessons in my sitting room that I didn't give it much thought until I was called out of discipline class one afternoon by a summons to Duke Francis's office.

My first thought was that he had somehow got wind of my ability, and I entered with some trepidation. However, he looked exactly as he had looked the day I came to ask him about hosting the ball, down to the pen in his hand and the parchment on his desk.

"Ah, Your Highness, thank you for coming. Please, have a seat." He gestured to one of the comfortable chairs facing his desk, and I sat.

"I'm sure you have considered the upcoming exams, and your rather...unique position."

I blinked at him, taking a moment to realize he meant my apparent powerlessness. I hadn't actually given it much thought, but I realized now that I should have. Without the ability to compose, I couldn't possibly pass a composition exam. Returning home having failed the Academy after my first year was hardly the triumphant homecoming I had been envisioning.

I sat up straighter. "I know it's not the Academy's practice to provide a modified exam."

"For many years it would not have even been considered," he said. "However, times have changed. We already have a modified program established for those energy mages who choose to complete their studies here. I have met with the other senior instructors, and it has been decided that a further modification would be acceptable in your specific situation."

I drew a deep breath, relieved to discover I wasn't facing imminent expulsion.

"The first year combat exam involves physical combat only, despite your occasional battles in the arena. I understand you will not need assistance in passing that."

"No, Your Grace," I said. "I hope not."

"Your composition and discipline exams will be theory only and will be timed, written exams conducted in a separate room to that of your year mates." He gave me a long look. "I recommend that you pay attention in class and study as much as you can. The Academy has already made an exception for you, and there are some who may not like it. We can accept nothing less than an exemplary result."

I swallowed, trying to remember the last time I had been properly listening in class. The duke's tone carried a clear warning, and I suspected I understood it. So far the Academy Head's neutrality had worked in my favor, but it might now prove my undoing.

The king's faction had decided they wanted to use the opportunity of my presence to build a greater connection to Ardann. They might even be preparing to negotiate a formal alliance. And so the duke had agreed to modify my exams to give me a chance to stay.

But General Haddon's faction must be growing increasingly

desperate to prevent any such connection between Ardann and King Cassius. And it seemed someone among their number was desperate enough to attempt to kill me. When compared to attempted assassination, it was all too easy to believe they might be placing pressure on Duke Francis to fail me. It would be a neat way to get rid of me with none of the blame on Kallorway.

And having already agreed to modify my exams, the duke's neutrality wouldn't allow him to make any more compromises. He would fail me if my performance was substandard in any way.

My status and believed lack of ability would protect me from the usual consequences of failing, but it would certainly mean my expulsion from the Academy. Such a thing would bring shame on my family and my kingdom.

And it would prevent me from completing my main assignment here. After nearly a year, I was finally making progress in understanding the crown prince, but our conversations rarely strayed into future politics. I still couldn't answer the question of which of his parents he meant to support once he had finished his training.

I needed more time. Which meant I needed to pass my exams and ensure the general had no possible excuse to force the Academy Head to send me away.

"Of course," I said slowly. "I completely understand."

"Excellent. In that case, I recommend you return to class with all speed. Who knows what valuable tuition you might be missing?"

The days seemed to speed up after that. I started paying attention in class again, listening intently and taking notes to review later. While I practiced with my new ability, I had almost entirely stopped visiting the library, but I began to haunt it again now. Hugh grinned whenever he saw me, full of jovial comments about trainees and exams.

Bryony had been infected with the same concerns and couldn't afford as many compositions for me to practice on anymore. I still managed to make progress, however, succeeding in working the composition faster and faster, and making slight modifications to the wording—much to my relief.

I no longer felt like such a fool, shouting, "That energy is mine," into the calm of my sitting room. Saying *come to me*, or some similar variation, carried more of my preferred subtlety—a particularly important trait when you were forced to work your compositions aloud rather than writing them down and rolling them up away from prying eyes.

The weather heated enough that combat practice became sticky and at times unpleasant. I had fewer days now that I excelled, but at least I didn't need extra strength from Bryony to be confident in my ability to pass my combat exam.

One particularly hot day at the beginning of summer, Mitchell sent us to the arena where I was one of those assigned to observe the day's battle. It was a relief, given the weather and the way my mind always seemed to be bursting at the seams these days, and I accepted the break gladly.

I watched the royal guard and the growers battle the creators and the armed forces/law enforcement pairing, each team with one energy mage in support. Only Isabelle sat out beside me, her focus intent on the battle.

Idly I watched a small breakaway group battle in front of me. A bolt of pure power from Royce burst against Frida's shield, which dissolved, overwhelmed at the onslaught. She had another one ready, though, waiting in her hands, and she managed to rip it before Royce could follow up the advantage with a further attack.

I considered the way the power hovered around her, the bubble enclosing her a familiar sensation after a lifetime raised in a palace. I had been shielded often enough that feeling one around me was like a comfortable second skin, despite it being a closed composition with no actual connection to my energy.

I had barely used shields in my months here since I was

unable to replenish my supply of them, and I missed the feeling of security they gave me. Without thinking, I imagined Frida's bubble around myself instead of her.

"Come to me," I whispered, as I had learned to do when stealing Bryony's energy composition.

So clearly could I imagine how it felt to have one around me, that it took a moment to realize it was a real sensation and not my imagination.

In front of me, power streaked out from Royce, going straight through Frida's non-existent shield and dropping her to the ground, her arms and legs clasped to her side by a binding composition. I gasped, and Isabelle gave me an odd look, her brow furrowing as her eyes flicked to either side of me.

She would be able to sense the power around me now, but she couldn't possibly guess where it had come from.

"The arena shielding will protect us from stray compositions," she reminded me, and I realized she thought I had gotten jumpy and worked a shielding composition of my own.

"Of course," I said, unable to think of anything more intelligible to say.

She looked back at the battle. "I thought Frida's shield would last longer than that. She'd only just released it. She needs to spend more time on her shielding compositions."

"I—yes," I muttered, getting more incomprehensible by the second.

My eyes flew to Frida as the battle ended, Royce's team declared the victors, having overcome their opponents in multiple places across the arena floor. He helped her to her feet, and I could see the two chatting. Neither looked in my direction or seemed in the least suspicious that anything had occurred other than Frida using a weak shield.

But the power still surrounding me reminded me that it had been nothing of the sort. I had thought my power was that of an energy mage and could only be wielded against an active, open energy composition. My few attempts to try against other compositions had certainly all ended in failure.

But I had just twisted a closed power composition, redirecting a shield that had been crafted to protect Frida toward myself instead. This discovery changed everything about my power, and I couldn't wait to tell Bryony and Darius about it.

Bryony joined me, chattering about the battle, her words washing over me unheeded. Of course she couldn't sense power, so she noted nothing unusual about me.

Even my abstraction was common enough these days as I ran over mental notes for the upcoming exams.

But Darius's steps faltered as he climbed past me to a higher seat, and he paused to throw me a single, confused look. He could feel the shield that still surrounded me, and I could see him searching our surroundings for any hint of a threat.

I met his eyes, letting a smile break over my face, and hoping it would be enough to relieve his concern. But I caught Jareth watching me as well, and the expression dropped from my face. He had taken to cornering me whenever he could manage it, asking me quiet questions about my progress with my ability. His smiles never faltered, but it made me increasingly uncomfortable, and each time he did so, my answers grew more vague.

Dellion sat beside me, tossing her head and wiping sweat from her eyes.

"It's far too hot to be running around and beating each other with swords," she said. "You were fortunate to be an observer today, Princess."

I nodded, only listening to her words with half an ear.

"Grandfather has promised that as soon as the Academy finishes for the year, we'll all make a trip down to his estate on the southern coast. And I, for one, can't wait. It will be cooler down there, and I intend to swim every day."

"All of you?" I asked, my attention caught as I imagined Darius slicing through the waves. "You mean your whole family?" My eyes wandered to where he sat, still watching me.

"Well, not *everyone*," Dellion admitted, sounding petulant. "King Cassius has important business in Kallmon and cannot be spared, apparently." Her wrinkled nose made it clear what she thought of such an excuse. "And I believe Darius has refused the invitation, which is hardly a surprise. But Aunt Endellion is to come. And Jareth, of course. He loves that estate, and he missed our last trip down since he was on the Sekali tour that Grandfather arranged."

"General Haddon arranged that tour?" I asked, concern seeping through me. "Why did Prince Jareth go and not Prince Darius?"

Dellion rolled her eyes. "The king could never spare Darius for such a lengthy expedition. Why, it took two years to convince him the poor boy had to be allowed to leave court to attend the Academy." She threw a sympathetic glance over her shoulder at her older cousin.

Her words would have sounded humorous, so obviously parroted from some older family member, if they hadn't filled me with alarm. It seemed that as far as the queen's family was concerned, Darius danced attendance on his father while Jareth was the general's golden boy. I didn't like the sound of that at all.

The concern shadowed me throughout the day, fighting against the buzz of joy at my expanded ability. Finally it seemed I might be able to do something of real value. But I found the discovery didn't weigh with me as it should when overshadowed by my worry for Darius's safety.

I did drag Bryony away at lunch, however, snatching a private moment in the entranceway to whisper what had happened in combat. She squealed so loudly, the sound hurt my ears, and a passing instructor issued us a stern warning.

As she passed on, I heard her mutter, "Exams," under her

breath. Apparently trainees were known for odd behavior the closer it got to that dreaded time of year.

"But this is huge," Bryony whispered, having recovered proper volume regulation. "Beyond huge. You're not an energy mage but some sort of strange hybrid. I guess that explains why you can feel both energy and power. So do you think you can take any active composition and twist it to come to you instead?"

"I don't know. The first one I ever tried was my own energy, and what could be more familiar than that? And now I've managed it with the power composition I find most familiar. I don't know how much that plays a part. Or maybe I have it all wrong and it has nothing to do with that at all." I shrugged. "I suppose we'll have to start experimenting all over again."

"I won't be able to help much this time," Bryony said. "I can't work power compositions for you to test with. Do you think you could do it to anything, though? There are so many different types of power compositions, and some of them aren't exactly attached to a mage at all. How would you claim them?"

I sighed. "If only it wasn't for exams! They're taking up all my time and mental energy. But it's no good unlocking my power only to fail the Academy—especially when I still haven't achieved what I came here to do. Perhaps I won't manage my triumphal return home this summer after all. I might need another year of experimenting before I have a handle on any of this."

Bryony gave me an odd look. "I hope you're glad for your own sake, and not just because you think your family will finally be proud of you."

"Of course," I said, dismissing her words. "But can you blame me for being excited to share it with them?"

"Nooo." She didn't sound entirely sure. "It's natural enough to feel excited. I just wonder, Verene, if you've really considered every aspect of your ability."

"What do you mean?" I frowned at her. "I've put so much thought into it, my mind spins in circles sometimes."

"It's this new ability I'm thinking of," she said, clearly hesitant but determined to share her thoughts anyway. "It's one thing to steal one of Frida's first year shields. But what would it mean if you could divert an enemy's attack—*no matter how strong*? Verene, you could turn away one of *your mother's* compositions. I'm not sure there's anyone else in the kingdoms who could do that if she's operating at full power."

"But I don't know if I can do anything like that," I said. "That's a fairly big leap. You just said yourself that most compositions can't be attached to me in the same way as a shield or energy siphoning."

"Yes, but even the possibility of you having that kind of power is going to interest a lot of people. I'm sure your aunt would like to know every detail about the extent of your ability. I'm sure she'd like to know very much. And do you think she'd let you return to Kallorway—to come back within Cassius's reach—if you might be the only person with the ability to stop your mother?"

"I…"

She waited, but I didn't finish the thought, so she continued. "You've always been so desperate to prove yourself useful to your family, Verene, and I understand that no one wants to feel useless, but…have you really considered just how they might like to use you?"

"My parents would never *use me*," I said weakly.

"Your father doesn't sit on the throne," Bryony reminded me, unwilling to let the matter go, despite the sympathy on her face. "And your brother has been raised as much by your aunt as by your parents. I don't doubt he loves you, but the crown is a heavy burden to bear. Everything else has to come in secondary to its responsibilities."

I didn't want to acknowledge the truth of her words, but I couldn't deny them either. One day, when Lucien sat on the throne, he would do whatever it took for the good of Ardann. No matter what that meant asking from his sister.

I had admired my aunt's sacrifices—I still did. She was the queen Ardann needed. And I had wanted to be like her. But was I ready to hand myself over to become a tool instead of a person? Even in the hands of someone I loved and admired?

"I can't tell them, can I?" I asked in a small voice.

"I'm not saying never." Bryony's voice now held a pleading note, as if asking for my forgiveness. "I just think it might be better to wait until we really understand the scope of your abilities. Because I think you just showed we're only beginning to understand them."

I squeezed my eyes shut. "You're probably right, but...I need to think about it. It's been so many weeks with no real progress, and now it all feels like it's happening too fast."

Thoughts of Darius pushed back to the front of my mind. My family wasn't the only royal family I had to worry about, either.

"Of course," Bryony said quickly. "I'm not trying to pressure you..."

"No," I said, "you're trying to protect me. My aunt and my brother have all of Ardann as their family—and I have you."

We embraced, huddled in the corner of the entranceway, tears running down both our faces. I had dreamed so many times of a triumphant discovery of some hidden ability. But I should have thought more about Bryony's situation.

I had been so fixated on all the heroic, powerful abilities in my family, that I had brushed off the other example in our midst. The example of Declan and Bryony. Some abilities weren't safe to be shared. Some abilities created only a burden.

CHAPTER 26

When the knock came behind the tapestry that evening, I flew across the room to open it. But Darius wasn't alone. My mood dropped, and my face with it, but for once I didn't care that my emotions were on open display.

I stepped aside and reluctantly let them both enter. Jareth moved into the room, but Darius stopped beside me, his voice and face urgent.

"What happened today in the arena? Why did you shield yourself?"

I glanced back at Jareth. "It was an accident. Of sorts. But you don't need to worry. No one attacked me."

Darius took a deep breath, tension draining out of him. With a start, I remembered that he always used to be tense when we interacted. But it had been different ever since the night I was attacked. The barriers between us had been broken down. And now I had gotten used to seeing the other side of him.

"I can understand you feeling twitchy." There was anger in his voice, although I knew him well enough now to know it wasn't directed at me. "I should have made more progress on discovering your attacker by now."

"I'm willing to call no one attempting to drain the life out of me progress." I smiled, but he didn't smile back. Apparently he couldn't see it as a joking matter.

"Are you sure there's nothing wrong?" Jareth asked. "You've been acting oddly all day."

"Have I?" My voice sounded cold, even to my own ears. "Maybe it's the exams."

"Yes, about that." Darius glanced at his brother, flicking his eyes toward a seat. Jareth flopped into it, an expression on his face I didn't like.

"About exams?" I looked back and forth between them.

"Well, not exams specifically. More the end of the year." Darius drew a slow breath. "At the beginning of the year you told me you wanted our two kingdoms to be united. I didn't believe you then, but I think we understand each other better now. And so I have a request for you to take to your aunt—if you think she would be open to hearing it."

"An alliance request?" I looked between him and Jareth again. "Surely your father can't have come around to the idea already? I know many in his faction seem to be in favor of such a move, but he seemed to positively hate me at Midwinter."

"Not exactly an alliance." Darius hesitated. "Perhaps you'd better sit down."

Bryony popped her head out from where she'd been lying on her bed reading, took one look at the scene in the room and disappeared into my bedchamber, closing the door firmly behind her. Part of me wished I could follow her. I didn't want to be having this conversation—or any conversation—with Jareth in the room.

But I obediently took a seat on one of the sofas, while Darius took the second chair. He leaned forward, his focus on me, tension back in every line of his body. I had known him for nearly a year now, and I had never seen him so nervous. In fact, I wasn't sure I had ever seen him nervous at all. What did he want to ask me?

I leaned forward as well. "What is it, Darius? What do you want to ask my aunt?"

"I want to know if Ardann would support me in deposing my father and taking the throne—without the aid of my grandfather."

I gasped, drawing back. "You want to take the throne…now?"

He shook his head sharply, his concerned eyes pinned on me, watching every change of my expression.

"Not now. When I graduate. I can't take the throne if I'm not a full mage—as my father knows well." Bitterness crept into his voice. "He played every trick he knew to keep me away from here, to delay the day of my graduation. But I prevailed eventually." He glanced across at Jareth with a small smile. "I couldn't let my baby brother come to the Academy without me."

Jareth managed the tiniest of answering smiles, but his attention was focused just as intensely on me as Darius was.

I took a steadying breath. "So you're not talking about an immediate coup. You want to know if Ardann will…what? Directly support a coup? With troops? Or just acknowledge your claim once you're on the throne? What exactly do you want me to take to my aunt?"

Darius shook his head. "No troops. My hope and intention is that this will be bloodless. My father has been promising for years that he will step aside when I reach full maturity, but I know he has no actual intention of doing so. I merely intend to… force his hand."

He smiled grimly, the danger back in his eyes.

"I won't bore you with the details of how that might be achieved, but it is a goal I have been working toward for some time. And I do not intend to be a puppet for my grandfather any more than I intend to be a puppet for my father. Kallorway has been divided long enough. I will be the king who unites us again."

His eyes bored in to me. "Ardann played its part in dividing us, and I can understand their reasons for doing so. But it is a new era now, and a new king will sit on Kallorway's throne. I want to know if your aunt really means the pretty words she sends through you. Is she ready to see a healed and strong Kallorway? Will she support me if I make it so? Or will she support my enemies, and seek to keep us weak and divided?"

I swallowed. Darius said he had been working toward this plan for some time. And yet no hint of it had reached any of our diplomats and intelligencers. He had perfected his cold mask and his act of careful neutrality. But he trusted me enough to tell me the truth and lay it all out before me.

I struggled to take in what such trust meant from someone like Darius who trusted almost no one.

"I believe she means it, yes," I said slowly. "And I will do all I can to convince her that when you sit on the throne in Kallmon, you will mean Ardann no harm."

His eyes burned with an almost feverish light, a small smile playing around his eyes. "I have every intention of doing all I can to make that message very clear."

Jareth stirred uncomfortably, but we both ignored him.

"Your father's promises will help your case," I said, speaking slowly as I rolled the issues around in my mind. "Especially if you can force him to follow through with them without bloodshed. It will be an abdication, not a coup. But what of your grandfather?"

With great willpower I prevented myself from looking in Jareth's direction.

"Once I sit on the throne, I will make it clear to him who rules," Darius said, his voice grim.

I swallowed, choosing my words carefully. "There are some who believe he would do almost anything to see someone loyal to him upon the throne."

"My grandfather will have to learn that loyalty goes both

ways. If he cannot swear loyalty to his king, then he will face the consequences of such treason."

Fear filled me, but I forced myself to nod calmly.

"I will take your message to my aunt, and I will plead your case. And when I return next year, I will do what I can to help you."

A hard smile swept across Darius's face, doing nothing to give him the soft edge that I loved best on him.

"I will not fail Ardann's trust." His eyes caught mine. "Or yours."

Jareth stood and began to pace around the room. "It's a dangerous road, brother."

"We're not having that conversation again," Darius said sharply. "It is finished."

Jareth ground his teeth together audibly, crossing over to my desk and flipping through the pile of blank parchments he found there, as if he couldn't make himself be still.

"Older and wiser heads than yours have failed at the task you set yourself."

"Then it is good I do not face this path alone," Darius replied, but he was watching me not his brother.

Jareth glanced over his shoulder at us, and something frighteningly like rage twisted his features. I drew back, my pulse racing.

But he looked back down at the desk, and I wondered if I had imagined the fiendish expression. It didn't fit his usual friendly mask. Was I just imagining his face reflecting what I feared lurked inside? His grandfather wanted me gone...did he have a willing puppet in his one dutiful grandson?

"We should be going," Jareth said.

"You can go." Again Darius spoke to his brother without taking his focus from me.

"Darius." Jareth crossed over to stand near him. "Brother."

"I said, *you can go*." Darius's voice was low, the edge clear.

Jareth set his lips together, spun on his heel and marched from the room, slamming the door closed behind him.

"Darius." My eyes lingered on the fluttering tapestry.

I tried to think how to raise my concerns. How did you tell someone you thought their brother might be involved in a conspiracy against them? But when I looked back at Darius, his expression drove all thought of Jareth from my mind. My breath caught in my throat.

"Verene."

He stood, and I stood with him, drawn toward him by a force I couldn't control.

"I should have trusted you sooner," he murmured, his voice strangely thick. "But trust is a rare and dangerous commodity in my world."

"I understand." My voice was hardly more than a breath.

"Of course you do," he said. "Just like I should have known you would."

He took the final step to bring us together, our faces a breath apart as they had been so often before. But this time he didn't stop. His arms wrapped around me, as strong and sure as they had been when they carried me to safety.

He paused for a moment, his eyes burning down into mine, no sign of the ice that so often entrapped them. But I could take the pressure and the waiting no more. I reached up and gripped his silken hair, pulling his face down toward me as I pushed up to meet him.

His lips crushed against mine, his arms tightening around me and lifting me off my feet. The fire I had glimpsed in him from our first interaction in this room engulfed me, burning away everything that had stood between us for so long.

I gripped him more tightly, desperate for this moment to never end.

When he did at last pull away, lowering me back onto my own feet, both of us were gasping for air.

"Verene." His hands dug into my hair, and for a moment I thought he meant to pull me in for another kiss.

I leaned toward him, but he just held me there, his eyes devouring my face.

"Darius," I said, gripped suddenly by terrible fear. I grasped the front of his robe, shaking it in urgency. "I'm afraid for you."

"I don't want you to waste your fear on me," he said gently. "I have strength enough for this. Especially with your support."

I shook my head. "No, I mean your brother."

"Jareth?" He pulled back slightly, although he didn't let go of me. "He's the only one I can truly trust in all this. Ever since we were the smallest children, we've only had each other. Don't let his outburst just then put you off. He's just scared for me too. Without each other, we would be alone with our family—and neither of us wants that."

"But I've heard your grandfather favors him," I said. "Is that true?"

This time Darius did let his hands drop, pulling back to frown at me. My own arms dropped to my sides.

"What is this? Who has been in your ear?"

"But is it true?" I asked.

He ran a hand through his hair. "It's true enough he's always had a preference for Jareth. Many people do. I'm quite used to it, I promise you. Jareth has the advantage of being free from the weight of political pressure that rests on everything I do."

"But if your grandfather believes Jareth is loyal to him and you are not, don't you think it's possible he might—"

"Try to put Jareth on the throne?" Darius barked a laugh. "He would find himself in trouble with such a plan. Jareth wants the throne even less than I do—he hasn't been raised with the weight of responsibility that makes me put my own wishes aside. Grandfather would have no luck in that direction."

"But are you sure?" I asked. "Jareth didn't seem at all happy about you seeking an alliance with my aunt."

"He doesn't know you like I do," Darius said. "He thinks it's too early to trust you."

"Or maybe he thinks that with Ardann behind you, he'll have more trouble taking the throne himself."

Darius frowned. "Next thing you'll be accusing Jareth of being the one to attack you!"

"Is it so impossible?" I shot back, swept up in my fear and frustration that he was brushing my concerns aside so thoughtlessly. "He was late to the meal my first night here. Maybe he was busy leaving me a message—at your grandfather's behest. And I saw them talking together at my ball. Perhaps they didn't like seeing how warmly your father's allies greeted me and decided to step up the attacks. The general once had an alliance—of sorts—with my family. Maybe he doesn't like the idea that you might form one of your own."

"Enough," Darius said, his voice harsh. "My brother is not trying to steal my throne, and he's certainly not going to kill you to try to achieve such an end. This is fanciful nonsense."

"But how can you be sure?" I asked, hating the pleading note in my voice, but desperate for him to consider the possibility.

"Oh Verene." Darius sighed. "Because I know him, almost as well as I know myself. My brother would never betray me. I understand that betrayal between brothers is a tale as old as time, but you haven't lived at the Kallorwegian court. The place is a pit of vipers, and Jareth and I have both always hated it. My brother takes every opportunity he can to escape. He has no desire to tie himself there forever."

I frowned, thinking of Dellion's words about Jareth loving their grandfather's southern estate, and even of his participation in the delegation to the Sekali Empire. It was possible I had misinterpreted his actions.

"You know what it's like to be royal and separated from everyone else around you," Darius continued. "We have only our family who we can be our true selves with. And for Jareth and me, we have only each other. We are all we have ever had. I am sure that without Jareth by my side I would not have survived my childhood—not sane at least. He has always been there to bolster me whenever the burdens got too great. My brother has only ever lifted me up."

"But his smiles don't reach his eyes," I whispered, unsure how else to enunciate the uncomfortable feeling he gave me.

Darius gave a pained smile at that. "All of us born royal wear masks, Verene. I wear one of impassive ice, Jareth wears one of friendly joviality. It's a less common choice, but it has served us both well enough. You can't blame him for doing the same thing the rest of us do and keeping his true self hidden from prying eyes."

He lifted a hand and rested it gently against my cheek. "It eats me up inside that there is someone here who would dare to raise a hand against you. Every day they go undiscovered makes me rage inside. But it is not my family that seeks to harm you. I mean to keep my promise. I will find whoever tried to kill you. And then you'll see."

"I just want you to be safe," I said in a small voice.

"As does Jareth," he said. "You two are not so dissimilar, you know."

I stiffened at that, and he shook his head.

"One day you'll see." His hand dropped from my cheek. "Goodnight, Verene."

"Goodnight, Darius," I whispered back.

CHAPTER 27

*B*ryony took one look at my face and knew not to ask any questions. It was only as I was slipping into bed that memories of my new ability resurfaced. Somehow, with everything else to distract me, I hadn't told Darius about my discovery.

I would find a chance to tell him tomorrow, and then we could celebrate together. I knew how pleased he would be for me.

He had kissed me, not declared his undying love, but I couldn't help the dreams that filled my mind. I had told my aunt I would do everything I could to secure an alliance with Kallorway, and there was one time-honored method of binding two kingdoms together. If Darius could win himself the throne with Ardann's support, perhaps my aunt might suggest a marriage alliance to seal our new unity. I knew my parents would let me go once they understood what Darius was really like.

It was a pleasant dream, one filled with more burning kisses and a lifetime of his strong arms around me and his support at my side. But eventually an insidious voice in my mind reminded me that marrying Darius would mean becoming queen of Kallorway.

I had seen his eyes burn for me, but I had also seen the inferno inside him when he spoke of taking the throne and unifying his people, of making them strong again. I had just decided that I couldn't be a tool for my aunt, my feelings motivated in part by the new life I had built here this year. This Academy, and Darius, and Bryony—an energy mage from the Sekali Empire—had become a second home and family to me. I couldn't dedicate myself to Ardann and risk being turned against them. But could I dedicate myself to Darius and risk being turned against my family?

Bryony's words from earlier haunted me. My ability might make me the one tool that could balance my mother's power. Bryony had said how valuable that would be to the king of Kallorway, although she had been thinking of Cassius. But the same was true of Darius. Could I hand myself and my powers—whatever they might be—to him so blindly?

He said he trusted me, and I trusted him. But the throne changed people. It required something from them that none of the rest of us could understand.

My dreams turned to ash, crumbling around me. I couldn't tell Darius the truth of my abilities. I couldn't bear to give him that temptation and see it change him toward me.

I had dreamed of proving myself powerful and useful, and now I was more powerful than I had ever imagined. And my aunt had sent me here to find out the truth behind Darius's mask, and he had just willingly handed me all the answers I sought.

And yet none of it brought me any joy or satisfaction. None of it was enough anymore. Darius was no longer just a tool to me, a means to help my kingdom. It wasn't enough to discover his intentions and use them for Ardann's gain. I wanted to see him succeed—I wanted to see him heal his own kingdom. And if I was honest with myself, I wanted to be at his side while he did it.

But the very power I had dreamed of possessing for so long now stood in my way. What good was great power if it didn't allow me to be useful? And yet my loyalties had become so twisted and confused that I could no longer blindly devote myself to proving my value to Ardann.

I could see only one way forward. I would take Darius's request to my aunt and plead his case as I had promised. But I would make no mention of myself or my own complicated feelings toward the prince. And I would keep my new abilities secret from everyone, as Bryony had advised.

Next year I would return to the Academy and continue working to uncover the extent of my power. Perhaps once I truly understood myself, I would have a better chance of knowing what good my power could do in the complicated balance of politics between Ardann and Kallorway—and the even more complicated balance of everyone who had a place in my heart.

It was a long night, but my pillow kept quiet about any tears I entrusted to it.

I attended classes the next day and tried to think about exams, but every time my eyes fell on either Jareth or Darius, my stomach tightened into knots that twisted and turned. I spent the whole evening in tense anticipation of a knock on the hidden door, but none came. And when I fell into bed that night, I couldn't decide if I was disappointed or relieved.

My dreams were deep and dark and suffocating. But something in me rose up, fighting against them, thrashing and kicking until I swam back to consciousness. And yet, when I left my dreams, my eyes opening, my breath didn't return.

I was suffocating in truth. Someone held a wad of material over my nose and mouth with a firm grip.

I bucked and writhed, my hands clawing out across the bed

until one of them found what it was searching for. Ever since my attack, despite the compositions on my bedroom door, I had slept with my naked sword hidden beneath the edge of my bedcovers. I thanked that foresight now and swung the blade blindly in the dark.

A male voice cursed, and the pressure lifted from my nose and mouth. I gasped and gasped again, continuing to wave the sword frantically through the air above me.

As soon as my breathing calmed, I scrambled from the bed, nearly catching myself in the covers and tumbling to the floor. But I steadied myself in time, landing on my feet and racing to rip the curtains from across the windows. Moonlight flooded into the room, revealing a man dressed in black from head to toe, a length of material wrapped around most of his face.

"Who are you?" I snapped, ready now with my sword held steadily in front of me.

He replied with another long string of curses. A shallow cut along one of his arms bled sluggishly.

I tried to edge around him toward the door, but he stayed stubbornly in place, blocking my access to it. I lunged at him, but a parchment had appeared in his hand, and he was already ripping it.

Power raced toward me, hitting me with force, and trying to rip the breath from my lungs for a second time. But my body fought it, my hand releasing my sword as I dropped to my hands and knees. The body always fought against death compositions, a natural defensive mechanism that required significant power to overcome.

But the assassin's composition was strong, and it fought back, my throat starting to close. I gritted my teeth.

"I control you," I managed to rasp out, and a new awareness flooded my brain, although I couldn't have explained where it came from.

I could see the exact makings of the composition, as well as its purpose. It had been formed and shaped to pull all the air from my lungs, and that was the task the power dedicated itself to achieving.

Instinctively I knew it wouldn't work to simply cut it off. The power had to go somewhere, and it wanted to interact with my lungs. So I gave it a twist, choking out the single word, "Fill."

Instantly air flooded into me, filling my chest before rushing out again in a mighty bellow, far louder than I could ordinarily manage.

"Darius! Darius! Attack!"

The assassin fell back, fear in his eyes now rather than rage.

"Impossible," he breathed.

I stooped to retrieve my sword, fury giving my limbs strength. How dare this stranger attack me in my bed!

He fumbled for another composition, ripping it as he stumbled backward toward the door.

But this time I was ready. I had finally realized my misunderstanding about my ability, and as the power raced toward me, I snarled, "You are mine."

As soon as I spoke the words, I could sense the shape and form of the working, just like the last time. It was a binding composition, meant to hold me long enough for the assassin to escape. A smile spread over my lips.

"Turn it back," I said.

The power sprang away from me, racing back to catch the wide-eyed assassin off guard. His arms and legs sprang together, and he crashed forward to land flat, his face against the floor.

The door behind him crashed open, and Darius lunged into the room, his sword raised, and his eyes burning with fury. He nearly tripped over the man lying prone on the floor, his eyes darting from my attacker to the scattered pieces of ripped parchment, and finally to me, standing there in my nightgown, my sword still raised in front of me.

He sagged slightly.

"You're all right. I was afraid…"

I nodded and then sank onto the floor, my legs no longer able to support me now that the danger was past.

Darius stepped forward, his free hand reaching for me. "You *are* all right?"

I swallowed. "Yes. Yes, I'm fine. I just need a minute." I drew several panting breaths. "He tried to suffocate me in my sleep. It was such a primitive method, and yet it nearly succeeded."

"Thank goodness you had both your sword and your defensive compositions to hand." He reached down to help me gently back to my feet.

He looked again at the scraps of paper on the floor. "Or were those his?"

"They were…" I hesitated, "…both." It was true enough.

He nodded, accepting the comment at face value, and no doubt assuming I had shielded myself. I longed to pour out the whole story to him, already missing the days when we worked together, but I forced myself to stay strong.

"Bryony!" I stiffened and lunged for my sitting room. In the panic of the moment, I had forgotten she now slept outside my bedchamber door.

If the assassin had merely snuck past her, she should have been well and truly roused by all our noise. I pushed past the screens and found her lying rigid on her bed.

I drew a shuddering breath, falling back against Darius's chest and letting myself enjoy his solid strength for one moment. Her eyes were moving, straining toward me and screaming the fury her mouth obviously couldn't. He had used a full binding composition on her, but she was alive.

I opened my mouth, intending to take control of the composition, but snapped it shut again, thinking better of it. Darius still stood behind me, and what would I do with the power?

I turned to him. "Could you…?"

He nodded, already drawing a composition from an internal

pocket. He ripped it, and Bryony sprang to her feet looking ready to spit fire.

"Where is he?" she asked. "Where is that no-good—"

"Bound," I said, cutting her off. "But I don't know for how long, so we should probably deal with him."

"*I* will deal with him," Darius said in an implacable voice. "I've been waiting a long time to have a few words with whoever is behind these attacks."

"I suspect he isn't the instigator," I said. "He didn't seem smart enough for that."

"Then he can tell me who is," Darius said, unperturbed.

Bryony looked at him a little doubtfully, but I nodded agreement, feeling only relief. Darius was the expert in law enforcement. They had compositions that could reveal the truth and compositions that could compel a man to talk. Darius would be far more effective than Bryony or I could hope to be.

I sank into the closest chair to hand—the one in front of my desk.

"I just don't understand how he got in," I said. "My doors are protected with a highly complex composition, and I should have had a warn…"

The word trailed off as I stared at what lay under my hand. A stack of parchments. But not blank ones as I had supposed. Bryony must have shuffled everything around at some point during our practices. These were the compositions from the drawer, the remaining ones from the supply Layna had given me for my door.

And Jareth had stood here only yesterday, flipping through them, reading all the limitations she had built into them. For a whole year, everyone had felt the power on my door, unable to probe its complexity, and I had been safe inside my rooms. And then the very day after Jareth saw the true scope of my protections, I was attacked in my bed.

"Jareth," I breathed. "It was Jareth."

Darius sighed. "Please, not this again. We'll have the truth soon enough."

I held up the stack of parchments, waving it at them both. "Jareth read these yesterday. He was standing right here, Darius. You saw him. These are the locks for my door. This is how he got his man past them."

Darius frowned. "I don't remember him reading your compositions."

"I didn't even realize it at the time myself. And now that I think about it, you weren't looking at him when he was at the desk. It was driving him crazy that he couldn't capture your attention."

"So you admit you didn't see him reading them?" Darius sounded frustrated. "Why are you so determined to believe he's the villain here? This man could have got in through a window, for all we know."

"A window? We're several floors up, remember."

Darius strode away from me, returning to my bedchamber and grasping the bound man by the material of his shirt. He dragged him unceremoniously behind him, hauling him through to my sitting room.

"Jareth is my brother." Each word fell like a shard of ice. "He is not trying to kill you. Mistrusting him is the same as mistrusting me."

Neither Bryony nor I said anything, and after a final charged moment, Darius dragged the man away toward his own rooms.

CHAPTER 28

*a*fter the door closed, silence reigned for a long moment.

"Thank goodness I didn't tell Jareth the extent of my abilities," I said. "Or that man wouldn't have tried to use power compositions on me."

"So you still think it's Jareth?" Bryony asked, glancing uneasily at the tapestry.

I sighed. "I don't know who else could have gotten through the shields on my door. I suppose we'll know the truth soon enough, one way or the other."

"But you used your abilities?" she asked. "To defend yourself?"

I nodded. "We've been misunderstanding them all along. I thought I was claiming the energy and the shield for myself, but that wasn't really what was happening. And since I didn't understand what I was trying to do, it only worked when I recreated the exact situation I had stumbled onto before. I've been bumbling along, waiting to accidentally trigger the right combination."

"So what should you have been doing?" Bryony asked, looking confused.

"I wasn't claiming the energy for my own, or the shield," I

said. "I was claiming the composition itself. I was taking control of it and then twisting it. I couldn't give your energy to Darius before when we tried because I skipped the step of claiming it myself and tried to send it straight to him. If we tried it right now, I could do it easily."

Bryony looked at the tapestry again. "So you've told him then? That you can take control of power compositions as well?"

I shook my head. "No. And I'm not going to. I said *if* we tried, not that we should."

"And you're sure…" She looked at me, worry clear in her eyes.

I nodded. "I can't tell Darius for the same reasons I can't tell my family. Not yet, at any rate. And especially not now that I realize just how powerful I've suddenly become."

The power I had always thought would bring me joy sat like a rock in my gut.

"I'm sorry, Verene," Bryony said quietly. "And I'm sorry I was no use to you in there."

I shook my head quickly. "I'm just relieved you're all right. That's all that matters. The assassin must have been forbidden to harm any other trainees." I bit my lip. "I suppose we should try to sleep. I don't know how long…" My voice trailed away, and we both looked toward the tapestry this time.

"I don't know about you," Bryony said, "but I was never very good at waiting."

Her words snapped something in me. "Personally, I'm sick of waiting. Waiting to turn sixteen, just in case I developed some sort of power, after all. Waiting for someone to find a way I could still be of use anyway. Waiting for the other trainees to accept me. Come on, Bree. We should be part of this."

I strode over to the tapestry and wrenched it aside. It came slightly loose from the wall. I didn't bother to knock, pushing the door open and stepping into Darius's sitting room for the first time, dragging Bryony through behind me.

A similar space to my own greeted my eyes, although it was

decorated in a deep burgundy rather than soft green. Darius stood in the middle of the room, his back turned to us, but he swung around at the unexpected intrusion, his eyes widening.

It occurred to me for the first time that Darius had shields on his door. Shields that apparently were specifically crafted to allow me through. I had told him once that I would visit him, but I had never actually done so. Apparently he had prepared for the possibility. I pushed away the thought of what that meant before it could cause my heart any more pain.

"We want to be here for the interrogation," I said, a hint of defiance in my voice.

"Certainly." Darius stepped slightly to the side, allowing me a full view of the assassin, who sat on the floor, his back propped against one of the sofas.

The man met my eyes, but his gaze was missing the anger or resentment I had expected. Instead I could see only fear.

"What have you done to him?" I asked.

Darius raised an eyebrow. "I have worked a composition that compels him to answer my questions, and another that reveals the truth."

He gestured at a ball of light that hovered near him. I had seen the occasional truth composition and knew it would go black if the man spoke a lie.

"And what has he revealed?" Bryony asked.

"Nothing yet." Darius looked at me. "You're the one he attacked. Perhaps you'd like to ask the questions."

I swallowed and licked my suddenly dry lips. Would Darius ever forgive me when I exposed his brother as a traitor?

I started with an easy question.

"Were you sent to kill me?"

The man ground his teeth together, eventually opening his mouth as if forced to do so.

"Yes."

The light of the truth composition didn't waver.

MELANIE CELLIER

I took a deep breath. "Who sent you?"

The man's eyes rolled frantically in his head as he fought to keep his mouth closed. But eventually he could resist the power that surged around him no longer.

"Cassius," he gasped out, and I fell back a step.

"Cassius? As in, King Cassius?"

"No." The man answered more quickly this time. "Not the king."

I frowned, glancing across at Bryony. There was some other Cassius who had reason to want me dead?

But Darius stepped forward, his posture rigid. "You mean my father?"

The man nodded.

"I don't understand," I said.

Darius kept his gaze on the assassin and the bright light of his truth composition.

"You weren't hired by the king, but by Cassius the man?"

My attacker gulped before nodding.

"Speak aloud," Darius barked, and the man reluctantly confirmed his nod.

Something slammed shut across Darius's face, surrounding him with the ice he usually shielded himself in. My limbs trembled as I tried to process what the confession meant. It was the king's faction who had warmed to me, so how could it be the king behind the attacks? I had become so certain it must be someone who supported General Haddon. Someone like Jareth...

Bryony sidled up beside me. "What's happening to him?"

"Who? Darius?" I whispered back.

"No, the assassin."

I frowned from the cowering man to my friend.

"What do you mean?"

"Can't you feel it? Where's his energy going?"

I spun around to examine the man again. He wasn't cowering, I realized, so much as slumping, his core of energy growing

266

dimmer by the moment. I concentrated and felt the trail of it trickling away.

I took an urgent step forward.

"Who else has been helping the king?" I asked. "Has Prince Jareth been—"

But the man's eyes bulged, and he toppled sideways before I could even finish the question. My hand flew to my mouth, and it was all I could do to stop myself from retching.

Darius whirled on me.

"What was that?"

"His energy," Bryony explained. "It all got taken. It was happening so slowly we didn't even realize until the last moment."

Darius knelt beside him, feeling for a pulse at his neck. "Is he...?"

"He's dead," I said in a shaky voice. "His energy is gone. It's all just dissipated away. If he was still alive, it would be straining to return to him."

No wonder he had looked so afraid. His fear hadn't been for us but for the composition he must have known already bound him. Had it triggered when he named Cassius? A built-in safety mechanism to ensure the assassin could never be used as evidence against the king?

"I still don't really understand," Bryony said hesitantly.

"I can explain," said Darius.

I pulled back at the formal note in his voice and the empty look in his eyes.

"I promised you it was not my family behind these attacks, but I have failed you. I thought I had little trust in my father's judgment, but apparently I still had too much. Even after all these years, he clings to his resentment. He will never forgive your mother for defeating him, or Ardann for forcing him to seal his power."

His words fell heavily between us. "He could not act as the

king, not when his actions betrayed those who still follow him. If he had been willing to do it openly, with the weight of the throne behind him, it would not have taken him a year to get this far. But he sought to take his revenge in secret."

"So what happens now?" Bryony asked. "Our witness is dead."

"It is no matter." Darius's flat voice sent chills up and down my spine. "There will be no public trial. I will deal with this matter myself. I can assure you, Your Highness, that my father will offer no threat against your life again. He may seek to control me, but I promise you I have influence enough for this."

He was every inch the prince I had first met, and I couldn't doubt his ability to keep his promise.

"You need not concern yourself about this matter any longer," he said. "And since you still seem to doubt, please accept my assurances that there is no possible reason for my brother to have been involved. We have our culprit, and he will not harm you again. I ask only that you not spread this story further than this room but trust me to deal with it."

"Of course," I said. "And thank you."

He bowed. "It is I who must thank you for your forbearance. You would be well within your rights to withdraw from Kallorway immediately and revoke any question of an alliance."

I blinked at him. "I will still take your request to my aunt, if that is your concern. You are not responsible for this, and if anything, it only proves the validity of your case."

He bowed again. "You are most gracious."

"Darius." I reached out a hand, taking a single step toward him, but he pulled back, stepping away from me, and I let the hand drop.

"If you will excuse me," he said. "There is still much I must do. Your Highness. Bryony." He nodded in the direction of the still open door back to my suite.

I hurriedly stepped back through it, nearly colliding with Bryony. She closed the door gently behind us, and for a long moment I couldn't seem to move. Darius's ice had invaded my heart, and now it was splintering in deep, rending cracks.

I had pushed too far. He had said that to mistrust his brother was to mistrust him. And yet I had pressed the assassin about Jareth anyway. Perhaps if I had been less desperate to accuse the prince, I might even have managed to act quickly enough to save the assassin's life. But I had spoken without thought, and now I might have driven Darius so far away there was no coming back.

Exams were held four days later. I had thrown myself into study in the meantime, hiding in my books and avoiding private conversation with anyone. Bryony seemed to understand, giving me as much space as she could without actually leaving me alone. And although I could often feel Darius's eyes burning through me, he didn't approach me in class or reappear in my sitting room.

Bryony told me he was giving me space to study, obviously thinking I was concerned about his absence. But in truth, I was relieved. Just the sight of him brought me pain, but I had realized the situation was for the best.

It was possible I might be able to talk him around, to apologize and bring his fire back. But if I was going to keep the scope of my abilities from him, then we couldn't possibly go on the way we had been before. This distance between us was necessary. So I hid in my books to try to distract myself from the pain.

After the intensity of my study, the exams themselves were an anticlimax. In combat, I was assigned to battle Dellion, and the two of us each managed to demonstrate several skilled moves before my eventual victory. She even smiled at me when the match was called in my favor, apparently feeling I had done my part to help her pass her exam.

Armand and Isabelle were the weakest of our year with a

sword, and Mitchell had mercifully paired them together. Their bout was unimpressive, but apparently more than sufficient for a passing grade.

After lunch, I was ushered into an empty classroom where a sour-faced Amalia presided over my two written theory exams. My hand was cramping by the end of it, but there hadn't been a single question I couldn't answer.

I stepped out of the exam room feeling a weight lift from me. Neither General Haddon nor King Cassius had any excuse to expel me from their Academy now.

But almost immediately a different weight slammed down to take its place. I had been using the exams as an excuse to put off thinking about my bigger problems, but I could put them off no longer. Without study to take all my time, I would have to find a way to experiment with my new ability to manipulate power compositions. It wouldn't be a simple task now I had decided I couldn't ask Darius for help.

At the evening meal, Duke Francis appeared and announced that the entire Academy had passed their exams. We all cheered and banged our cutlery on the table, as the fourth year trainees stood and took a ceremonial lap around the room to our raucous encouragement.

I threw aside my royal dignity for the moment and banged and shouted with the rest of them. It was surprisingly cathartic.

When we returned to my suite afterward, Bryony surprised me by producing a chilled bottle of juice and a cake which she had somehow managed to procure from the kitchen.

"Tonight is a night for celebration," she told me. "There is to be no talk of compositions or abilities or exams," she paused and gave me a stern look, "or princes."

"Yes, ma'am," I said meekly. "I'll drink to that."

We spent the evening eating and drinking and reminiscing about the various times Bryony had visited Ardann during our childhoods, laughing until our sides hurt at the pranks we had played on my brothers and our parents.

On impulse, I asked her if she would return with me to Corrin for the summer.

"Perhaps your parents could come and spend time with us there?" I suggested. "I know my parents would love to see them. And Stellan always enjoys any time he can spend with energy mages."

For a moment I thought I was asking too much and that Bryony must be longing for her own home. But she brightened at the suggestion.

"Of course I'd like to spend the summer in a palace instead of a small village." She laughed and clapped her hands together. "And I'm sure I can convince my parents to come."

I smiled in relief. If I was going to keep a secret this big from my parents, it would help to have a buffer of distraction between us. Plus, with my friend around, I was less likely to spend the summer thinking endlessly about Darius.

Bryony immediately launched into her many plans for our break—of which the most pressing seemed to be shopping—and I joined in the conversation with as much interest as I could muster.

And when I collapsed into my bed later that evening, it really did feel like a weight had lifted from my shoulders.

I still had to master my abilities. And my heart still ached every time I thought of Darius's icy face and the barrier of mistrust that had somehow grown between us on both sides. But I had survived my first year as a trainee—despite my lack of power and being surrounded by my people's traditional enemies—and I had emerged from the year far stronger than I could have dreamed.

Darius had promised that his father would not attack me again, and despite everything that now lay between us, I believed he would be true to his word. Just as I believed he had the strength and will to take his father's throne in three years. Despite everything that had happened, I could return next year to the life I had built for myself here.

And while I didn't have all the answers yet, and I still didn't trust Jareth, I would have time enough to seek the truth next year. In the meantime, it was summer, and I was finally going to see my family again.

I couldn't wait. It wouldn't be the triumphal return I had envisaged, but perhaps I would still get to have that one day. Perhaps I would find a way to be of use to my kingdom while still staying true to myself. It was a dream worth holding onto.

NOTE FROM THE AUTHOR

Read about Verene's second year at the Kallorwegian Academy in Crown of Danger.

If you missed it, you can also read about the adventures of Verene's mother, Elena, when she attends the Ardannian Academy as a commonborn and becomes the Spoken Mage, starting in Voice of Power.

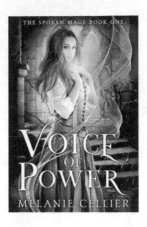

To be informed of future releases, as well as Hidden Mage bonus shorts, please sign up to my mailing list at www.melaniecellier.com.

And if you enjoyed Crown of Secrets, please spread the word and help other readers find it! You could start by leaving a review on Amazon (or Goodreads or Facebook or any other social media site). Your review would be very much appreciated and would make a big difference!

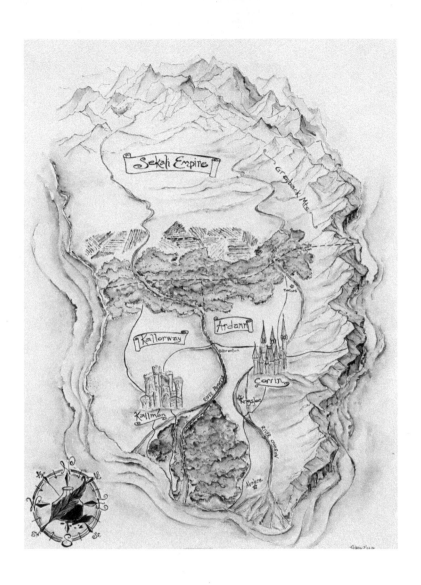

ACKNOWLEDGMENTS

It has been both a joy and a challenge to return to the world of Ardann, Kallorway and the Sekali Empire. The world has grown considerably since I wrote the first book about Verene's mother, but there is still plenty left to explore. I'm so grateful to all the people who have been with me throughout this journey as well as the new ones I'm acquiring along the way. And, of course, I'm especially grateful to my readers and the enthusiasm so many of them have shown for this world. Without that excitement, the Hidden Mage series would likely never have existed.

A big thank you to my new beta reader, Naomi, as well as my usual loyal and talented crew, Rachel, Greg, Ber, Priya and Katie. And, of course, my editors, Mary, Deborah, and my dad.

It was a long process to decide on a new cover look for this new series, and I'm grateful for the patience and skill of my cover designer, Karri. I'm so pleased with the way we were able to experiment with a different style while still incorporating elements of the Spoken Mage covers.

It has been a time of high stress in my life lately, and I'm so grateful to all those family and friends who continually support me and who somehow have the patience to listen to me pour out my thoughts whenever I need an outlet. I am also, as always, grateful to God for sustaining me no matter what.

ABOUT THE AUTHOR

Melanie Cellier grew up on a staple diet of books, books and more books. And although she got older, she never stopped loving children's and young adult novels.

She always wanted to write one herself, but it took three careers and three different continents before she actually managed it.

She now feels incredibly fortunate to spend her time writing from her home in Adelaide, Australia where she keeps an eye out for koalas in her backyard. Her staple diet hasn't changed much, although she's added choc mint Rooibos tea and Chicken Crimpies to the list.

She writes young adult fantasy including books in her *Spoken Mage* world, and her three *Four Kingdoms and Beyond* series which are made up of linked stand-alone stories that retell classic fairy tales.

CPSIA information can be obtained
at www.ICGtesting.com
Printed in the USA
LVHW040005200123
737476LV00001B/83

9 781925 898491